MW01133243

DARK WARRIOR'S PROMISE

THE CHILDREN OF THE GODS
BOOK EIGHT

I. T. LUCAS

NATHALIE

"*D*amn it!" Nathalie slammed the oven door shut.

"What happened?" Jackson poked his head into the kitchen. "Need help?"

"No, get back to the register," she snapped at him.

He arched one blond brow before doing as he'd been told.

With a sigh, Nathalie braced her mitt-covered hands against her work table and let her head hang down from her neck.

She was short-tempered as hell this morning, and it wasn't only because she had slept less than three hours last night. Ever since Andrew's peculiar comment from yesterday, her mind had been churning with questions. She could no longer look at Jackson without wondering what his and Bhathian's agenda was, and by that, she meant what was Andrew's.

Why had none of them mentioned being related to each other before?

"Number two sandwich, mayo on the side," Jackson

called out from the other room, instead of coming in or just sticking his head in to announce the new order. Her irritated response must've come out nastier than she'd intended, to scare off a guy who seemed to be afraid of nothing.

Good. Today, she really wasn't in the mood for seeing his pretty face and his fake charm.

Her father had had one of his episodes last night, waking her up sometime around two in the morning. He'd come into her room, saying that he couldn't sleep in his bed because there was some random guy already sleeping in it. No amount of arguing had managed to convince him otherwise. In the end, she'd given up and had moved his blanket and pillow to the couch in the den.

She'd been up since then.

You should have found him a place months ago.

Oh, hell, Tut. He was back.

What else could go wrong? Why couldn't she get one damn break in her stupid, miserable life?

She thought she'd found in Andrew the perfect guy to share her life with, only to discover that he'd been hiding things from her—like the fact that Bhathian and Jackson were part of his family. And she couldn't shake the suspicion that he'd gotten closer to her only to find out information about her missing mother.

She thought she'd found in Jackson the best helper for her shop, only to discover that the kid was part of the conspiracy.

She thought she'd found in Bhathian a great new friend, one who was selflessly helping her out of the goodness of his heart, but he was with them, and obviously had an ulterior motive.

But the last straw was Tut. After such a long stretch of silence, she thought she'd gotten rid of him. All that remained was to banish Sage as well. It would've meant that she was getting better. But her hopes had been shattered.

She was still as nutty as ever.

Damn it. Even if her suspicions about Andrew were nothing but paranoia, what kind of a future could someone as bat-shit crazy as her hope to have with a man like him?

Nutty Nattie would never have a normal life. She would never get married and would never have kids. She would grow old alone with only a bunch of cats for company.

Trouble was, she was allergic to them, and an old dog lady didn't work as well as an old cat lady.

With hot tears flooding her eyes and sliding down her cheeks, she fled the kitchen, afraid someone would come in and see her crying like a loon. And if the tears weren't bad enough, she was losing the battle against the sobs that were pushing up her throat.

Shit, she couldn't breathe.

The downstairs bathroom was the closest, but it served the coffee shop and didn't offer much privacy, especially since she was about to bawl her eyes out and sob uncontrollably. Which left only the second-floor bathroom. Dropping the mitts at the foot of the stairs, Nathalie ran up and locked herself in her cramped sanctuary.

Dramatic much? Tut's sarcastic tone was like a kick to the gut. Dirty, underhanded bastard, kicking her when she was already down on the floor.

"You're such an asshole." Nathalie dropped the toilet lid and sat down.

And you're overreacting because you're tired. It's happened before. You get depressed when you're sleep-deprived.

"Shut up. Just shut up. I can't deal with all this crazy right now." She dropped her head to her hands.

You're not crazy, you have a gift, he said softly.

"Says the crazy voice in my head."

What if I can prove it?

"How?"

Tell you something that no one else knows.

"Go ahead, I'm listening." Tut was so full of shit. For years he'd claimed that he could tell her nothing because it was against the rules.

Columbus didn't discover America.

Nathalie rolled her eyes. "Everyone knows that. Some Viking explorer got there first."

Tut chuckled. *The truth is that America had always been known, and various peoples had been crossing the Atlantic Ocean for thousands of years. It just wasn't known to the Europeans of Columbus's time.*

"Maybe yes, maybe no. It's not something I can use. There is no way to prove it. You need to give me something more concrete, something personal, not something anyone can dig out of obscure history books."

Sorry, I've been dead for far too long. All I have are anecdotes which are history to you.

"Bloody convenient excuse."

Ask the new guy, he's fresh.

"Sage?"

Whatever he calls himself. He's a newbie so there is a good

4

chance that he died recently and can remember stuff to tell you that you can still verify. Except, time doesn't work the same on this side, so even though he might think he'd been alive only yesterday, he could've been dead for many years of your time.

This was more information than Tut had ever shared with her. "Why are you telling me this only now?"

I had no reason to tell you any of this before. But as I said, my time here is limited, and I don't want to leave you vulnerable.

"Fine. If Sage comes back, I'll ask him."

He will. You're like a beacon of light to those of us who cling to this existence for one reason or another. That's why you were bombarded with so many voices when you were little. I helped shield you, and as you got older, becoming more guarded and skeptical, that beacon of yours has dimmed. But some desperate souls will still find you, I have no doubt of that.

"Why? What do they want from me?"

Think about it. If there were only one person in the world who could hear you, wouldn't you fight for a chance to be heard?

He had a point. It must be awful to be all alone in the big void with no one to talk to. "Yeah, I guess I would."

Okay, now that we are clear on this subject, you need to get up, wash your face, and get back to work before they come looking for you.

For a change, Tut had sounded sincere and had actually made sense. If there really was an afterlife—and she tended to believe that there was, even though she wasn't religious like her father—communication with the dead must be very limited. Otherwise, instead of esoteric, it would be a commonplace occurrence. Perhaps she really was one of the *lucky* few who possessed this dubious talent.

But as disturbing as it was to accept that she was talking

to actual ghosts, thinking of herself as psychic certainly beat thinking of herself as crazy. So why not adjust her belief system and change the story she was telling herself? How different would her life have been if she had been embracing her psychic ability instead of doubting her sanity all the time?

It was so simple—just a matter of a change in perspective, a change in attitude, a new storyboard. There would always be doubts; there was no way around it given the supernatural nature of the interactions, but she could choose to brush them off instead of letting them take over.

"You're right," she told Tut.

Invigorated by the shift in logic, Nathalie pulled down a long piece of toilet paper and dabbed her eyes dry before blowing her nose into it. Getting up, she lifted the lid and flushed the paper down the toilet. As she watched it get sucked down the small whirlpool, she hiccuped once, then turned around to examine the damage in the mirror.

God, she looked awful—blotchy nose, puffy eyes, the works. How on earth was she going to erase the signs of emotional meltdown from her face?

Makeup, and lots of it.

When she was done, her skin tone was flawless thanks to several coats of foundation. Her eyes were still red-rimmed, but the black eyeliner and mascara she'd applied liberally helped them look less puffy.

The downside was that she was painted like a hooker.

Whatever, it would have to do. She was going to spend most of her day in the kitchen anyway.

ANDREW

"*S*on of a bitch." Andrew slammed the phone down.

It was four in the afternoon, and he had to drag his ass all the way to the airport, in rush-hour traffic, to investigate a supposed prank. A baggage handler had shown up to work wearing a padded vest, which in itself wasn't all that unusual, but a coworker had noticed that the padding looked odd. That, combined with some troubling comments the handler had been spewing lately, prompted the coworker to approach security.

The guy had been detained, and his vest had been checked. It turned out that a bunch of empty matchboxes had been sewn into the padding, creating the square outlines his coworker had noticed.

Strange? You bet.

The excuse was that he'd been pulling a prank on his buddies.

Yeah, right. Andrew had a strong suspicion that it had

been a test to see if the guy could get away with a dummy before attempting the real thing.

There were gaping holes in airport security that had to be plugged before something worse than 9/11 hit the United States. Problem was that the TSA and Homeland Security couldn't come up with a solution that didn't cost millions to implement, or create additional holdbacks. Airport personnel moved between secured and unsecured areas many times during their workday, and it wasn't feasible to screen them every time they re-entered the secured areas.

The only solution, in Andrew's opinion, was to screen everyone entering the airport.

Expensive? Sure. New checkpoints would have to be built at the entry points, and they would have to be numerous to facilitate fast processing of the inbound traffic.

Necessary? Absolutely. And if it meant that airfare would get even pricier to cover the additional costs, Andrew was willing to pay a few extra dollars for a ticket so he could fly safely and get rid of the anxiety even he felt every time he boarded a plane. And he was pretty sure that most travelers would gladly pay it as well.

Not that anyone had been paying attention to him or his suggestions at that fucking summit in Washington. No one listened to the field people. It was all about department politics and the bureaucrats covering their own pampered asses.

God, he hated politicians. Hell, he hated all bureaucrats.

They should each serve a few years in the armed forces before being allowed to run for office. Not that it was guaranteed to produce better judgment calls, but it would no doubt be an improvement. Fighting on the front lines and risking their own bloody lives would definitely make them rethink their priorities.

"Where to?" Kravitz asked as Andrew passed his desk on his way out.

"The fucking airport. I have a suspect to interrogate."

The agent glanced at the clock hanging on the wall behind him. "I don't envy you the drive. Traffic will be murder."

"Isn't it always?"

Kravitz nodded. "Can't argue with that. See you tomorrow, Spivak."

Andrew gave the agent a two-fingered salute. "Say hi to Lora for me."

Six months ago, Kravitz had married an intern from the accounting department and hadn't stopped smiling since. Evidently, marriage agreed with the guy.

"Will do."

Would he be as stupidly happy as Kravitz if he married Nathalie? Probably not. Even though he loved her passionately and saw himself spending the rest of his life with her, Andrew just wasn't the cheerful sort. All he could hope for was a measure of contentment, some peace for his restless soul.

He hated keeping things from her.

Hell, who was he kidding? Andrew was guilty of worse. He was plain out lying to her. But even if he disregarded the clan's directive of keeping its existence secret, it wasn't his place to tell her the truth—it was her real father's. Except, he just couldn't help thinking that the duplicity would blow up in his face at some point.

It had taken him a while to figure out why Nathalie had been upset last night, and why she'd lied about the reason for her tears. Clearly, she must've gotten suspicious after his stupid blurt about Bhathian and Jackson being related to each other and through his sister to him. The woman was far from stupid, and it didn't take a genius to figure out that he must've had a good reason not to mention this before.

God only knew what she was imagining. Women had a tendency to blow up every little thing into monstrous proportions even without having a good reason. And lying was a fucking big one.

Driving up the levels of the underground parking of his office building, Andrew waited until he cleared it before hitting Nathalie's number.

"Hi, Andrew," she answered in a flat tone.

Fuck, now he was sure he was screwed. "What's up, sweetheart, you sound off."

"I'm just dead tired. My dad had an episode last night, and I've hardly gotten any sleep."

She sounded truthful, but his gift wasn't as good when limited to audio clues. "Perhaps I should let you sleep and come over tomorrow. I'm on my way to the airport to interrogate a suspect, so I would be running late anyway."

Andrew held his breath as he waited for her response. If she agreed with him, he was screwed. But if she still wanted to see him tonight, it would mean that he hadn't screwed up as badly.

Or that the woman was a saint.

"No, I want you to come. I'll ask Jackson to stay a little longer and keep an eye on my dad while I take a nap. Wake me up when you get here."

Feeling the muscles in his jaw relax, Andrew let out the breath he'd been holding. "Are you sure?"

"Of course, I'm sure, you silly man. I miss you."

A big grin split Andrew's face. "Your wish is my command, sweetheart."

She giggled. "Duh, of course, it is."

Suddenly, the drive didn't seem as daunting, and as he hummed along to the tune of a popular love song on the radio, Andrew realized that he was still smiling.

Damn, he was turning into a fool just like Kravitz.

BRUNDAR

P *athetic.*

Brundar rubbed his neck as he observed his students' clumsy attempts at toppling their opponents down to the mat. After two weeks' worth of intense drilling, he'd finally paired them up to see how well they had internalized what they'd learned.

Apparently, not very much.

And out of this bunch of losers, he was supposed to pick candidates for the advanced class. It was embarrassing to admit, but Michael, who had started training as a lowly human, had shown way more promise than this group of inept immortals. As of now, he was the only serious candidate they had for the Guardian training.

It had to do with attitude. Michael was an athlete who loved to challenge himself. On the other hand, most of these trainees had signed up just to learn basic survival skills. They loved their cerebral day jobs and had done nothing athletic in ages. Their motivation was marginal at best, and their attitudes sucked.

Surprisingly, the only one who had shown some aptitude was none other than Carol—the airhead with the drinking problem. Not that this was her only vice. On more than one occasion, he'd smelled weed on her. But she was trying, probably because she had no job to speak of and was most likely bored. Physically, she had a long way to go. Short and chubby, she lacked muscle tone, and her endurance was shit. But she was aggressive and had a decent aim with a handgun. In fact, she was the best shooter in his class—a dubious title considering who she was competing against.

He clapped his hands to get their attention. "Okay, people. That's enough."

Just as they'd been taught, his students lined up and bowed from the waist.

"When I call your name, you may leave."

"Yes, Master," was the response from the group of twenty-two immortals.

At least they had gotten this part down. Whipping some discipline and proper etiquette into the bunch of newbie civilians hadn't been easy, but it had been necessary. Their obedience and respect were the only things that made teaching the class bearable for him.

When those he'd called had departed, there were only four people left: Carol, her likewise unemployed buddies, George and Ben, and Roland.

Slim, slim pickings.

"You are the best in this class."

Smug looks and high-fives followed.

He grimaced. "That's not a great achievement. Being better than bad doesn't make you good."

The smug looks wilted.

"But I'm giving you a chance to get better. I've chosen the four of you for an advance class from which the best will be selected for the Guardian training program."

Carol and her buddies looked excited, Roland looked down at his bare feet.

"A problem, Roland?"

"I'm not interested in the Guardian program. I just want to learn self-defense."

"No problem. It's voluntary. Do you still want to join the advanced class?"

"If I don't have to join the Guardian training later? Then yes."

"The advanced class starts tomorrow at seven."

"Do we still need to come for the six o'clock beginner class too?" Carol asked.

Poor girl, not the sharpest tool in the shed. "No, Carol, just the seven o'clock."

"Yes, Master." She bowed her head, the mass of her strawberry blonde curls fanning around her cherubic face.

Lucky for her, Carol was beautiful—in that fragile sort of way that males found irresistible. They couldn't help but feel protective of her, and that perceived weakness was what drew them to her like moths to a flame. He wondered if she used it to her advantage, and her dumb act was just that—an act.

Still, even if she wanted to join the Guardian Force, he wasn't going to recommend her despite her talent with a gun. It wasn't about being a chauvinist. After all, he had no problem with Kri, but Carol was an irresponsible airhead, soft and weak. Definitely not Guardian material.

"Dismissed." He waited until they exited to turn off the lights.

Originally, the place had been designated as a classroom, but more space had been needed for training, and the room had been turned into a makeshift training area by removing the chairs and desks and covering the floor with rubber matting. There was another one just like it next door, and that was where he was heading next.

Bhathian was finishing up with his own class, and Brundar was curious to see how many students he'd chosen for the advanced training. Eleven left the room, and a few moments later five more headed out. Not bad. Together they had harvested nine.

"Are they any good?" he asked as he entered the classroom.

"Nah, not even one. If you ask me, it's a big waste of time. Basic self-defense is one thing, and training for the Guardian Force is another. Kian and Onegus are deluding themselves if they think these guys will amount to anything."

Brundar shook his head. "I don't remember it being like this when we were young."

Bhathian snorted as he turned off the lights. "Different times. Lads were stronger then, used to working with their hands. We carried a sword even before our voices changed, and learned how to use it even before we transitioned."

"We have to get our old friends to come back." Brundar followed Bhathian into the elevator.

"Talk to your brother."

"What for?"

Bhathian shrugged. "He has a way with people. Maybe

he could convince some to reconsider. Kian is not having much success in luring them back, but then he's not the best guy to try and sell something to someone that doesn't want to buy. But Anandur, well, you know him, he is a charming bastard."

Not a bad idea. Anandur had always been the glue that had held the Guardians together. The fun guy, the prankster, the one everyone liked. Perhaps reminding the guys of the good old days would do the trick.

"I will. Listen, I want you to take over both of our beginner classes, and I'll take the advanced one. I don't want to waste any more of my time than I already have on this."

"No problem. How many of yours moved up and how many are left?"

"Out of the twenty-two, I chose four for the advanced course."

Bhathian rubbed his chin. "Your eighteen plus my eleven makes twenty-nine." He shrugged. "I'll manage."

"Good." Brundar nodded as the elevator stopped at the gym level. "I'm going to look for Anandur."

NATHALIE

"*I* made you a cappuccino." Jackson came into the kitchen with a peace offering.

Smart boy. He would do well in a relationship. Instinctively, he was trying to appease her even though he had no clue why she was angry. Nathalie wondered if he realized that he was partially responsible for her peeve and was trying to get back into her good graces.

Nah. Andrew had just blurted the newsflash of them being related yesterday, and she was pretty sure he hadn't informed Jackson yet.

"Thank you, I need it." Nathalie took it from him and sat down on the stool he'd brought for her from the front. It was hard to be mad at such a thoughtful guy. Jackson had noticed that she'd given up the only chair in the kitchen for her father to sit in and had nowhere to rest, so he brought her the stool.

"When you're done, I would like you to meet my friend Vlad."

God, not another one of his endless string of friends.

She was grateful for the additional clientele Jackson was bringing in, and most days she enjoyed interacting with them, but today she was too tired for socializing. "Perhaps some other time. I'm barely keeping my eyes open, and I'm counting the minutes until closing time. As soon as I flip the sign to closed, I'm going upstairs and collapsing on my bed."

"But that's exactly why I want you to meet Vlad. You need help in the kitchen, and Vlad needs a job."

"That's very thoughtful of you, but even with the extra business you're bringing in, I can't afford another salary."

"I know, but he is willing to work for free until you can pay him."

"Why on earth would he want to do that?"

Jackson smirked. "Because I sold him on the idea that you'd teach him to bake."

"He wants to be a baker?" A highly unusual career choice for a teenager.

"Not necessarily, but he wants to make money."

Nathalie snorted. "Then he's choosing the wrong profession, that's for sure."

Jackson patted her shoulder as if she was a little slow. "Let's go sit down with Vlad and negotiate a deal. You're practically swaying on your feet."

"We can't take a break at the same time. What if someone orders something?"

"It's ten minutes to closing, and we can say that the kitchen is closed. You're done for today." He tugged on her apron strap.

Bossy kid. But whatever, he was right.

"Papi, are you okay here by yourself for a couple of minutes?" she asked her father.

When he nodded, she took the apron off, washed her hands in the sink, and followed Jackson out while drying them on a dish towel.

"Nathalie, this is Vlad."

She lifted her head to say hello to Jackson's friend and almost ran back to the kitchen. No wonder the kid was willing to work for free. Who in their right mind would want to employ him?

He'd scare the customers away.

Dressed all in black, with numerous chains and buckles for decorations, he was totally into the goth style. But that wasn't what was so disturbing. Vlad was very tall, probably close to six and a half feet, and so scrawny that she doubted he weighed more than her, probably less. Hunched over, with a face pale as a white sheet of paper and stick-straight black hair that fell over one eye, he looked like a cross between Dracula and his servant Igor.

The kid must've been wearing colored contacts because the blue of the one eye that was visible wasn't like any kind of blue Nathalie had ever seen before.

Her startled response had him hunching even further, and he dropped his head—the long swathe of hair covering most of his face.

"Hi, Miss Nathalie," he whispered from under the curtain of his glossy hair.

Shit, now she felt like a jerk. Poor kid. Being seventeen and looking like this must be hellish. She of all people should know.

"Hello, Vlad." She offered him her hand. "Is it short for Vladimir?"

After a moment of hesitation, he shook what she'd

offered, holding her hand with gentle, slim fingers that were tipped with long nails.

"No, it's just Vlad." His murmur was barely audible.

"Come, let's sit over there." Jackson pointed to an empty booth.

"Okay, so here is the deal." Jackson addressed her as soon as they were seated. "I was thinking about your mode of operation and how you can make more money and work less."

Nathalie rolled her eyes. Kids and their dreams of money falling down from the sky. "Go on. I'm curious to hear what brilliant plan you've hatched."

Jackson smirked. "The coffee shop is already working at full capacity, so we can't expect to be making more money out of it. Your baked goods are in high demand, but you can't make more by yourself, and we can't sell more in this small shop."

"I'm not moving."

"That's not what I'm building up to. My idea is to sell directly to offices. I can have a bunch of my friends peddle your baked goods door to door, working on commission only. And as to production, we could start with Vlad, and if the thing takes off, we can hire additional helpers."

She had to hand it to Jackson, the boy was a natural entrepreneur, but he hadn't taken into account her kitchen's limited capacity. "First of all, I'm not set up for mass production. I don't have the right equipment or even space to put it in. Second, I have to wonder, what's in it for you?"

A big grin spread over Jackson's handsome face. "Money, of course. I manage and organize the door to door sales, and we split the profits from it. And as to your kitchen, we start with what we have, and when we outgrow it, we'll worry about the solution then."

Nathalie couldn't really find fault with Jackson's plan. On the face of it, his idea seemed good. But was she up to the extra hustle?

"I'll sleep on it. Right now I don't want to even think about extra work. And as for you, Vlad. Can you be here tomorrow at four in the morning?"

Vlad perked up, flipping his long hair back and away from his face. "Yes." He smiled a little, showing a pair of incisors long enough to be considered fangs. Was he wearing some kind of prosthetics? Nah, looked too real. But what was even more disconcerting were his eyes, which were both visible now—the eerie blue one and the glowing green one.

Fate had been cruel to the boy, more so than to her, and Nathalie was doubly glad that she'd offered him the job. It was on the tip of her tongue to tell him—welcome to the freak show—so he'd know she was a kindred spirit, but she managed to refrain. Vlad would've taken it the wrong way. Instead, she extended her hand to him with the biggest smile she could muster in her exhausted state. "Good. Come round the back and knock."

He shook on it vigorously. "I will. Thank you. You won't regret it, I promise."

"I know. Welcome aboard." On the inside she added, *Us freaks have to stick together, dude.*

To Jackson, she said, "I'm going up to sleep. Can you finish here and keep an eye on my dad until Andrew shows up?"

"Sure thing."

ANANDUR

*A*nandur grimaced as Brundar walked in with an expression more dour than usual on his pale face. Not bothering with pleasantries, like saying hello to his only brother, he headed straight for the fridge, pulled out a beer, and sat down on a stool next to the counter.

"Nice of you to show up, brother mine." Anandur couldn't help the sarcastic tone. Lately, Brundar had been gone most nights, turning up for work and a change of clothes and hightailing it right after.

They hadn't talked in days.

Not that Brundar was much of a conversationalist, but he was a good listener, and Anandur needed someone to talk to about the situation with Lana. Even if only to hear himself talk. He had stuff he wanted to get off his chest, and Brundar was better than a priest in a confessional at keeping things to himself.

Brundar swiveled the stool around to face Anandur. "What can I do for you?"

His brother knew him too well. "Nothing. I just feel like

I'm living here alone. Should I start looking for a new flat mate?"

"Not yet."

What the hell was that supposed to mean?

"Are you serious? You're planning on moving out?"

Brundar raised his beer bottle in a salute. "Just messing with you."

Brundar? Joking? Not likely. The guy had no sense of humor whatsoever. But if he was set on keeping his plans to himself, there was no force known to man, mortal or immortal, that could pry it out of him.

Anandur wasn't going to even try. "So what's new with you?"

"The trainees suck."

"Oh, yeah?"

"Out of the twenty-two in my class, I barely scraped four for the advanced training, and one of them is Carol." Brundar's thin lips twisted in distaste. He lifted the bottle and took a long swig.

"That bad, eh?"

"You have to help Kian and call some of the old Guardians, using that famous charm of yours to persuade them to come back. We need them."

"Kian didn't ask for my help. He said he would handle this."

"Yeah, but I bet you'll have better results."

Anandur scratched at his beard. "Probably. I can start with Uisdean and Raibert. Last I talked with Raibert he was telling me about the construction company the two of them started. My impression was that they weren't doing that great."

"You should also give Niall a call. You guys used to be tight. You can pull on those old friendship heartstrings."

Not likely. Niall was happy with his successful antique dealership, wearing fancy suits and pretending to be related to royalty while shagging all the bored rich housewives who wandered into his showroom. Anandur doubted Niall would agree to leave his cushy lifestyle for that of a simple Guardian. Even if only temporarily.

Unless…

"I have a great idea. I can bait them—dangle Amanda's success with identifying Dormants. Tell them they'll be first in line for any females she finds."

Brundar gulped down what remained of his bottle. "That should work." He got up and pulled another one from the fridge.

Something was bothering the bastard, but asking him about it was futile. Brundar didn't share.

Anandur rubbed the back of his neck. "Anyway, I have this problem…"

Brundar reopened the fridge, pulled out another beer, and put both on the counter. "This one is for you." He pointed.

It was annoying, the way Brundar could read him like an open book while Anandur had no idea what was on the bastard's mind.

"It's about the Russian girl I'm supposed to seduce."

Brundar arched a brow. "And you need my advice? The self-declared chick magnet lost his touch? What happened?"

"It's not about the seduction part, you bastard. I don't need anyone's advice on that. My problem is that I don't want to thrall her. The scumbag Alex is screwing all of his crew, and he's probably thralled them numerous times. I'd hate to add to the damage. And anyway, you know me, I'm not all that good at thralling. If Lana has been subjected to it so many times, she might've built up a resistance. What if I fail to thrall her?"

Brundar shrugged. "Easy. Tie her up and blindfold her."

"And how is that supposed to help? It's not like she won't be able to feel my fangs sink into her neck, or ignore the euphoria that will follow."

Brundar sighed. "You've never engaged in BDSM, have you?"

Anandur cringed. "No, not my thing. And I'm sure it's not Lana's either."

Was it Brundar's? Or was he talking theoretically? And if it was, on what side of it did his brother play?

There was no point in asking. He wouldn't get an answer.

Brundar shrugged again. "Do whatever you want, but you asked my advice, and that's the only way you can bite a woman without having to thrall her afterward. Do you want me to tell you how to do it or not?"

If only to satisfy his curiosity, Anandur was eager to hear Brundar out. This was a rare opportunity to get some insight into the mystery that was his brother.

"Sure, why not. Tell me. I want to know. I'll decide if I want to try it or not after I hear what's involved." If Brundar brought up whips and chains, then it would be a definite no-no.

"First of all, you don't have to bite her neck. You can bite her inner thigh. The advantage being that it's less sensitive than the neck, and it will be less obvious what you're doing.

Especially with your beard and mustache confusing the sensations. After all, once you remove her blindfold, and she takes a look, there will be no marks left. And if she happens to be really into it, she'll attribute the euphoria to subspace. But if it's only a game for her, then you have to make sure that she orgasms so many times that she can barely remember her own name."

Anandur smirked. "That I can do, no problem. But what is subspace?"

"It's very similar to the venom-induced euphoria. An intense scene can trigger the release of endorphins and other hormones that produce a morphine-like effect. It numbs the pain and creates an ecstatic floaty feeling."

Anandur cringed. Pain wasn't a word he liked to associate with sex. "Can it be achieved without hurting the girl, only with loads of pleasure?"

Brundar shook his head. "Not really. But again, if you exhaust her with plenty of orgasms, she can come close enough."

"Yeah, I think I'll stick to this. I'm not comfortable with what you call an intense scene."

A rare smile lifted the corners of Brundar's lips, and he clapped Anandur on the back. "I know, you're too soft." Then he got serious again, pinning Anandur with hard eyes. "A word of caution. If you decide that you want to play, there is much more to it that you need to learn. What goes up must come down, and the high always ends up in a low. The drop in endorphins and adrenaline produces symptoms similar to shock, and it's extremely important to help the sub come down gently. A warm blanket, a bottle of water, and something sweet to eat are a good start. Cuddling and reassuring, that's another part of it. Look it up before trying anything."

Damn, the guy was serious, and it was clear that he knew what he was talking about. But cuddling and reassuring? Brundar? Somehow Anandur couldn't picture his brother doing this for someone, or even being on the receiving end. Brundar didn't like to touch others or be touched. But then that was with males. He probably didn't mind it with women.

Anandur saluted with his beer. "Got it. And don't worry, I have no intention of playing this hard. I'm okay with pretend play, nothing more."

Brundar nodded, and then in a rare gesture of brotherly affection he squeezed Anandur's shoulder. "Good luck." He emptied his second beer and headed for the door.

"Where are you going?"

"Out."

"I figured that much. Where to?"

Brundar lifted a brow and opened the door, then closed it softly behind him.

Anandur sighed and brought the bottle to his lips. *I guess that was as much brotherly sharing as I'm ever going to get.*

6

NATHALIE

*I*t was dark outside when Nathalie opened her eyes, the weak moonlight drawing a wavy pattern on her blanket. Damn, Andrew wasn't there. Could he still be stuck at the airport?

What time is it?

She turned on her bedside lamp and glanced at her watch. Nine twenty-two. He must've decided to go home.

How disappointing.

But then, as a sound of murmurs reached her, coming from the direction of the den, an excited flutter stirred in her belly. She couldn't tell for sure, but one of them sounded like Andrew's.

He'd come after all.

Nathalie got up and shuffled to the door. The voices became clearer as she opened it, and she recognized one as Andrew's and the other as Jackson's. For a moment, she contemplated standing out in the hallway and listening in. Perhaps she could catch them talking about whatever they were hiding from her. But then the name Vlad was mentioned, followed by Andrew's masculine laughter.

God, she loved to hear him laugh. He didn't do it often enough. She should make it her mission from now on. Perhaps she could subscribe to a website that delivered a daily dose of jokes. There must be something like that, and if there wasn't, there should be.

"Hi, guys," she said as she entered the den and walked over to the couch.

"Hi, sweetheart, what are you doing up?" Andrew asked as he opened his arms.

Gladly accepting the invitation, Nathalie sat on his lap.

She sighed as Andrew wrapped his arms around her, surrounding her with his warmth and his strength. It felt so good, and she wanted to stay like this forever. Closing her eyes, she rested her cheek on his hard chest.

Andrew kissed her forehead. "You should have stayed in bed. Jackson told me you were swaying on your feet from exhaustion, and that you almost fainted."

She turned her head and opened her eyes, casting Jackson a questioning look.

He shrugged. "I just tell it as I see it."

"It wasn't from exhaustion. It was because of Vlad."

That earned her another hearty laugh from Andrew, his big body shaking under her. "Jackson told me about him. Poor kid."

Nathalie felt a slight pang of guilt for using Vlad to amuse Andrew. "Yeah. What I don't get, though, is why he makes it even worse by dressing like a goth and growing his nails like that. Maybe if he wore jeans and a T-shirt like a typical teenager and cut those claws, he wouldn't be as scary. And that emo haircut isn't helping him either."

"Vlad is the guitarist of our band. The nails and the look are part of the gig."

"That explains a lot. But does he have to dress the part all of the time?"

Jackson sighed. "It's better to look as if he's doing it on purpose. Looking like an emo goth beats looking simply like the tall, thin, creepy kid."

"I guess you're right." Being a teenager sucked. Thank God she was no longer one.

Jackson pushed up to his feet. "I'm going. See you tomorrow, Nathalie. I hope Vlad will make himself useful."

"I'm going to make sure that he does."

"See ya, Andrew." He waved before disappearing into the dark hallway.

Nathalie listened to Jackson trot down the stairs, then open the front door and lock it behind him. It was amazing how quickly she'd trusted him with his own key and the code to the new alarm Andrew had had installed.

The kid had gotten under her skin, which was to be expected considering how helpful he was, especially with her father. And although she couldn't completely ignore the niggling suspicions as to his motives, she found it hard to believe that there could be something truly sinister hiding under that charming façade. He was just a kid on the cusp of manhood. With the enthusiasm and naïveté of youth, Jackson was looking for a way to prove himself as some big shot entrepreneur and to make money.

To Nathalie, he was a godsend. She should be grateful

that he'd come into her life. And the dangerous vibe he emitted, the one that occasionally made her uncomfortable, must be due to his emerging masculinity. This one was going to grow into the ultimate alpha, but in a good way, hazardous only to the young girls' hearts he was going to break.

And Andrew? There was no way he could feel so good and so right while harboring some nefarious intentions toward her or her mother. It must've been all in her head.

Nathalie burrowed closer into Andrew's chest. "When I woke up, all alone in my room, I was afraid you decided not to come."

"I told you that I would be here. I would never dare disobey direct orders from my queen."

She loosened his tie and popped the first button on his shirt. "Your queen, eh? I like the sound of it."

He bowed his head. "I'm your humble servant, your majesty."

She was going to have fun with that. Andrew had no idea what he'd started. "Kiss me," she commanded in a haughty tone.

He kissed her nose. "Like this?"

Nathalie giggled. "Nope, try again."

He kissed her forehead. "Like this?"

"Nope, a little lower."

Andrew smirked and planted one on her chin.

"I think you need a demonstration." She looped her arms around his neck and pulled him down.

With his palm cradling the back of her head, he took over and kissed her, his tongue slipping into her mouth and coaxing hers to join the dance.

When he drew back, his hooded eyes belied his smirk. "Like this?" he taunted.

"Exactly."

He closed his mouth over hers, his previous playfulness replaced by a hot, demanding hunger. With his shaft growing harder beneath her, Nathalie's hips moved as if they had a mind of their own, rubbing against it.

"You're driving me crazy," he groaned into her mouth.

"And you're wearing too many clothes."

"What do you want to do, love?"

"Let's go to my room."

"What about your father?"

"I'll lock the door, and if he wakes up, I'll stall for time while you duck into the closet."

Andrew shook his head. "Alright. I guess beggars can't be choosers." He pushed to his feet with her still in his arms.

"Ohh, you're so strong," she husked.

Andrew grinned, the smugness practically oozing from him.

Evidently, her guy wasn't immune to compliments.

"Go on..." he encouraged as he carried her down the hallway to her room.

"I like how you can lift me so effortlessly, as if I weigh practically nothing. I can feel your chest and arm muscles flexing against me, and I can't wait to have my hands all over that bare hardness."

"Woman, I'm gonna do such wicked things to you tonight," he said as he laid her down on her narrow bed.

"Lock the door."

"Yes, ma'am." He turned the key in the lock, already loosening his tie on the way back. "We'll have to be very quiet."

He toed off his shoes and unzipped his slacks, pushing them down together with his boxers. "Which is going to be a problem since I'm going to drive you wild with pleasure." He shrugged off his shirt and sat on the bed to remove his socks. Foregoing the careful folding and draping he usually did, Andrew dropped his clothing in a messy pile on the floor.

Nice, she liked that he was impatient to get to her. She was impatient too.

Nathalie was still dressed when Andrew joined her in bed.

Stretching her arms over her head, she arched her back. "Could you help me out of my clothes? I'm still so tired," she teased.

"With pleasure." Andrew pushed her T-shirt up, stopping to cup her breasts for a moment before pulling it over her head. "Just checking that my beauties are still here."

She grinned. "I think you should make sure. Maybe those are imposters hiding under the bra."

He chuckled and snapped the front clasp, letting the cups fall sideways. "Nope, these are mine. But just so there are no doubts, I'll have to taste them."

Nathalie giggled as he caught one nipple between his lips, gave it a thorough licking, then repeated on the other. "Yep, the taste is unmistakable. These are mine."

"What do they taste like?"

His eyes were smoldering as he answered. "They taste like my woman and love."

Impatient with the game she started, Nathalie pushed down her stretchy jeans and kicked them off. A moment later, they were lying on their sides facing each other, skin to skin. It felt amazing. "I wish I could fall asleep naked in your arms every night, and wake up like this every morning."

Andrew ran a gentle hand down her back and cupped her ass. "Me too. This is my definition of bliss."

A beautiful dream, but for now an impossible one. There was no way Andrew could move in with her. Aside from the problem of Fernando's aversion to change, there was simply not enough room. And moving to a bigger place where the three of them could be comfortable wasn't feasible either. For Nathalie to work and take care of her dad at the same time, living above the shop was an absolute necessity.

Nathalie felt tears prickling the back of her eyes. "Make love to me, Andrew."

"Your majesty's wish is my command."

7

ANDREW

*H*e'd promised Nathalie wicked things, but all Andrew wanted was to make slow and gentle love to her. To show her how much he cherished her with every touch, every kiss.

"I love you," he whispered as he palmed her face, looking into her tear-misted eyes. There was so much longing in her gaze. Andrew wished he could satisfy all of it, give her everything, solve all of her problems. But all he could manage for now was this suspended moment in time, a bubble of carefree pleasure that would provide her with a temporary distraction.

He kissed her, his tongue sliding into her welcoming mouth as his palm closed over her breast. Nathalie's eyelids slid shut, and he felt her body going soft in his arms. She was letting go of her stress, enjoying what he was doing to her.

Her hands brushed over his chest, caressing, following the contours of his muscles. "I love your body. You're so hard... all over."

"And you're so soft." One of her bra straps still clung to her shoulder, and Andrew pulled it off, touching the sexy lacy thing to his nose before throwing it down to the floor. He loved that she'd bought the front-closing bra especially for him, so he could get her naked faster.

His sweet Nathalie was a lustful woman. And he was one lucky bastard.

"You're so luscious." He plumped one breast before taking her nipple into his mouth.

Nathalie moaned softly and arched into him, her fingers digging into his hair as she held him to her. He licked and sucked until she pulled his head off and brought it to her other nipple.

Bossy ex-virgin.

When he lifted his head, he looked with satisfaction at her taut little peaks, reddened and pebbled from his attentions.

"You're so beautiful," he whispered.

She was still wearing a pair of lacy white panties that provided no cover whatsoever, and Andrew's shaft sprung to painful attention when he realized they had become transparent because they were soaked through.

Nathalie followed his gaze, and a soft blush colored her cheeks. "Take them off."

"Not yet, sweetheart." As he ran a finger over the gusset, Nathalie hissed in a breath. And as he pushed the fabric aside and slid his finger over her wet folds, her torso shot up, and she groaned.

"Shh, you need to stay quiet." He reminded Nathalie that her father was sleeping on the other side of the thin wall separating their bedrooms.

"Shit, I forgot," she whispered, and bit down on her lower lip.

"I'll tell you what." He drew lazy circles around her most sensitive spot. "For the next twenty minutes or so, I suggest you hold on to a pillow." He ran his finger down her slit. "Because you'll need it to muffle the screams." He winked and then dove between her legs.

With a giggle, she snatched a pillow. Spreading her thighs wide, she gave him better access to her center, where her little wet panties were wedged between her swollen lower lips. The view was sexy as hell, but Andrew doubted it was comfortable. God forbid this most sensitive area of her body would get chaffed.

Slowly, he pulled her lacy panties down her legs and threw them on the floor where they landed on top of the rest of the pile. Eyeing the mess, Andrew had the passing thought that he should push everything under the bed, or into the closet, to avoid a mad shuffle in case Fernando came knocking. Except, there was a naked beauty sprawled before him, her glistening sex too tempting to spare time on practicalities.

For a moment, Andrew just gazed, admiring the perfection and beauty of the female anatomy. Well, not any female's, his Nathalie's. He was still amazed at how quickly she'd taken to sex and how uninhibited she was. In fact, he was pretty sure that exposing herself to him like this was turning her on. Her hips were restless on the mattress, and she was teasing her own breasts, thrumming the nipples with her thumbs.

Fuck, he could explode just from watching Nathalie arouse herself. But she was getting impatient.

Lying on his belly, Andrew buried his face between her legs and inhaled deeply. Her fragrant womanhood was intoxicating. As he took his time luxuriating in her unique feminine musk, he rubbed his cheek on the soft flesh of her inner thigh, watching her arousal intensify.

Yeah, having his eyes on her most intimate flesh was definitely turning her on. It was like watching a flower bloom, the soft petals swelling to reveal the magic center where her dew was growing more copious by the second. With a groan, Andrew extended his tongue and lapped it up.

She hissed. "You're killing me."

He lifted his head. "With pleasure, I hope."

"I'm empty and needy, and you're taking too long."

Well, well. Gone was the shy virgin, replaced by an outspoken and demanding vixen.

And how hot was that?

Parting her soft pink petals with his thumbs, he pushed his tongue inside her, giving her what she wanted. Sort of. He knew she longed for a different part of his anatomy inside her, but if his goal was to give her multiple orgasms, he needed to start with his mouth.

Nathalie's fingers clawed at his head, holding him to her as if she feared he would stop. He had no intentions of leaving this heavenly place, not until he felt her falling apart and screaming into that pillow she'd dropped to hold on to his head.

Folding his tongue so it formed a spear, he kept thrusting it in and out of her at an ever-increasing speed, grunting with pleasure when he felt the walls of her channel start rippling around it.

It took no more than a minute of tongue fucking before she let go of his head to grab the pillow. Her pleasure cresting, Nathalie squeezed it hard over her face as she orgasmed violently, the sound of her screams muffled as her hips thrashed on the mattress.

And he hadn't even tongued her clit.

He should propose to her, like right now, because this woman was indeed a unicorn—one of a kind and magical.

Magically orgasmic, that is.

"Shit, I'm sorry," she mumbled into the pillow.

He stretched on top of her and tugged the thing away. "What for?"

Nathalie smiled shyly. "For coming too soon. It's supposed to be something guys worry about, right?"

He kissed her cute little nose. "Precisely. You, sweetheart, can climax as many times as you want. This was just a little one to whet the appetite."

"Oh, yeah? What have you planned next?"

"I wanted to spend some time with my ears squeezed between your thighs, eating you up, but now that I got you under me, I changed my mind." He nudged at her entrance.

She lifted her hips, and he gripped his shaft, guiding it inside her.

"Oh, God, Andrew, this is so good," she breathed as he glided inside her slick sheath. "I love the way you feel, so hard and yet so smooth and velvety. You fill me up so perfectly."

Did she have any idea how sexy she sounded? And how much he loved it?

Not dirty sex talk per se, it was nevertheless enough to

make his cock rock-hard and ready to shoot. But he gritted his teeth and commanded the bad boy to behave himself.

After all, he was supposed to be the older, experienced man who was teaching the innocent girl about the art of sex. Not a young buck who suffered from premature ejaculation.

8

NATHALIE

*A*s Andrew made love to her slowly, tenderly, Nathalie cherished every second of it. It wasn't that she hadn't enjoyed their previous lovemaking, which had been more intense. She had—tremendously—even that first one, which had been quite painful. But this was special, because it felt like so much more than sex.

Her heart swelling with love, the powerful emotion was overwhelming, and tears—the happy kind—were stinging the back of her eyes. For Andrew's sake, though, she managed to hold them back. The experience would be ruined for him if he saw her tearing up, and it wasn't like she could explain things while he was thrusting in and out of her.

"I adore you," he whispered, the emotion reflected in his eyes.

Nathalie clutched him to her as if she was never letting go. "I love you and adore you too."

Andrew slanted his mouth over hers and kissed her long and hard. Soon, though, his shallow thrusts deepened, becoming more urgent, and he buried his face in her neck, groaning into her skin to muffle the sounds. She held on tight as the pounding became furious, and as her pleasure swelled and then exploded, she bit down on Andrew's shoulder to stifle her own desperate cries.

Breathing hard, Andrew remained sprawled on top of her. Nathalie ran her hands up and down his muscled back and tight buttocks, closing her eyes as she concentrated on the powerful beat of his heart and the heavy weight of his sweat-slicked body.

She was officially blissed out.

When he regained his breath, Andrew pulled out and rolled onto his back, pulling her with him to lie on top of him.

"Your father must be sleeping like a rock if he didn't wake up from the racket."

"What racket?" Nathalie thought they'd been good about keeping it quiet.

"Towards the end, the bed frame was banging against the wall so hard, I wouldn't be surprised if your neighbors across the alley heard us."

"Oh, God." Nathalie buried her face in Andrew's warm chest. "It's so embarrassing."

She felt Andrew's chuckle reverberate through her body. "Forget about the neighbors. As long as your dad slept through it, we are fine."

"I hope our luck extends to the shower." She slid off him and went to her closet for a robe. "I should get you one too." She was going to order Andrew a robe first thing in the morning. Why hadn't she thought of it before? She should've done so already. The poor guy was spending nearly every night at her place, leaving in the early hours of the morning to go shower and change at his house. The least she could do was get him a robe and maybe a few changes of underwear.

Damn, she was such a lousy girlfriend.

Andrew sighed as he swung his legs down the side of the bed and picked up his trousers. "It's a shame the bathroom is out in the hallway."

Nathalie felt her cheeks heat up. She wished her living conditions were better. An en-suite bathroom that she didn't have to share with her father seemed like the epitome of luxury to her. Andrew's big bathtub had been so nice. His home was just an average house in a middle-class neighborhood, and yet it was several steps above her own. All she had to offer was a builder's grade shallow tub and a small shower.

Later, when they came back from their quick wash up, she put on her nightgown, while Andrew had to dress back in his slacks and dress shirt, making her feel guilty as heck.

"Could you stay and cuddle a little?"

"Of course." He plopped down on the bed and pulled her down, wrapping an arm around her and holding her tight against his body.

She snuggled into him, laying her cheek on his chest. Poor guy, he deserved to sleep comfortably in a decent sized bed, not to mention a clean pair of boxers or conversely nothing at all. She wondered if Andrew slept in the nude. Yeah, he probably did.

"I hate it that you're so uncomfortable."

He dipped his head and kissed her forehead. "To be with you, I'll sleep on the floor. But eventually, we need to find a solution. I want to spend my nights with you and wake up with you in my arms."

Nathalie sighed. "The only thing that is even remotely possible is for you to move in with me. Which I know is a step down from the standard of living you're used to. You have such a nice and spacious house, with a yard and everything."

"Wouldn't it be better if you moved in with me? Other than the master suite, I have two more bedrooms with a Jack-and-Jill bathroom between them—perfect for your father and a caretaker."

God, this was so tempting. And so generous of Andrew to offer. But even if she were willing to subject her father to the turmoil of getting used to a new house—which he probably never would—she and Andrew were not married.

Nathalie believed their commitment to each other was solid, but it was not the same as marriage. Not that an official certificate was a guarantee for a lasting relationship, but still, to move into your boyfriend's house together with your mentally disabled father—and his caretaker—was a big no-no with a capital N.

Even though she was convinced they would end up together, this would be a mistake of monumental proportions.

"That's so sweet of you. But I can't. For many reasons."

His arm tightened around her as if to let her know he wasn't going anywhere until they got to the bottom of this. "Let's hear them. One at a time."

She shifted a little, trying to get some space. But there was nowhere to go on her small bed. "Moving my dad away from his familiar environment may send him into a downward spiral, and I can't take the risk of his condition deteriorating because of this."

Andrew had no intention of letting her slink away and pulled her back, holding her tight against his body. "We can try to do it gradually. I can come and pick you up after work, and the three of us will spend some time at my place. Then I'll drive you back home. This way, Fernando can get used to my place one little step at a time, and if he shows signs of distress, we retreat a little, then resume the offensive. But each time we gain some more ground, and before you know it, you'll realize that the objective has been achieved."

Nathalie chuckled. "You sound like you're strategizing for battle. You're such a military guy."

Andrew shrugged. "Same principles apply. If you want to achieve a difficult goal, you have to come up with a good and detailed plan."

"We can try a couple of times, but we both work hard, and this will soon become exhausting."

"Now that you have some help in the kitchen, I hope that you won't be as pooped at the end of the day."

"Let's not put the cart before the horse. Vlad is just starting tomorrow. I was incredibly lucky with Jackson, but I can't expect this new kid to be as good. And anyway, I probably need one more helper if I really want to take it easy. But I can't afford it, not unless Jackson's new scheme works."

Andrew frowned. "What scheme?"

"He wants to sell my baked goods door-to-door to offices, roping in a bunch of his friends to do it on a commission-only basis. That's why he brought Vlad. If I'm to produce more than I already do, I need help in the kitchen."

Andrew harrumphed. "This kid is something else, I have to hand it to him. But I think he's on to something here."

"What do you mean?"

"Think about it. Your baked goods are delicious, and I'm not just saying it because I love you. If you can scale up production without compromising quality while maintaining reasonable costs, you can have a profitable business. Instead of doing everything yourself, you can manage others."

This sounded like a dream come true, but that was all it was—a pipe dream.

"There are a lot of ifs in this scenario. And I'm not a risk taker, I can't afford to be. First of all, I don't have the money to invest in equipment for something that may or may not work, and second, I don't have the time or the energy to pursue this."

"That's why Jackson's idea is so brilliant. He is conducting a small-scale test that doesn't require extra expenditure or investment of time on your part. He and his friends are willing to do the work free of charge."

Nathalie shifted in Andrew's arms so she could look at him. "Okay, so let's assume that Jackson's idea is a success. How does it help with our problem?"

Andrew smiled and leaned to kiss her nose. "It solves the issue of you being exhausted all of the time. When your workdays are more manageable, you can bring your father over to my place for an hour or two a day to get him accustomed to it."

"Sounds like a plan to me." Especially since it didn't

require any immediate action. First, Jackson had to execute his plan, then it had to be successful before the visits could commence. All of that would take a while, and even then there was no guarantee her father would respond well to the exercise.

Andrew yawned and pulled the comforter over them. "By the way, I spoke with my sister about the poor quality of caretakers we've been seeing, and she suggested we put an ad in the university's paper. As it's not going to be a full-time job, a student can be an inexpensive option. We might even get lucky with a psychology major."

As Nathalie's eyelids drooped and eventually collapsed over her eyes, she snuggled up closer, wrapping her arm around Andrew's middle. "Good idea, but can we talk about it tomorrow? That yawn of yours knocked me out."

He chuckled. "No problem, love. Goodnight."

9

ANANDUR

"*A*re you ready?' Anandur asked.

Shaking his head from side to side, Dalhu rubbed his neck. "As ready as I'll ever be."

"Okay. One, two, three!" Anandur let his pants drop.

He wasn't wearing underwear.

Dalhu groaned. "I don't know how you managed to talk me into it."

"Oh, don't be such a baby. I'm sure you've seen your share of naked men. I doubt there were private showers in the Doomers' camp. Though I bet none were as well-endowed as me."

"That's different. In the showers, men mind their own business and don't stare at each other's equipment. Just assume the pose and sit sideways on that stool, so I don't have to look at yours."

"Can you turn the portrait around? I don't remember the exact pose."

Carefully, holding it by the edges, Dalhu lifted the canvas off the easel and turned it so the front was facing Anandur.

"Got it." Anandur extended one leg to brace himself as he turned his torso to the right angle. "That's not the most comfortable position, just thought I should mention it."

"You wanted me to showcase your 'impressive musculature.' That's the best pose for it, so shut up and stop complaining."

"I'm not complaining, just stating a fact."

Dalhu rolled his eyes. "This must be punishment for my many sins. Never, like not in a thousand years, have I imagined myself drawing a naked man. And I've lived for nearly eight hundred already. So yeah."

"Not a man. A god."

Dalhu arched a brow but refrained from answering. Smart man. He was no match for Anandur who could carry on like this endlessly. Instead, the guy got busy with mixing oil paints on his palette.

Dalhu was getting better with those, and Anandur took credit for talking him into giving oils a try. At the start, the guy had been drawing exclusively with charcoal, refusing to touch oils—just because he'd been too big of a chicken to try. But then Anandur had bought him an Internet course on the subject and Dalhu had taken to the stuff like fish to water. He wasn't great at it, not yet, but Anandur had confidence in the guy.

"How is Annani's portrait progressing?" he asked, to banish the uncomfortable silence.

Done with the mixing, Dalhu paused, his gaze lingering on Anandur's thigh for a moment, before he touched his brush to the canvas. "I'm still working on it. Trying to get the right shades of red for her magnificent hair. But I'm afraid I'm not good enough to do justice to her ethereal beauty."

"I thought you said you're going to make hers in charcoal."

Dalhu paused with the brush in mid-air. "I started with black and white, but as hard as I tried, I couldn't get the results I wanted. It's impossible to express her magnificence without colors. But I'm just not good enough with them. Not yet."

"Maybe you should wait? Paint a few of the others before you tackle hers again."

"That is what I would like to do, but I'm afraid she'll be offended if I don't deliver her portrait soon."

Anandur smiled. Dalhu seemed to be still terrified of the goddess, in spite of all she had done to help Amanda and him. Without her help, the ex-Doomer would've probably been still rotting in a small cell down in the basement.

"Let me take a look. Maybe it's just in your head."

Dalhu put his palette on the counter and walked over to another easel, which held a canvas draped with what looked like a bed sheet.

Amanda must really love her Doomer to tolerate his mess and the destruction of her luxurious bed linens.

Despite her best efforts to keep it a surprise, the cat was out of the bag about the studio she was building for him. That kind of thing could've—maybe—worked on a human, but there was no fooling an immortal's sense of smell. Between the dust and the fresh paint he'd figured out that she was remodeling, and Amanda had given up on keeping it a secret—which in Anandur's opinion had been a foolish idea to begin with.

As Dalhu lifted the sheet off the painting, Anandur thought that he had never seen him looking more apprehensive. A whipping and an entombment hadn't fazed the dude as much as having his work critiqued.

"It's beautiful, but you're right, it still needs work." The image was true, and the lines were graceful. In fact, everything looked right, but it was just missing the something extra Anandur couldn't put his finger on. He wasn't an artist, so he couldn't even try to explain what it was. Maybe Dalhu was right, and it was impossible to capture Annani's beauty on canvas.

Dalhu's shoulders sagged, and he nodded. "I know. But what do I tell her when she asks about it?"

"The truth. Tell her you're not happy with how it's coming out, and that it needs more work. She'll understand."

Dalhu seemed doubtful. "She is a goddess," he said as if this fact explained everything.

"Yes, and she is a diva. But Annani is also kind and compassionate. She'll never throw a tantrum if there is a valid reason for her wishes not being met at the exact time and in the exact manner she would've liked them to. Don't worry about it; you will not fall out of favor with her because you're still struggling as an artist."

Dalhu closed his eyes momentarily and took a deep breath. "Thank you. For that alone, for the peace of mind you just gave me, your portrait is on the house. I'm not going to charge you for it, even though I deserve extra hazard pay for having to look at your naked ass."

Say what?

51

Anandur had never expected to pay for it in the first place. "Since when are you charging money for this?"

"Since Andrew has talked some sense into me. This is the only *job*—" he made air quotes—"I have right now, and I'd rather be embarrassed about charging for the pictures than about freeloading off Amanda. Who do you think pays for all the supplies? And now she builds a studio for me, which I'm sure is costing her a lot of money. I need to carry my own weight around here, and in my current situation, this is the only way I know how."

Well, Anandur couldn't argue with that. Dalhu's decision to charge money for his work was not only valid but necessary. It wasn't as if the guy was just passing the time during his recovery. For the foreseeable future, and probably indefinitely, this was going to be his only occupation, and therefore, his only source of income. He couldn't fault the guy for refusing to be a kept man.

"How much were you going to charge for it?"

Dalhu rubbed his neck, and Anandur could've sworn that there was a hint of blush in the guy's cheeks. "Five hundred?" he asked.

"Sounds reasonable enough. And when you get better, you could charge more. I'll tell you what. I'm going to drum up some business for you, spread the word about your talent." This was the least Anandur could do for getting his nude for free.

"I appreciate the offer, but don't, not yet. I'm in over my head with what I have. I'm putting the finishing touches on Syssi and Kian's wedding picture, I have yours and four other portraits, and I have Annani's. On top of that, tomorrow, I'm moving everything into my new studio, and I promised Amanda that I'd have the living room looking the same way I found it before I made it into my workspace."

"No problem, I'll wait a couple of weeks before I start harassing everyone and their mother to have their portrait done."

"That would be great."

For the next half an hour or so, Anandur shut his yap and let Dalhu paint. Because every time he engaged the guy in conversation, Dalhu would stop and hold the brush suspended in mid-air. Anandur wanted this session to be over sooner than later. His muscles were getting stiff from holding the unnatural pose.

Kian and Syssi's wedding portrait was right in his line of sight, and staring at it, he couldn't help thinking how happy Syssi had looked. Seeing her every day as he did, he hadn't noticed the change in her. But compared to her expression in that wedding portrait, he realized that lately she looked worried, preoccupied. It wasn't Kian; the guy still looked at his wife as if she was everything to him. Perhaps working for Amanda was stressing her out? Come to think of it, neither of them had mentioned discovering potential Dormants, and even Amanda's cheery disposition had been off lately. Yeah, that must be what was bothering the two.

The clunk of Dalhu's palette hitting the counter signaled the end of the session. "Okay, I think this is enough for today. Your face has started to look as if you're pushing out a load, so I assume you are cramping."

Thank you, sweet Fates in heaven.

Anandur pushed up to his feet and stretched, first up, and then side to side.

With a grimace, Dalhu turned his back to him and

grabbed his brushes and palette off the counter, dumping them in the kitchen sink. "It's good that Amanda is at work. She would have a conniption seeing me doing this. I'm supposed to wash them in a bucket first," he said with his back still turned to Anandur.

It was hilarious to hear the ex-Doomer use the word conniption, just another indicator of how well he was acclimatizing. Anandur pulled on his pants and pushed his feet inside his boots, then joined Dalhu in the kitchen. He opened the fridge and grabbed a beer.

Dalhu arched a brow. "Isn't it too early for that?"

"Yeah, but you don't have a coke, and I hate drinking plain water."

Dalhu shrugged. "That reminds me, how is it going with your Russian?"

"Not too great, but I have to ask, what's the connection between my aversion to drinking plain water and my Russian friend?"

Dalhu rinsed out the brushes and put them on a stack of paper towels to dry. "The few Russians I've met didn't like drinking water either. But as to your investigation, is there anything I can do to help? Not that I can offer much more than advice."

Anandur grimaced. "No, thank you. I've already gotten all the advice I need from my brother."

BHATHIAN

"William, my man, you've outdone yourself." Bhathian put his hand on the guy's shoulder.

Less than a week ago, after he'd started training the advanced class, Bhathian had had the splendid idea of building a makeshift simulator for weapons training. They had a shooting range down in the underground complex, but aiming at a stationary target was easy and not all that practical for what they would be facing in the field. Because unless he wanted to train them to be sharpshooters, which, of course, they could choose to do later if they wished, he wanted to train his students for hitting a fast moving target while in pursuit—like in real life situations.

With only a vague idea of what he wanted and basically no clue how to go about building something like that, he'd approached William, asking him to come up with a solution.

As always, William delivered, quickly and brilliantly. First, he and his geek squad had roped off a large part of the clan's second parking level. Then they'd scattered around a bunch of big planters, which in addition to the plants they were housing had been outfitted with life-sized cardboard cutouts of random pedestrians; males, females, and children. But the real kicker was the large remote-controlled toy trucks, each rigged to carry a cutout of a big man. William had devised a computer program to move them at the pace of a fast runner, but he'd thrown in the mix a few that were slower and didn't look like Doomers.

William puffed out his chest. "Glad to help. Have fun with it." He handed Bhathian the tablet with the program to run the thing and turned around, heading toward the bank of elevators.

"When are you going to join a class?" Bhathian called after him.

William didn't even turn around when he waved a hand and called back, "Never!"

Bhathian chuckled. Frankly, there was no need. As far as he knew, William never left the keep. But he sure as hell could've used the physical exercise. On second thought, though, the guy's time was too valuable to spend on anything other than technology and computers, and as health wasn't a concern, William's excess weight and lack of movement was nobody's business but his own.

Pulling out his phone, Bhathian group texted the students to meet him in the parking garage.

Today, he had the perfect opportunity to put the simulator to the test with the advanced class, which was smaller, with only nine trainees. Brundar had asked him to teach it today, and in exchange, he was going to take over Bhathian's tomorrow.

Damn, he would've loved to try out the obstacle course himself—

Wait, this was actually a great idea. He could get the Guardians together, and they could have some fun with it. Man, they were going to love this. Besides, it would be interesting to see how the trainees compared to the pros.

A few minutes later, the elevator burped out the nine students he'd been waiting for. Carol and eight guys. The woman was an ace in the shooting range, and he was curious to see how well she'd do with the simulator.

"Gather around, people." He waited until they formed a semicircle and fell silent.

"Today, instead of the shooting range, we are going to try something new." He handed each one a laser gun. "These look like toys, but they are not." He hefted one in his palm, demonstrating that it was weightier than it seemed. "These are specifically made for training and are designed to act and feel like the real thing. They weigh as much as an average handgun, and the recoil is just as forceful. The laser is, of course, harmless, but the targets are wired to respond, so when you hit them, a light will go off at the exact point of impact as if it were a real bullet."

"That's so cool," Ben said, and a murmur of assent followed.

Carol was the only one who frowned. "Aren't we supposed to have our own weapons? Fitted specifically to each of us so we can take into account the heft and the recoil? Brundar said that it was crucial for us to train with our own weapon."

"This is true. But you are not there yet. When you're ready and we have the equipment, we will train with it, but

57

for now, this will suffice. It's just too much work to replace all the targets after each of you makes the run and destroys them with real bullets. We will save it for the final stage."

Carol pouted. "I thought we were getting our own guns already."

"Next week, Brundar will decide what each of you gets, and you'll start training with it at the shooting range."

George aimed his gun at one of the stationary cutouts and fired.

Bhathian saw red. "If you ever fire a weapon again without permission you're out of the program, is that clear?"

"Yes, sir. But this is just a toy–" George shut his yap when Bhathian got in his face.

"Does this look like a game to you?"

Actually, it did, but George knew better than to say so.

"No, sir."

"Good." He turned to the rest of the class. "We follow the same safety protocol as in the shooting range, no matter what training instrument we use. It could be a wooden carving or a plastic toy. We treat it with the same respect we would if it were a live weapon. It needs to become an ingrained habit, second nature, not something you need to stop and think about. When the heat is on, an automatic response could mean the difference between life and death for a soldier. The split second slower response, the debili- tating panic, all of those can be eliminated by falling back on the power of habit. Even a bunch of civilian newbies like yourselves should be aware of how crucial this is. Hell, a class of human fifth graders would've already understood this."

"I'm sorry, sir. Won't happen again."

Bhathian nodded, letting George off the hook. He had to remind himself that this wasn't military training, and that these people were civilians, most of whom had no aspiration towards joining the Guardian Force. Still, the same rules applied to self-defense, so he couldn't go easy on them just because they weren't going to become soldiers. He knew for a fact that proper training and ingrained responses could one day save their lives.

"Carol, you go first. Please stand right here." He pointed with his shoe to the X he'd drawn with chalk on the concrete floor.

"Yes, sir." She stepped on top of it, holding her gun down by her side.

He pointed toward the obstacle course. "The stationary cutouts are bystanders. You don't want to hit any of those. When I activate the simulator, a bunch of Doomer cutouts will start zooming around, but not all of the moving ones will be enemy targets. You need to focus and shoot only at those who look like Doomers and carry weapons. You need to hit the heart or to the head, anywhere else doesn't count for points. And any civilian hit will cost you points."

"Will they be shooting at me?"

Bhathian chuckled. "No, but that's a good point. Maybe I'll have William make modifications for next time."

"Like Laser Tag, we can wear vests and shoot at each other," Ben offered.

"That's also a great idea." Or maybe not. If it felt too much like a game, they wouldn't take it seriously. Bhathian hoped Brundar would have better luck than him at whipping these people into shape. As it was, after two weeks of

59

basic training and one of advanced, the bunch still behaved like they were at summer camp. Trouble was, they also thought that they were battle ready.

Fools, they would get eaten alive by anyone with a shred of experience.

Bhathian still remembered his own training. Oleg had treated them like maggots, calling them names and making sure that they knew they were worthless. He'd hated the guy, but now he was starting to think that maybe Oleg had had it right. The worst thing for a trainee was to think he was better than he actually was and rush into danger unprepared. Better they underestimate their abilities than overestimate them. Perhaps he should adopt some of Oleg's attitude. Problem was, his students would just leave. They were here out of their own free will, and none of them felt bound by honor or some lofty aspirations to stay. The reality was that he needed to tread carefully if he didn't want them hightailing it out of his classroom and running to complain to Kian.

Bhathian shook his head. Things had definitely changed since he was a young man. And not all of them for the better.

"Okay, Carol, get ready, and go!" He pressed start on his tablet and Carol shot forward, her curls bouncing around her face as she jerked her head from side to side, following the erratically zooming toy cars.

Damn, he'd forgotten to tell her that she had three minutes until game over. Oh, well, she'd figure it out.

11

NATHALIE

"*Y*ou look lovely today, my beautiful girl." Her father kissed her cheek before going back to his newspaper.

Nathalie couldn't remember the last time she had so much energy by the end of her workday. She felt like a whole new person, fantastic. Even Papi had noticed.

Problem was, now that Vlad had practically taken over the kitchen, and Jackson was manning the register, she was spending most of her time up front—either waiting tables or taking orders. Her father, however, had to remain in the kitchen because the place was always packed and she couldn't have him take up a booth. Surprisingly, he had no problem sharing space with Vlad. He simply ignored him as if he wasn't there.

From time to time, Fernando would have more lucid days, and Nathalie suspected that during those times, he was aware that not everyone he saw was real.

Perhaps he thought Vlad was one of his apparitions.

God knew the kid looked like a character from a vampire or a zombie movie. And earlier today, she'd discovered that he was also freakishly strong, which given his stick-like limbs was more than surprising. This morning, her earring had caught in her hair, and when she'd pulled to get it loose, it had fallen off. She'd watched it bounce off her work table and disappear behind the sheeter. But as she grabbed the broom to try and sweep it from under the thing, Vlad had lifted the two–hundred-pound machine with one hand, holding it up while reaching for her earring with the other. He hadn't uttered a grunt, hadn't broken a sweat, and once the retrieval had been accomplished, he'd lowered the machine slowly and carefully. The touchdown had been barely audible.

Though this incident had been the most notable, there was more. Vlad worked from six in the morning until eleven, took a break for three hours and then returned until closing. He never looked tired, and he never complained about his feet or his arms hurting, though they had to, at least at the beginning. After all, the only manual labor he had done before coming to work for her was playing the guitar.

Not that she was complaining. Vlad was the reason she could start her day at six in the morning instead of four. Now that he was in charge of preparing the dough for the next day, which he was doing every evening by the end of his shift, her morning routine had been cut in half. A huge improvement.

This new generation sure had better work habits than all of those that came before them. She'd never employed people as dedicated and hardworking as Jackson and Vlad.

And judging by the cars they drove, it wasn't as if the teenagers were hurting for money.

Hell, how did she become so lucky?

Or was she?

"Hey, Nathalie, should I flip the sign to closed?" A tray piled with dirty dishes in his hands, Jackson passed her by on his way to the kitchen, flashing her that disarming smile of his that was charming the customers into leaving him big tips.

Shit, was it closing time already?

Her days sure seemed shorter and, preoccupied with her thoughts as she'd been, Nathalie hadn't noticed that it was done. Not that one could tell by looking at the booths—most were still occupied.

"I'll do it," she told him and hurried to the door. Nathalie hated when people came in and she had to tell them the coffee shop was closed.

Jackson was back with the empty tray, clearing another table. And as she watched him from her station next to the register, the insidious doubts started crawling around her brain again. There was something off about these guys, but she couldn't put her finger on it. And she still had her suspicions about Andrew and Bhathian's motives.

Funny how her doubts always flew out the window when she was with Andrew, only to return when he wasn't there. She glanced at her watch. What was holding him up? Was he stuck in traffic? He should've arrived by now. As worry squeezed her heart in a vice, she berated herself for imagining worst case scenarios—like his car mangled on the side of the road and paramedics loading him onto a gurney.

She hadn't been like that before meeting Andrew. With

how deeply she used to be inside her own head, conversing with voices only she could hear, there hadn't been enough cerebral space left to imagine catastrophes. It hadn't happened immediately after she'd fallen in love with Andrew either. This was recent. A feeling of unease that wouldn't go away.

She lasted about a minute before pulling out her phone and calling him.

"Hi, sweetheart. I'm just parking the car. I'll be there in a moment."

"Okay." She clicked the call off and sagged against the counter. God, she was such a worrywart. How would she manage to be a mother and let her kids out the door? She'd have panic attacks on a daily basis. Or hourly. She really needed to work on this.

As Andrew burst through the door, Nathalie's face split into a big smile.

"Sorry that I'm late, love." He reached for her over the counter, pulling her toward him for a quick kiss.

"Traffic was that bad?" she asked.

"Nothing out of the ordinary, but I stopped by Syssi's place to pick up the resumes she collected for us. She says there are at least two she really liked, and she marked them with a red pen."

That's right, Andrew's sister had offered to post an ad in the university's newspaper, but Nathalie hadn't expected her to do it so promptly. And to interview the prospects as well.

"It's so nice of her to put so much effort into it. I would've thanked her in person, but you haven't introduced us yet." She made a face.

For some reason, Andrew was in no hurry for her to meet his family. So yeah, there were many extenuating factors, and arranging a meeting considering her limitations was difficult. And yet, if Andrew had really wanted them to meet he would've found a way.

With a sheepish expression on his handsome face, he walked around the counter and pulled her into his arms, fusing his mouth to hers in a smoldering kiss. His underhanded tactic worked, and as desire coursed through her, hot and molten, it robbed her of reason, and Nathalie forgot that she was supposed to be peeved at him.

When Andrew let go of her, she swayed on her feet a little, and he quickly wrapped his arm around her waist. "What's wrong, sweetheart? Are you feeling okay?"

She slapped his shoulder. "I'm perfectly fine. You just didn't let me breathe. Probably figured that asphyxiation will make me forget all about your stalling tactics. I don't understand why you haven't introduced us yet."

"Let's go upstairs and have this conversation there, shall we?"

"Fine." Nathalie turned toward Jackson. "You're okay closing up by yourself?" she asked.

He rolled his eyes. "It's the same answer I give you every evening when you ask; yes, I'm okay."

"No need to get snappy. Just don't forget to lock up."

"I won't."

In the kitchen, she said goodbye and thank you to Vlad, and then collected her father. "Come, Papi, your show starts in less than fifteen minutes. You don't want to miss the beginning."

Fernando folded his newspaper, put his coloring pencils

away in their box, and followed her and Andrew upstairs. He ducked into his room to turn on the television, while she and Andrew continued into the den.

"What did you get?" She eyed the brown paper bag Andrew was holding.

"A bottle of wine."

"Did you stop by the supermarket as well?"

"No, this is a gift from Syssi's husband."

"Aha."

Andrew rubbed his neck before taking her hand and pulling her toward the couch where he insisted she sit on his lap.

"It's not that I don't want you to meet my sister. On the contrary, it's just that I don't know how to make it work. You'll feel awkward about having your father drag along, and telling Syssi to come see you at your shop doesn't sound like the right thing to do either. But now that you can take off earlier, leaving Jackson and Vlad to take care of things, maybe we can invite Syssi to dinner at my house or at a restaurant, and then you won't feel weird about having your father there."

"What about her husband?"

Andrew grimaced. "I guess we have to invite him too."

"I was under the impression that you like the guy, so what gives?"

"I do like him, it's just that I'm not too thrilled about you meeting him."

"Why?"

"Because he is an incredibly handsome bastard, and if you start drooling all over him, I'll be tempted to make my sister a widow."

Nathalie giggled. "First of all, I'm sure he is not handsomer than you. He can't be, not to me. But in any case, I promise to save all my drooling for you."

12

ANANDUR

"Still nothing?" Anandur scratched his beard as he looked at William's computer screen. Not that he knew what he was looking at. A quick sidelong glance at Onegus reassured him that he wasn't the only one. His boss seemed just as dumbfounded by what the guy was showing them.

Good, so Anandur wasn't a complete moron for not getting it. Onegus was supposedly a smart guy, so he was in good company.

"Look at the patterns. Obviously, they have a device on board that interferes with transmissions." William pointed to the graph. "There is talking, but it's impossible to understand with the interference. I'm running it through one more program to see if I can filter it out."

"I don't get it. The boat must communicate with the shore, doesn't it?"

"They can either turn it off when they need the channel open or use cellular through a private satellite like we do. The bug is a radio transmitter."

"Damn. What about the detective monitoring the marina? His people must've seen something by now. Don't tell me that nothing suspicious happened before the boat left."

Onegus shook his head. "Nope. The captain and one other crew member went shopping for supplies and returned with a bunch of paper bags, nothing big enough to carry a person. Not unless they chopped him to pieces. And later Alex came on board carrying a briefcase. So as far as we know, there is no one other than Alex and his crew onboard. The only other possibility is that someone swam up to the boat and boarded it during the night. But that doesn't fit our scenario, so it's of no interest to us. If he smuggles drugs or criminals, I'm happy to leave it up to the human police to catch him."

"Fuck."

Lana had been gone for a week, and Anandur had hoped that the bug he'd planted would provide the information they needed. He was tired of keeping up the charade and wanted to end the thing with Lana. It wasn't that he didn't enjoy spending time with her—she was a hot piece of ass— but he was going nowhere with her. Getting Lana to talk about her boss, or talk at all, was like pulling teeth. Her poor English aside, the woman was more interested in screwing him than talking to him.

"How are you doing with your Russian?" Onegus asked.

"Getting nowhere."

"Keep pushing. As long as she doesn't get suspicious and dump your ass, there is no reason to stop."

"Yeah, I figured that much."

With a grimace, Anandur pulled out his phone and texted her. *Are you back?*

Lana had warned him not to call her while she was gone. Apparently, Alex had a strict policy about his crew fraternizing with other males. She was fine with breaking the rules—she just didn't want her boss to catch her.

The burner phone she used to communicate with Anandur had a shitty reception, so unless the Anna was back at the marina, the text wouldn't go through. But the excursion was supposed to be only a week long, so by now the boat should be sitting pretty in its dock.

He had to wait for a good ten minutes before she answered.

Come at 8. Dock.

Damn, he wasn't looking forward to another evening with the Russian. He was growing tired of her. With a sigh, Anandur pushed his phone back into his pocket. "I'm on for tonight."

"Good luck." Onegus clapped him on the back before leaving William's office, or lab, or whatever the guy wanted to call the cavernous room that was strewn with assorted desks and enough equipment to open a RadioShack.

Later, when Anandur got back to his apartment, he wasn't surprised to find it deserted. Damn, he hated how empty it felt. Not that Brundar was such great company when he was there, but still, it wasn't as lonely with him around. And besides, he needed the bastard to help clean the place. It was filthy, and Anandur had no intention of tackling the job by himself.

Okidu, who'd been keeping their place from turning into a pigsty, had stopped showing up lately. Probably Syssi's doing. She was treating the butler as if he were a real living breathing guy, making sure he wasn't taken advantage of or overworked.

Anandur loved the girl, he really did, but this was beyond nice and into the realm of stupid.

It was like worrying about the working conditions of a vacuum cleaner—one of those disk-shaped ones that were programmed to work on their own while the owners were gone. Actually, he should get one. Problem was, the thing couldn't pick up dirty clothes off the floor or swallow empty beer cans.

Oh well, it wasn't like his apartment needed to be presentable. After all, he never used the place for hookups. With a shrug, he headed to the bathroom and got in the shower. After he was done, he sprayed his face with cologne, even though he hadn't shaved, then sprayed a little more under his armpits and down his crotch. Smelling good all over never hurt.

The ladies loved it.

Looking over his modest clothes selection, Anandur chose an old pair of Levi's and a short-sleeved button-down that had seen better days. The thing had shrunk in the wash, and he couldn't even button it over his chest without it gaping in between the buttons. He left it partially open with his chest on full display.

As he examined his reflection in the mirror, Anandur had the passing thought that he was intentionally dressing up like a man-whore.

Did it bother him, though?

Nah, it was all good. Playing the gigolo was fun. After all, a guy had to have an awesome physique, well-polished charm, and impressive skills in the bedroom to be successful in that profession.

Anandur prided himself on all three.

Whistling to the tune of David Lee Roth's *I'm Just a Gigolo*, he grabbed the keys to the loaner truck and headed out to the marina.

13

SYSSI

"*L*ily, can you take a look at this? I need you to double check it." Syssi called the new postdoc Amanda had hired.

When she'd return to the lab, Syssi had been overjoyed to see the new face that had replaced David as their computational researcher. Lily was just as good, if not better, and Syssi no longer even bothered to try fixing things herself. At the first hint of a problem, it was Lily to the rescue.

"Let me see," Lily said as she took Syssi's seat.

Syssi left her to do her thing and walked over to Hanna's desk. "So, Hanna, you need to tell me your secret. How did you manage to lose so much weight while I was gone? Don't tell me the protein bars and the shakes were what did the trick."

Hanna smiled and pushed to her feet, then struck a pose, one leg forward and a hand on her hip. She must've gone down from a size eighteen to a size twelve since Syssi had last seen her. Pretty impressive.

"Wow, you look amazing."

"I do, right?" Hanna turned around in a slow circle, showing her backside. "Just look at this butt, I can wear jeans now. And I'm not done. I want to lose at least another ten pounds."

"So, how did you do it? Or is it a secret?"

As Hanna sat back down, her brows dipped low on her forehead. "Don't tell me you're thinking about going on a diet…"

Syssi chuckled. "I could lose a few pounds, but I figure it's not worth the effort. Though I'm still curious about how you did it."

Hanna sighed. "After I got so sick of the shakes that I couldn't stomach going one more day drinking that shit, I finally decided to shell out the money for a visit with a dietitian. I've already tried every diet on the planet, and nothing ever worked. The most I've managed to lose was five to ten pounds, and then I'd gain them back with interest. So my mom heard about this lady and made an appointment for me. And guess what was her brilliant advice?"

"What?"

"Eat less and move more. Like I didn't know that already. But she managed to drive it home that all those books and magazines with their fad diets of food combinations, food exclusions, supplements, timing and so on are just a huge money machine and that there are no tricks and no shortcuts. Her whole approach is eating small quantities of good unprocessed food, mainly plant-based, combined with daily physical activity."

"I'm sure there is more to it. If it were so simple, we wouldn't have an obesity epidemic in this country."

"You're right. The secret is planning, measuring,

preparing, scheduling, and monitoring." Hanna reached behind her and lifted her purse off the back of her chair, then pulled out a medium-sized red journal. "You see this? This is my bible. In here, I write down my weekly plan. I do it every Sunday. It includes everything; a list of meals, recipes, grocery shopping list, an exercise schedule, and so on. I prepare and freeze all the meals that I can make ahead of time on the weekend, so I can just grab a container and go. On Fridays, I meet with the dietitian and she weighs me, checks my journal, making sure that I followed up on everything I wrote, and makes adjustments as needed to next week's plan."

"Don't tell me you don't cheat."

Hanna rolled her eyes. "Come on, I'm only human. But just a little."

"I'm so proud of you. I don't know if I could've been this disciplined. It requires so much focus. But thanks for telling me. I'll pass along your newfound wisdom."

"Please do. If I can do it, anyone can. And I hope that, in time, it will become a habit, so I won't need to weigh and measure and plan everything—just eyeball it and get it right."

"I'm sure you will."

Now that she understood how hard Hanna was working on this, Syssi felt bad about going out to lunch with Amanda and just ordering whatever she wanted. Out of solidarity, she should order a small salad and skip dessert.

But Gino's lasagna was so good…

Oh, boy, she was one lucky girl to get away with eating something as decadently delicious and fattening as that dish without worrying about gaining weight. Though on second thought, being immortal didn't guarantee a svelte figure, as evidenced by William.

That was it. Tonight, she was going to hit the treadmill down at the gym. Lately, her physical activity had been limited to sexcapades with Kian. Pleasurable, numerous, and often exhausting, they nonetheless weren't enough to keep her in shape.

"Are you ready, darling?" Amanda sauntered over and handed Syssi her purse. "I'm starving."

She slung it over her shoulder. "Yeah, me too. I was just thinking about Gino's lasagna."

"One of the best items on his menu." Amanda opened the door, and they headed down the corridor to the elevators.

As they passed by the heavy door leading to the emergency stairs, an involuntary tingle of anxiety rushed down Syssi's arms. It happened every time, reminding her of how it all started. She wondered how many times she would have to pass by this door before having no reaction to it. Except, the fear was puzzling. After all, despite the scary events surrounding her first encounter with Kian, it was still the best thing to ever happen to her.

The drive to Gino's was short, and when they arrived, Syssi was glad that they got there after the lunch hour rush was over, so a table was available out on the porch. It was a beautiful day, sunny but not too warm, the smell of freshly cut grass carried by a gentle breeze. The perfect weather for sitting outside.

Amanda accepted the menu from the waiter but didn't even open it. "Where is Gino?"

The waiter smiled. "Sitting at the hospital and waiting for his eleventh grandchild to arrive."

Amanda clapped her hands. "This is wonderful. Do you know if it's a boy or a girl? I want to buy a present."

The guy shook his head. "Sorry, I don't."

Amanda waved a dismissive hand. "Don't worry about it, I'll find something to buy for the baby that works for either gender."

"That's very nice of you, thank you."

They placed their orders, a lasagna and a big garden salad to share, and Amanda added a bottle of wine.

"What are we celebrating? Other than Gino's new grandkid, that is."

Amanda shrugged. "I don't know. I just need something for a pick-me-up."

"You too? I've been having a bad feeling lately, and I don't know why. Like something terrible is going to happen. It's not a vision or a foretelling, so I'm not freaking out, but I am worried."

"Maybe it's hormonal." Amanda smiled her wicked witch smile. "Maybe you're pregnant?"

Syssi snorted. "I wish. It's so embarrassing. When I didn't get my period on time, I was sure I was. Luckily, I didn't say anything to Kian before having Bridget check. Imagine how I felt when she explained that immortal females don't ovulate every month like humans. That it's a random, on demand kind of thing. You might have thought to mention it to me before I made a fool of myself."

"I'm sorry. It just didn't cross my mind. It's not something that I think about. But now you know."

Syssi sighed. "Yeah, now I know. I was a little bummed. But on the other hand, I'm not ready to be a mother. So what's your problem? Is it adjusting to living with Dalhu?"

Amanda waved a hand. "No, I love having him around, even with all his mess, which I tease him about mercilessly. It's not that. Have you noticed the lousy subjects we are getting lately? I haven't seen even one with as much as a hint of talent."

"I know. I even raised the hourly pay in our ad to lure more test subjects. Who knows, maybe that's why we are getting people without any talent. They come for the pay, not out of curiosity to see if there is anything special about them."

Deep in thought, Amanda tapped a manicured fingernail on the glass table. "We should venture outside the university," she finally said.

"Can we? Is it okay to recruit from the outside?"

"Sure it is. You can put an ad on Craig's List, or some other internet site where people look for odd jobs."

The friendly waiter showed up with a basket of Gino's famous fresh rolls, still steaming from the oven, and the wine.

Syssi waited until he was gone. "So let's do it. At the rate it's going now, we are never going to find new Dormants."

Amanda lifted the napkin covering the rolls to let the steam out. "Yeah. There are a couple of problems with that. First, we might get some unsavory characters we don't want to deal with. Second, with the scarcity of jobs that's going on now, we might get inundated with applications. We won't be able to handle it."

"Can we hire another assistant? If we have the budget for it, that is. Someone who will be in charge of only that. Screening the applicants, making sure to schedule only the most promising ones, handle the paperwork… God, I hate the paperwork. With the stacks of legal documents each one has to sign, you'd think we subject them to open brain surgery." If she could hand that to someone else her workday would be much more enjoyable. She liked conducting the testing and interviewing most of the applicants. In general, the people who applied were friendly and polite, but occasionally she would get someone who wasn't.

"Do you think we should hire one of ours for this?" Amanda poked one of the rolls to check if it was still hot.

Syssi considered it for a moment. "That's a good idea. But who would want an entry job like that? It's not as if any of you—sorry, us, I keep forgetting—needs to work for money. Those who work do it either because they want more than what their shares in the family business provide, or to do something they like doing. I can't imagine anyone getting excited over boring paperwork."

Amanda took a bite of the roll and chewed for a moment, her brows doing a little dance on her forehead in sync with her thoughts. On anyone else, it would've looked funny, but Amanda didn't have an expression that didn't look gorgeous. "Maybe one of the teenagers on summer break would want the job. They don't get their share until they reach twenty-five. Even though a high school student will be inexperienced, the upside is that we can tell her the truth about what we are looking for."

Syssi arched a brow. "Do we know exactly what to look for?'

Amanda sighed. "No, not really."

14

NATHALIE

"The dough for tomorrow is ready in the fridge, and I also pounded the butter inside the large Ziploc bags like you showed me." Vlad removed his apron and hung it on the peg with his name on it.

On a whim, while ordering extra aprons for the guys, Nathalie had also ordered three wooden pegs, each with its custom-carved name plaque. One for Vlad, one for Jackson, and one for herself. She'd chosen a spot by the back door on the small stretch of wall before the staircase began, and Andrew had done the drilling and hanging part.

It was official now. Jackson and Vlad were part of her team, and all was right with the world. Well, not really, but she couldn't help the buoyant mood. There was definitely something to be said for the extra shuteye she'd been getting lately. Since Vlad had arrived about a week ago and had taken over most of her kitchen chores, she was waking up later in the morning, and feeling more rested and ener-getic with each passing day. Heck, she didn't remember when was the last time she had felt so good. So happy.

Not that good sleep and hardworking teammates were the only reasons for her happiness. She had so much to be grateful for. Jackson already felt like part of her family, and once she'd gotten over Vlad's vampiric appearance, she had discovered that he was a sweet guy under his goth garb, and had adopted him too.

And then there was Andrew. Nathalie smiled. Today they were going to take her father to Andrew's house for the first time. Papi had been having a good day so far. There hadn't been much talking to people that weren't there, and he'd even said hello to Vlad. Which was a big improvement because up until today he'd been ignoring the kid—refusing to acknowledge his presence.

"Come on, Jackson; we are going to be late." Vlad called his friend who was still collecting dirty dishes from the tables.

"Go on, Jackson. I'll finish up. You guys need to get moving."

Finally, they had a gig lined up, opening for some heavy metal rock band that she'd never heard of but according to the guys was a big deal.

Jackson dropped the dishes in the sink, then took off his apron and hung it next to Vlad's. "I wish you could come see our performance."

"I wish it too. But unless you and your friends come play in my shop, I'm afraid it will have to wait." She couldn't take her dad to a rock concert. Come to think of it, even if they played right here in her shop, their music would probably upset him. Jackson had had her listen to a recording, and although she'd like it, Papi certainly wouldn't. He would call it noise.

Jackson stopped in his tracks. "That's a cool idea. I'll run it by them."

"Jackson!" Vlad held the door open.

"Coming! Bye, Nathalie, see you tomorrow."

"Break a leg!" she called after them.

"Thanks."

Nathalie finished washing the dishes and wiped clean the two tables Jackson hadn't gotten to before leaving. Done for the day, she took a satisfied look at her little café. Profits had been good lately, and she appreciated the added peace of mind of finally having enough money not only to cover her monthly bills but to start paying off some of her debt.

Thank you, God. She offered her gratitude to a God she'd been staunchly proclaiming not to believe in.

Aware of the irony, Nathalie shook her head as she flicked the lights off before climbing upstairs to join her father and Andrew in the den. Last she'd checked on them, they'd been sharing the couch and watching a game. It was nice to think that they were forming some kind of a connection, but the truth was that Papi didn't always remember who Andrew was, or even recognize him as someone he'd already met. Some days, he called him son; others he clasped his hand with a polite smile, looking up at him as if he were a stranger.

"Hi, guys, ready to go?"

"Go where?" her father asked.

Damn, he'd already forgotten. "We are going to Andrew's house."

As Fernando cast Andrew a sidelong glance, she was relieved that he at least remembered who Andrew was.

"Why?"

"He is inviting us to dinner. Remember? We talked about it this morning."

"Ah, Okay." He pushed to his feet, clearly having no recollection of the conversation but pretending that he did. "I'll just put my shoes on."

"We will wait here."

As Papi shuffled to his room, Andrew got up and pulled her into his arms. "One day at a time, sweetheart. It's going to be alright. After several visits, he'll remember it."

Trouble was, she knew he wouldn't. Most days, Fernando still believed that this wasn't his home and that for some reason she was keeping him away from his real one—the old house they'd sold years ago. So the chances of him remembering Andrew's home were nil. All she was hoping for was that he wouldn't freak out. This would be progress enough for her.

She lifted her face and kissed Andrew, just a little peck on the lips, saving her passionate kisses for later. "What did you make for dinner?"

Andrew chuckled. "Make? Me? Did I ever give you the impression that I can cook?"

"You've been a bachelor for so long; I would think that you'd know how to prepare something simple for yourself."

"Sorry to disappoint. But all I've learned is how to buy frozen meals and put them in a microwave. Dinner tonight is going to be the Chinese takeout I have in my car, reheated and served on nice porcelain dishes."

"Well, at least there is that. Though I'm surprised you have bothered to buy porcelain dinnerware."

"It was a gift from my grandma."

"Aha, that makes more sense. When was the last time you used them?"

Andrew looked a little embarrassed when he said, "This is going to be the first."

She was touched. Evidently, he'd never invited any of his other girlfriends to an elegantly served dinner at his house. But then another thought flashed through her mind as she imagined the heirloom china accumulating dust in some forgotten kitchen cabinet. "I hope you washed them."

"I may not be a great housekeeper, but I'm lucky enough to have one. Usually Milly comes only once a month, but I asked her to clean the house again yesterday, including the dishes."

"You never told me that you have a housekeeper." Nathalie put her hands on her hips and cast him a suspicious look. "Is she attractive?"

He nodded. "Milly is beautiful."

Was he messing with her? By the way his lips were twitching, he was. She was going to pay him back. With interest. "You'll have to fire her. I'm a jealous girlfriend, and the idea of you alone in your house with a beautiful woman infuriates me."

"That's why you need to move in with me. You'll keep an eye on me so I'm not tempted by Milly." The twitch turned into a big grin, and a chuckle escaped his throat. "Sorry, I can't keep it up. Milly is beautiful, for a sixty-something-year-old grandma, who's been happily married to her high school sweetheart for the past forty-something years."

"So why is she cleaning houses?"

Andrew shrugged. "I don't know. Maybe she's bored, or maybe their pension money is not enough. Not something you ask a person. All I know is that I can trust her with a key and that she gets the job done. I'm not a messy person, and I'm hardly ever home, so it's not like she has a lot to do."

Nathalie slapped his arm. "Did you have fun tormenting me like this?"

Andrew pulled her into a hug. "Yes, and I like that you're jealous. But you have nothing to worry about. You're the only one for me. And you know it."

Sweet man.

She might not be an expert on relationships, but a guy who was investing so much time and energy into making theirs work was a keeper. "I love you," she said and kissed him again.

Definitely husband material—

Except for the secrets that she was sure he was hiding from her, and all the other things he conveniently forgot to mention.

15

ANANDUR

"Come." Lana grabbed Anandur's hand and pulled him behind her.

"Where are you taking me?"

"It's a surprise."

"Should I close my eyes?"

"No need, we are here."

They were standing on the dock next to an old, rather small boat. Anandur cocked a brow. "So where is the surprise?"

She pointed at the yacht. "This is the surprise. The owner ask me to look at boat for the next five days when he go to New York. So it's all ours until he come back."

"Sweet." Anandur followed her inside.

The layout of the boat's interior was similar to that of a motorhome, compact and functional, and it seemed that Lana had been busy since she'd gotten back. Something smelled delicious. The table had been set with disposable plates and flatware, and the source of the smell was a big oval platter hosting a grilled chicken surrounded by baked potatoes. Other than the main course and a bottle of vodka, there was no other food or beverage on the table.

Anandur smirked. A typical Russian meal.

He pulled Lana into a hug. "You cooked for me. I'm touched." He kissed her plump lips.

"Not me. Renata cook."

Anandur lifted a brow. "You told her about us?"

She shrugged and took a seat. "It's okay. She say nothing to boss."

That was a good little nugget of information. The women were more loyal to each other than to Alex. It was an opening he might use to his advantage. "Thank you for arranging this, and give Renata my thanks for the food. It smells amazing."

Lana surprised him when she mumbled something under her breath that sounded a lot like grace. A hurried sign of the cross followed before she attacked the chicken with a pair of poultry scissors.

Interesting.

Anandur had heard her say *Jesu* several times, but he'd thought nothing of it. A lot of people did it without being religious in the slightest, but it seemed that Lana was.

"You want I put on your plate or take yourself?" Lana paused with half of the chicken skewered on a carving fork.

Anandur lifted his plastic plate with his palm, propping it from below, so it wouldn't collapse under the weight of the chicken. "Thank you."

She smiled and pushed the halved bird off the carving fork with her finger, dropping it on Anandur's plate. The thing held, even when she added a generous portion of potatoes. He wasn't a big fan of poultry, but the chicken was

87

done perfectly, and as he chased his first bite with a chunk of potato, Anandur gave Lana the thumbs up and nodded his appreciation.

Satisfied, she poured vodka into the two plastic tumblers and handed him one. "Salute!"

"Salute!" he mumbled with a full mouth as he touched his tumbler to hers.

Lana was as much of a hearty eater as Anandur, and as he shoved the last tasty morsel into his mouth, she wasn't far behind.

"This was good." He rubbed his stomach, pretending to be full. A whole chicken wouldn't have filled him, but it wasn't as if he wanted to flaunt his excessive appetite. The more normal he managed to appear, the less suspicious the cagey Russian would be.

Damn, no matter how good his boy-next-door act was, she would be suspicious as hell if he tried the stuff Brundar had suggested. She'd probably kick him out. Unless she was into that kind of shit. Problem was, he couldn't think of a clever way to casually weave it into the conversation so he could observe her response.

"I'm happy you like. I'll tell Renata." She leaned to refill his tumbler.

The bottle was almost gone, and Lana wasn't showing any signs of loosening. He hoped she'd brought more than one.

She followed his gaze with a smirk. "Don't worry, I have more."

"Phew, I was worried for a minute." Anandur pretended to wipe away sweat from his brow.

Lana pushed to her feet, walked over to one of the wall

cabinets, and pulled out a bottle. "Here," she said as she put it next to Anandur.

"Don't you think the owner would notice that his stash of vodka got smaller while he was away?"

Lana shrugged. "I buy him new bottles."

Without thinking, Anandur lifted up to pull his wallet out of his pocket. He took out a couple of twenties and handed them to Lana. "My contribution."

She shoved the two bills back. "No. You keep your money. You need it. I make more money than you."

Who could've known that the tough iron lady was hiding a heart of gold? Which made him feel even worse about his deception. *Just remember what's at stake, buddy. Women's lives are ruined forever with this one's help.*

"I may be a lowly deck boy, but I have my pride." He pushed the money back.

Lana took it, separated one bill and tucked it into her pocket, then handed him the other. "The vodka is cheap."

He could live with that. "So, I guess your boss is a nice guy if he pays you top dollar." Anandur returned the twenty to his wallet and stuffed it back in the pocket of his jeans.

Lana harrumphed. "Alexander is pretty, but not nice."

"Why? Because he doesn't allow you girls to bring guys onboard?"

"This too." Lana grabbed the plastic plates and tossed them into a paper bag. She took the empty platter to the sink and started washing it.

"So, tell me what other naughty things your boss does. Is he into kinky sex games? Does he tie you up and blindfold you?"

This was probably his best and only shot at the subject,

and Anandur inhaled deeply to catch any changes in Lana's scent. But it seemed that kinky games were not her thing because there was no change in her level of arousal, which had been basically neutral throughout their meal.

So much for Brundar's brilliant plan.

Damn.

"He likes more than one woman in bed. Sometimes two, sometimes three, and sometimes more. Is that kinky?"

"No, that's living a dream."

Lana angled the spigot so the water spray hit Anandur in the face. "My mama say all men are pigs. She is right."

Anandur laughed as he wiped his face with a paper napkin. "Your mama is wise. Men are despicable creatures who think about nothing other than sex, but women are not always better, true?" He pinned her with a hard stare.

Lana seemed to shrink under his gaze, and her face twisted with guilt. She turned her back to him and continued washing the platter that was probably already clean.

For a moment, the silence hung heavy in the cramped space, and Anandur thought Lana had shut the door on that conversation, but then she said, "Some people so stupid and weak. They are like cows, and the bad wolves catch them. This is how the world is." She turned around to face him, drying the platter with a dishtowel. "I'm strong. I'm not a cow like the stupid American girls. I never fall into the trap of the pretty wolf."

"So there are cows, and there are wolves. Any other animals?"

She pursed her fleshy lips. "Snakes, people who see the wolf and hide from him but not say something to cows.

Weasels help the wolf. And the lion who eat the wolf and the cow."

Anandur chuckled. Her analogy was spot on. "And what animal are you?"

Lana shrugged, but he could smell the stench of guilt coming from her. "I am weasel. I help the wolf because wolf keep me safe from lion."

"Aha, but here is the thing, baby. The wolf will gladly feed you to the lion to protect its own hide. You can never count on the son of a bitch not to betray you."

"I know." She put the tray into a clean paper bag. "And I watch wolf carefully, but I have no other way."

"How about helping the lion? That must be better than helping the wolf. And I don't think lions eat weasels."

She laughed, but it was a sad laugh. "I don't know any lions."

"Sure you do." With a roar, Anandur leaped out of the chair and pounced on her. He threw Lana over his shoulder and went searching for the bedroom.

16

CAROL

"*H*ey, guys, you want to go out tonight?"

The class was over, and Carol didn't have any plans, which sucked. Her bestie had bailed on her, using finals as an excuse. Why the hell had Sharon decided to learn accounting of all things? It was so boring, and it wasn't as if Sharon was starving for money. With her income from the clan's share, she could've managed just fine. Working was entirely optional for clan members, and Carol had no intention of seeking employment unless she found something really exciting to do. Unfortunately, the only occupation she'd ever found fulfilling was no longer available. And besides, being a courtesan had lost its appeal a couple of centuries ago, and she hadn't done it for the money anyway. Not that working for a living hadn't been a necessity back then, the clan hadn't been as wealthy as it was now, but she'd really enjoyed the lifestyle.

Nowadays, she could get sex almost anywhere, but without a girlfriend to accompany her on a club run, she was stuck with Ben and George. It wouldn't be the same

92

with the guys, their presence might deter men from approaching her, but it was better than going alone.

Someone had to keep an eye on her so she wouldn't overdo it with the booze.

"I'm game," Ben said.

"Me too. Do you want to go home first and change, though? Personally, I'd rather shower and put on something decent." George was a clothes whore, so there was no way he was going to go as is.

"I'm with you. You can't expect me to go looking like this." She waved a hand over her training outfit.

Ben shrugged. "Where and when?"

"Eight, Harvee's," Carol offered.

"It's not safe. Harvee's is not a members club. Let's go to The Basement."

Easy for George to suggest, he was a member. Carol wasn't. It was too pricey. And as far as she knew, Ben wasn't a member either. "Don't be ridiculous, George. It's not like we are defenseless."

"Yeah, we are badasses." Ben pumped his fist.

He was right. The guys were getting pretty good at hand to hand combat. Unfortunately, Carol was still too out of shape to be any good. Per Brundar's instructions, she was supposed to hit the gym every morning and do an hour of cardio and another half an hour of weight training. She'd done it twice. Every evening for the past two weeks she'd been promising herself that the next morning she was going for sure. And every morning she'd pressed snooze on the alarm and had gone back to sleep. Fates, she couldn't understand people who actually enjoyed exercise. Weirdos, one and all.

Damn, Brundar would be furious, and he wasn't the kind of guy she wished to aggravate. But even though he scared the crap out of her, the fear wasn't a strong enough motivator.

Perhaps the problem was that at the back of her mind, she entertained a hope that he'd go easy on her because she was such a badass with the gun. Not everyone was meant to be an athlete, right? Trouble was, they didn't get to take their weapons home. She would've felt much safer carrying.

Still, living in fear was no way to live. She needed to get out and have fun, find a decent guy to screw, or she was going to go nuts.

She would never admit it to anyone because it was so damn embarrassing, but she even tried to look for hookups at Starbucks because it was supposedly safe. Except, she'd found out that the place was crawling with nerds. Carol loved simple guys, tall and heavily muscled, and didn't care much for intelligence. After all, she wasn't looking for a good conversation, was she?

"What are the chances of Doomers showing up at Harvee's out of all the clubs? We'll be fine," she said, feigning confidence.

An hour and a half later, showered and ready for conquest, Carol pulled up to the valet in front of Harvee's and left her Prius with the attendant.

Armed with killer four-inch spiky heels, a skirt that barely covered her ass, and a slightly sheer blouse that showcased her designer bra, Carol felt unstoppable. The bra had a matching thong, but only one lucky guy would get to see it tonight.

Naturally, heads turned as she wended her way between

the tables to reach her friends—who apparently hadn't been waiting for her idly. Each already had a little hottie glued to his side. Good for them. But if she didn't want to feel like a fifth wheel, she'd better work fast.

"Hi, guys, want to introduce me to your new friends?"

"I'm Wendy." The one sitting on Ben's knee offered her hand.

"I'm Carol, nice to meet you."

"Monica," said the other one and waved.

Done with the introductions, Carol took a seat, crossed her legs, and began scanning the sparse crowd for the kind of guy she liked. It was still early, so there wasn't much of a selection, but the place was going to fill up in the next hour.

In the meantime, she ordered a drink, and another one, and another...

"What's your sign?" Monica tapped her shoulder.

"Capricorn, why? What's yours?" Carol loved talking about that shit. The first thing she read in the fashion magazines she subscribed to was the horoscope.

Monica's eyes sparkled with excitement. "So you're stubborn, determined, and loyal. It's a great sign, mostly for a guy. I'm a Libra, and I love Capricorns. Best boyfriend material. Have you had your astrological chart done yet?"

"No, I just read the horoscope."

Monica snorted. "Those are too general. If you really want to know your future and who is your perfect match, you need to have your chart done. But it's crucial to have the exact time of your birth. I can't make a chart without it."

Carol laughed. "I have no idea. I can call my mom and ask, but I doubt she remembers." It had been a couple of centuries...

"I'm sure she does. Call her up, and when you have it, I'll do your chart."

"Thanks. I will." She probably wouldn't, but there was no reason to be rude to the girl.

Monica twirled a lock of her dyed red hair around her finger. "Are you into tarot cards?"

"As in reading or being read?"

"Both, I guess."

"I don't know enough to read someone else's fortune, but I love to have mine read to me." Not that anyone today was as good at it as the gypsies of her youth.

The girl rummaged in her purse. "Shit, I forgot to bring them. I have a miniature pack I take with me everywhere I go. I must've left it at your place, Wendy."

"I'll check when I get home and call you."

"Thanks. But anyway, all is not lost. I also read palms. Give me your hand."

Carol finished her drink before offering Monica her palm.

The booth they were sitting in was dim, and Monica had to bring Carol's hand so close to her face that her nose was practically touching it. And still, it wasn't enough. Her brows riding low on her forehead, Monica traced the lines with a finger. "A big change is coming. There is a fork in the line that indicates a new path. It might be a new job, or a new boyfriend, or even marriage, but whatever it is it's going to be big."

For some reason, Monica's stupid foretelling, one that Carol was giving no credence to, sent chills down her spine. She yanked her hand out of the girl's grasp. "Thanks, but I don't really believe in any of it," Carol said with a tight smile.

Fates, she needed a drink. But there was scarcely anything left in her glass, and she waved the waitress over.

George covered her hand with his palm and leaned closer. "That was your fifth, you should stop."

Damn, six wouldn't get her drunk, but she'd told them to stop her after five. Fine, there were other ways to get rid of a bad humor.

She leaned into Ben and whispered into his ear, "Do you have any weed on you?"

"Plenty."

"Good. Let's go find a private spot."

On the sidewalk outside of Harvee's, several clubbers were enjoying a smoke—some of the tobacco variety, and some of the cannabis one. Carol went searching for somewhere secluded and dark. With a medical card in her wallet, she wasn't worried about getting arrested, but after years of smoking joints in hiding, she just couldn't derive pleasure from doing it in public.

The alley behind the parking lot looked secluded enough, but thanks to the floodlights that kept the lot illuminated it wasn't completely shrouded in darkness either.

Carol leaned against the block wall that separated the alley from the building on the other side, waiting for Ben to finish rolling the smoke. When he was done, he licked the paper to close it and pulled a lighter from his back pocket. "Do you want to light up? Or do you prefer for me to start?"

"You do it."

He nodded and lit the thing. After taking a big inhale, he

handed it to her, keeping the smoke inside him for as long as he could.

Carol took a puff, then another, before handing it back to Ben. Already the tight feeling in her belly was starting to ebb, and as soon as Ben was done, she took it from him and took several more.

"We should be getting back," Ben said as she passed him the joint, and lifted his foot to extinguish the thing on the sole of his boot.

"No, not yet. Let me finish it."

Reluctantly, he gave it back, but his eyes darted from side to side, and he tucked his hands under his armpits as he shifted from leg to leg. "It's damn freezing out here. Be quick about it."

Carol frowned. What was he talking about? Ben was wearing jeans and a long-sleeved shirt, while she was in a miniskirt and a sleeveless top, and she wasn't cold. Was he coming down with something?

"Maybe you should go inside. I'll be done in a minute."

"No, I'll wait. I'm not leaving you alone out here."

She rolled her eyes. Even in her less than superb shape, Carol doubted an average human male could subdue her. But if they ganged up on her, well, that was a different story. With that in mind, she dropped what was left of the joint and put it out with her shoe. "Let's go."

As they crossed the alley and entered the well illumi-nated area of the parking lot, Ben released a relieved breath. A minivan rolled into one of the few remaining spots, and a moment later the side door slid open, which struck her as odd because she was expecting the valet to jump out from the driver seat then rush back to the front.

Instead, a tall, muscular guy got out, the kind that immediately caught her interest, and right behind him came two more, just as yummy.

My personal buffet.

As she started sauntering toward them, Ben grabbed her arm and yanked her back against his body. She was about to say something, but he twisted her around and clamped a hand over her mouth.

What the fuck?

"Walk slowly. Don't make any sudden moves. Pretend we are a couple," he whispered in her ear so quietly that even she had trouble hearing him. "Don't look back, and don't say a word when I remove my hand. Nod if you understand."

She did, even though she had no idea what had gotten into him. Yeah, those guys were built, but that didn't mean they were looking for trouble, right? But just in case Ben had seen something she'd missed, she followed his lead.

Listening to what was going on behind them, Carol waited breathlessly to hear the minivan's door slide shut, and then four sets of shoes hitting the concrete in the opposite way. Time stretched into infinity as she and Ben took one step and then another, waiting for those sounds so she could finally exhale. But those sounds never came. Instead, Carol heard them getting closer.

"Run!" Ben grabbed her hand and broke into a sprint, dragging her behind him. She did her best to run as fast as she could on her four-inch heels, but they never had a chance.

It all happened so fast that she barely registered what was going on. One moment she was holding Ben's hand, the next someone was grabbing her by the waist and lifting her up with a force that was clearly not human. As much as she flailed and fought she couldn't gain an inch. The arm wrapped around her felt like an iron band.

"What do we have here?" the Doomer holding her rasped in her ear. "A succulent little immortal female."

Carol fought harder, twisting and kicking, but it was no use. "Let me go!" she screamed.

He clamped a hand over her mouth. "Thank you, darling, for all that thrashing. It got my fangs primed and ready for this." She felt the excruciating burn of them sinking into the soft skin of her neck, but a moment later the pain subsided. With euphoria spreading through her brain and her body like a wildfire over parched brush, Carol sagged in her captor's arms.

Through her foggy brain, she forced herself to open her eyes and look for Ben. Did he manage to escape? Or did they get him too? But with the Doomer's fangs still embedded in her neck, and his hand holding her head immobilized, she could only see what was ahead of her, and Ben wasn't there.

As the Doomer's venom kept sliding into her vein, Carol had the passing thought that he was pumping her with too much and was going to finish her off.

Please, merciful Fates, make it so. Let death set me free.

17

SYSSI

"It's so nice to get out of the keep for a change of atmosphere. We should do it more often." Syssi stuffed another piece of an avocado egg roll into her mouth. "God, I missed these," she said as she cut off another piece and dipped it in the cilantro sauce that came with it.

Tonight, she had taken Kian out, choosing to revisit her favorite restaurant from her previous life as a human. Syssi felt as if decades had passed since that pivotal moment in Amanda's lab when she'd first met Kian. It had been the start of an incredible adventure, one that, hopefully, would last the rest of her very long life. Everything was perfect. She had an adoring husband, a warm extended family, and a job she loved. It should've felt idyllic, a fairytale, and yet she was restless.

Hopefully, this slice of normal would restore her equilibrium. It felt as if it had been ages since the last time she'd tasted her favorite appetizer, when in fact the actual time elapsed could be measured in months, not even years.

Strange, how the perception of time didn't follow a linear path.

At first, Kian had felt ill at ease in the bustling restaurant, mainly because of the cramped seating arrangements that put him in close proximity to mortals, but little by little he was starting to relax. The ogling looks he was getting from females were kind of annoying, but he was either oblivious or chose to ignore them. Even the guys were paying more attention to Kian than to her.

Oh, well, this was a price she was willing to pay, especially since Kian had eyes only for her. While she was sitting across from him, the rest of the world might as well not exist as far as he was concerned.

But he was certainly paying attention to the egg rolls, picking them up with his fingers and stuffing them whole in his mouth. "You're right, these are good. And the tamales too, although I have to scrape off the sour cream. We should order another round."

Syssi chuckled. "Only if you plan on eating everything yourself. I'm done."

He glanced at the small appetizer plate she'd been using, then back up at her. "You must be kidding. We didn't even order the main course yet."

"I've had enough. These are very filling. When I used to come here before, I would often order just the appetizers. Their portions are huge. I swear, each one can feed a family of four."

Kian took the last egg roll off the platter and placed it on her plate. "Eat," he commanded.

So bossy, but in a good way. "Are you going to order more?"

"Yes."

Syssi nodded and cut a piece of the green delight, swearing it was her last. She hadn't hit the gym after work as she'd planned because her insatiable husband had had other ideas. Unfortunately, sex didn't count toward her goal of weekly exercise, which she'd set at minimum of half an hour a day.

"Tomorrow morning I'm coming with you to the gym. Don't let me stay in bed."

Kian arched a brow. Syssi wasn't a morning person, and while he started his day with a session at the gym—after their morning romp that is—she preferred to laze in bed with a cup of coffee or two, reading the news and some of the more interesting articles along with some mindless browsing on her tablet.

"What's going on, Syssi? Did you get it into your head that you need to lose weight? Because I assure you, you're perfect the way you are."

She dabbed at her mouth with a napkin. "Thank you, I appreciate the compliment. But I can't count on my super-duper genes to keep me looking great forever. You look the way you do for a reason." She waved a hand over his muscular upper body. "Your vegan diet and your dedication to a daily exercise routine keep you in shape. And conversely, William looks the way he does because he is eating indiscriminately and avoiding the gym like the fiery pits of hell."

Kian smiled and took her hand, bringing it up to his lips for a kiss. "I would love to have you join me in the gym every morning. I treasure every moment I get to spend with you. But I'm curious about the impetus for this resolution."

"You remember Hanna?"

"Sure, the postdoc at Amanda's lab."

"She managed to lose a lot of weight and looks amazing. She said it was all about eating less and moving more while being mindful of what and how much. It got me thinking that I need to be more disciplined with my eating habits and physical activity."

His eyes flared with the supernatural gleam she was so familiar with, and he hissed, "I can help keep you disciplined."

Syssi rolled her eyes. "Is everything about sex with you?"

"Obviously." He smiled, his fangs making an appearance.

She leaned forward. "Don't smile."

Kian's hand flew to cover his mouth.

"Want me to talk about disgusting things?"

He laughed from behind his hand. "Please don't. I don't want to hear about little kids puking all over themselves while I'm eating."

He remembered. How sweet.

"Fine, so I'll update you on the new plans Amanda and I have for the lab."

"That's better."

"I put an ad on Craig's List for subjects with para-normal abilities, offering to pay twenty an hour for their time."

"This will guarantee that you'll have a lot of people with no talent wasting your time."

"I know. That's why we decided to hire an assistant to do the initial screening. That way we will get to test only those with potential."

Kian shook his head. "I don't know. Doesn't seem to me

like the best way to go about it, but I have nothing better to suggest."

"You want to hear some of the crazy ideas that I've played around with in my head?"

"Of course."

"Asking William to develop a computer or arcade game that will somehow test for abilities, and then lure the winners into some final competition for a big prize."

"That's actually not so crazy…"

"You must be kidding."

"Not at all. The game can be based on the random images program you use in the lab. It seems like a simple enough thing to do."

"Kian, you are a genius. I don't know why I haven't thought of it myself. It's so obvious."

"It would have never crossed my mind without you mentioning a computer game first. I wasn't thinking in that direction at all."

Syssi smiled and raised her hand. "High five for teamwork."

He slapped her hand, and then lowered it for a kiss. "This calls for a celebration. Champagne?"

She wasn't a fan of that particular bubbly. "How about a Mojito instead?"

"Mojito it is." He waved down a waiter and ordered two, together with another serving of avocado egg rolls.

Syssi leaned back in her chair and tapped her lower lip with the tip of her finger. "The trick will be to disguise it as a game and make it enjoyable for both young men and young women."

"I think you can leave this part to William and his

'Genius Squad'—that's how they asked to be called. They objected to us calling them the geek squad."

"Can't blame them. Though I thought it was kind of cute."

"Apparently not to teenagers."

The waiter came back with their Mojitos and Kian's egg rolls. "Are you ready for the main course?" he asked.

"Not for me, thank you," Syssi said.

Kian flipped the menu closed and handed it to the guy. "Please bring us the mango salad, without the chicken, and two plates. We're going to share."

"I told you I'm stuffed," she said as the waiter left with their order.

"Just in case you change your mind. If you don't want any, I have no problem eating everything by myself." He raised his tumbler. "To great minds working together!"

"To us!" She smiled and clinked his tall glass.

But as she brought it to her lips to take a sip, her hand began trembling, and her vision blurred, becoming a swirl of colors. Her head spinning, she felt herself slide down in her chair.

Oh, no, not now...

A vision was coming, and there was no stopping it.

"Syssi! What's wrong?" in a split second, Kian was out of his chair and on his knees beside her. The tumbler began sliding out of her hand, but he caught it in time and put it on the table, then clasped her hands. "Talk to me, sweet girl. You're scaring the shit out of me."

By now her whole body was trembling uncontrollably. "We need to go home. Now."

"Of course." Kian's beautiful face was pinched with

worry as he pushed up to his feet and lifted her up. "Are you feeling sick?"

"No. It's not about me. Something bad is going to happen, and we should be home when it does. That's all I know for certain."

18

NATHALIE

"Some more orange chicken?" Andrew hovered with the serving bowl over Fernando's shoulder, ready to heap some more on her father's plate.

"Maybe just a few pieces. I'm full, but this is very tasty. Could you give me the recipe? I'm a baker, not a cook, but I know my way around a kitchen."

Andrew shot Nathalie a look that said, 'help!'

She patted her father's wrinkled hand. "You know, Papi, that we can't cook Chinese in the coffee shop. It will stink up the place. Customers want to smell coffee and baked goods when they come in, not something deep fried."

"Yes, you're right, of course. Can't cook Chinese in a coffee shop. What was I thinking? I'll tell you what I was thinking. That we have a perfectly good kitchen at home, where we can cook whatever we want, but you never let me go back there!"

"Papi, we've been over this before. We sold that home a long time ago. There is somebody else living there now."

"So you've been saying." He speared a piece of orange chicken with his fork and stuffed it into his mouth.

Nathalie sighed. She couldn't complain, it had been going well up until now. And as Fernando's tantrums went, this had been a mild one. Nevertheless, it was a sign that they should head home.

"Finish your dinner, Papi. We need to go."

"What's the hurry?" Andrew put the serving bowl on the table and sat down. "Let the man eat in peace, Nathalie. It's not healthy to rush a meal." He winked at her.

Fernando shot her a worried glance, checking to see if she'd gotten angry over Andrew's remark.

"It's okay, Papi. Andrew is right. There is no hurry. I want you to enjoy the meal."

Her father shook his head as if puzzled by something. "You can cook." He pointed his fork at Andrew, then at Nathalie. "And she listens to you and doesn't hold every word you say against you. I say it's a match made in heaven."

Andrew looked guilty, no doubt feeling bad about deceiving Fernando. But his little Chinese takeout deception aside, Nathalie wanted to jump on the opportunity and finally tell her father that she and Andrew were a couple. Problem was, in order to do so in a way that would be easiest for him to understand, she needed to twist the truth too.

"You are absolutely right, Papi. This is why Andrew and I decided to get engaged." She shot Andrew a glance, hoping he wouldn't look like a deer caught in the headlights of an oncoming truck. But the man was smiling from ear to ear as if he'd heard the best of news and couldn't be happier.

"Well, it's about time. I was wondering what was holding you kids back."

Nathalie glanced at Andrew, who was still smiling broadly as if all of their troubles were solved and all was good in their world. But she knew better. "How long have you known Andrew, Papi?"

Her father's brows dipped down as he concentrated. "Many years, I think. Didn't you kids start dating in high school?"

She wanted to correct his misconception, but Andrew put his hand over hers and shook his head imperceptibly. "It's time we settled down, don't you think, Fernando?"

"Absolutely. I want grandkids, and my Eva, she is going to be so happy."

God, how Nathalie hated moments like this. She was so angry at her mother. For leaving her father, for abandoning her and disappearing to God knew where. Such a selfish woman. And yet Fernando still loved her, still pined for her. It was so unfair.

"I'm sure she will," Andrew said. "Let's make a toast." He poured a little wine into each of their goblets. "To a happy marriage."

Fernando lifted his glass and clinked it with Nathalie's, then with Andrew's. "And fruitful," he added with a wink.

Andrew nodded solemnly. "And fruitful."

LATER, when Andrew had driven them back home, Fernando clapped Andrew on the back and congratulated them again before retiring for the night.

Nathalie's shoulders sagged as soon as his door closed, and the fake smile she'd been fronting for his sake dissolved from her face. "God, this was so awkward."

Andrew pulled her into his arms. "I think it went well. In fact, it was better than I'd expected."

She pushed at his chest, and he let her go. "Oh, yeah? Which part? The one about us being engaged? Or the part about getting married and having kids? Or maybe the one about his long gone ex-wife he still thinks he is married to?"

Nathalie plopped on the couch and let her head drop back on the cushions, feeling exhausted and depressed. Damn, was she becoming bipolar in addition to her other abnormalities? This morning she'd been floating on a happy cloud, and now she couldn't muster one positive thought. What was wrong with her?

Andrew came to sit next to her and lifted her legs so her feet were nestled in his lap. "You're just tired, baby. This was a stressful evening for you." He started massaging her feet.

A ghost of a smile hovered over her lips as Andrew's expert fingers began working their magic on her toes. "You may be right. Though I hate lying to my father like this."

"You're not lying."

"Twisting the truth is the same thing as lying, Andrew."

"Look." He pressed his thumb to the arch of her foot, and she let out a moan. "We never set dates or made official proclamations, but I plan on spending the rest of my life with you. And, hopefully, you feel the same way about me. So, if these were our intentions all along, then we weren't lying to your father or misleading him in any way. True?"

She sighed. If there was one thing about Andrew that

wasn't perfect, it was that he didn't have even one romantic bone in his body.

Nathalie regarded him with a mock sternness. "Andrew Spivak, this was the lamest proposal I've ever heard."

The poor guy looked so stricken that she just couldn't keep up the pretense. "But I loved it anyway." She leaned up and kissed his lips.

"I'm sorry. I should have planned this better."

"I'll tell you what. I still want you to propose on one knee or both, but I'm thinking along the lines of both of us naked while you do it."

"Woman, I like the way you think."

Andrew was up on his feet and lifting her up in his strong arms before even finishing his sentence. In several long strides, he closed the distance to her room and lowered her gently to the floor, then turned around and closed the door behind him, locking it.

Curious to find out what he was going to do next, Nathalie stood on the area rug next to her bed and waited for Andrew, a flurry of excited butterflies taking flight in her stomach.

With a predatory smirk, he sauntered up to her and knelt on the carpet. His hands reaching around to cup her ass, his nose was pointing at the junction of her thighs, almost touching.

"Let's get you naked, baby," he rasped as he tugged at the stretchy fabric of her pants and pulled them down without bothering with the button or the zipper. Next, he lowered her panties down her thighs, and she braced a hand on his shoulder to keep steady as she stepped out of them, one leg at a time.

Andrew got up to divest her of her blouse, pulling it over her head, then unsnapped her bra and let it fall down to the floor. Dropping back to his knees, he lowered all the way down to his haunches and looked up at her with a worshipful gaze.

"God, Nathalie, you're so beautiful that you take my breath away. My own, personal Aphrodite."

The love in Andrew's eyes, in his words, was shining so brightly that she felt tears stinging the back of her eyes, and a corresponding powerful wave of emotions burst out from her heart. She needed to touch him, to feel his strong body against hers. Nathalie went down to her knees in front of Andrew, and with a lurch flung herself into his arms, almost toppling them both.

She clung to Andrew as if her life depended on it, not caring if she was crushing him with her hug. "I love you so much," she whispered into his neck.

"I love you too, and you'll make me the happiest man alive if you agree to become my wife."

Her chuckle was accompanied by a sniffle. "I wanted both of us naked when you asked me."

"So is it a yes, or a no?" he teased.

Nathalie hesitated for a moment. Could she really agree to marry a man who was keeping secrets from her? It could've been absolutely perfect if not for her suspicions. But as she was well aware, life wasn't perfect, and neither was Andrew. Eventually, he'd have to trust her enough to tell her everything or there would be no marriage. But that didn't mean that she couldn't say yes to him now. They had plenty of time before any talk about a wedding was even possible, and, hopefully, by then all would be revealed.

"Of course it's a yes. But I hope you don't mind a very long engagement."

"I'm not getting any younger, you know. But there is no rush."

Nathalie let go and pushed back up to her feet. "I still want you naked as you kneel for me."

"Another fantasy?" He was teasing her for wanting to enact every item on the list of fantasies she'd collected over the years.

"Yes, but this is a new one."

"Now, this is exciting." He smirked as he started on the buttons of his shirt. "Is it a wicked one?" He shrugged the shirt off, exposing his mouthwatering muscular torso.

Nathalie shrugged, her lips twitching with the need to smile. "Maybe a little."

Andrew lifted up on his knees and unbuckled his belt, then pushed his pants down his legs. His boxer briefs went next, and then he was kneeling in front of her, fully erect, his shaft rising up from his groin like a flagpole.

With a slight incline of his head, he said, "I'm at your service, my queen. Awaiting your command."

Damn, she'd hoped he would guess what she wanted, and the wily man probably had, but he wanted to hear her say it.

"Pleasure me," she commanded.

"You need to be more specific than that."

Damn, he was pushing her to say things she was still too embarrassed to voice, which was kind of silly since she had no problem with the actual doing.

With one hand cupping a breast, she lowered the other to the juncture of her thighs, her finger hovering lightly over the seat of her pleasure. Andrew's breath intake was audible, but still, he hadn't made a move to touch her, waiting for her to tell him what to do.

"I want your tongue, right here." She tapped her finger lightly over the spot.

His smile was positively predatory, hungry, as if he was eyeing a tasty treat and was about to devour it.

"With pleasure, your majesty." Andrew's hands cupped her butt cheeks and pulled her closer, his tongue snaking out and flicking over that most sensitive bundle of nerves.

"Oh, yes…" she moaned and could swear he was smiling with satisfaction just from the way his tongue moved. The scene she had engineered was incredibly arousing, but a few moments into it, her legs started quivering, and she was having trouble staying upright.

19

KIAN

"*P*ut me down, you're making a scene," Syssi hissed.

Reluctantly, Kian let her legs drop down but held her up with an arm wrapped around her waist. Bhathian, their designated bodyguard for this evening, had rushed ahead to get the car. He'd been sitting a few tables away to give them privacy. The idea was to provide Syssi with the illusion that they were just a normal couple going on a normal date. A bodyguard sitting right next to them would have spoiled the effect.

She'd seemed a little off lately, and Kian had hoped this outing would improve her mood. But apparently something more serious than missing her old life was causing her unease, and had been a prelude to the fucking vision that had hit her like an epileptic seizure. He'd never seen her like that, and it had scared the crap out of him. There was nothing more terrifying than watching the woman you love gripped by some mysterious force you were powerless to fight off.

It reminded him of how desperate and inept he'd felt during her transition, when he'd thought he was losing her. Not a good memory

As they pushed through the restaurant's door and stepped outside, the Lexus was parked right by the entry, thanks to the generous tip Kian slipped the valet so it could be quickly retrieved. With one glance at Bhathian's expression, the guy dropped the keys into the Guardian's palm.

As they got into the back seat of the SUV, Kian wrapped his hand around Syssi's shoulders. Her slight form trembled against his body as if she were cold. He rubbed her arm. "How are you feeling, sweet girl?"

"I'll be fine. You should call the keep and find out if anything happened."

He kissed the top of her head. "Someone would've called me already. Don't worry. Everything is going to be okay. Whatever it is, we'll deal with it."

"Call. I just want to make sure."

"I can do that." He pulled out the phone and selected Onegus's contact. "Anything going on?"

"No, why?"

"Syssi had a premonition that something bad is coming. Soon. And even though she doesn't know where or what, I suggest you put security on high alert."

"Will do."

Clicking the phone off, he glanced down at Syssi. The poor girl looked so shaken, clutching her purse in a white-knuckled grip and tapping her foot. He tucked her closer under his arm, holding her tight against his side and rubbing her arm until he felt her shoulders relax. Only then he asked, "What exactly have you seen?"

For a long moment, she just chewed on her lip, her brows pinched in concentration. "It's hard to describe. The input wasn't visual, or rather not visually clear. There was a darkness that started as a mere fog, evolved into a swirling mass of wispy dark tendrils, and then coalesced into a terrifying blackness. There were sounds. Again, nothing that I can make sense of. A cross between the roar of a turbulent wind and that of a pack of hyenas. But I felt a sense of urgency, of immediacy, as if there was something we needed to do to either prevent it or do something about it after it happened." She exhaled a breath. "I hate it. Hate that I get these premonitions of doom, but not enough information to do anything about them. What's the point of having them if all they accomplish is to make me miserable?"

Regrettably, she was right. For the first time, he had gotten a taste of what she'd been dealing with for most of her life, and it was absolutely infuriating. To wait impotently for the unknown disaster to strike, unable to do anything to prevent it or even prepare for it, was worse than having no forewarning at all.

He bent down and kissed her forehead. "It's damn frustrating, that's for sure. But when it comes we'll just have to deal with it, the same way we deal with any disaster that strikes. The only difference is that now both of us are stressed."

"I shouldn't have told you. It's bad enough that I'm burdened with these useless premonitions. You have enough real stuff to worry about without being bothered with this nonsense. In the absence of specifics, there is nothing you can do about it anyway. Shit happens all the time with or without my vague warnings."

"Don't be ridiculous. Of course, you have to tell me. Even if it's for the sole purpose of having someone to share it with. And don't even think about trying to hide it from me. We are a couple, a family, and we face shit together."

Syssi sighed and slumped in his grip, putting her cheek on his chest. Damn, even after all this time, it still got him every time she did something like this. The implied trust, the fact that she took solace in his arms and was willing to lean on him for support was precious to him.

"I love you, my sweet girl," he whispered and nuzzled her hair.

When Syssi didn't respond, Kian realized that she'd fallen asleep. Evidently, these damn premonitions were draining—emotionally and physically.

To keep it from disturbing her, he put his phone on silent and spent the rest of the drive staring at the screen, waiting anxiously for the bad news to arrive so he could get moving and do something about it. The wait and uncertainty were torturous.

As Bhathian eased the Lexus into its parking spot, Kian lifted Syssi into his lap and waited for the guy to open the door for him so he could slide out with his precious load.

She opened her eyes and smiled, then leaned up and kissed the underside of his jaw. "I can walk, you know."

"I do. But I like carrying you." He kissed her nose and gathered her closer.

With a sigh, she put her head on his chest and closed her eyes. "Did I tell you lately how much I love you?" she whispered into his neck.

He chuckled. "A couple of times. But not nearly enough."

"Really? My poor baby."

"Let's make a schedule. I think every five minutes will do fine. I just love hearing you say it to me."

"I love you."

"That's my girl."

When they got back into their penthouse, he lowered her to the couch. "I'm going to get myself a drink, and I suggest you have one too."

"Yeah, I need it. A simple gin and tonic, though easy on the gin."

He kissed her cheek. "Coming right up."

It had been good to joke around with Syssi for a bit, and during these lighthearted moments, he'd even managed to silence the countdown clock ticking in his head. But now the damn thing was back and louder than before.

Drinks in hand, Kian returned to the couch and sat next to Syssi. "Here, try it. Tell me if this is the way you like it." He handed her the tumbler.

She took a sip and nodded. "Perfect."

Taking a long one from his whiskey, he savored the burn in his throat, knowing that he'd be refilling his glass in short order. More than once. The fucking wait was killing him.

Kian got up, went to the kitchen, and grabbed a can of peanuts from the pantry. Syssi would have wanted him to pour them into a nice serving bowl, but he had no patience for that and brought the can to the living room, half expecting her to send him back for it. She said nothing, though, and as he offered her the container, she dipped her hand in it and pulled out a fistful.

A few moments later, his glass was empty, and he got up to refill it. "Would you like another one?" He glanced at Syssi's. She'd gone through half of it, but the melting ice cubes had probably further diluted the alcohol content that hadn't been much to begin with.

"No, thank you."

By the time he'd emptied his second serving of Macallan, Kian was ready to punch the walls—the prospect of Syssi's disapproval the only thing holding him back.

With a loud intake of breath and then a forceful puff through pursed lips, Syssi put down her glass and pushed to her feet. "This is nuts. I can't take it anymore. I'm going to fill up a bathtub and soak. You're welcome to join me."

As tempting as her invitation was, he knew he wouldn't be able to relax enough to enjoy it. "Go on. I'll stay by the phone and let you know as soon as I get any news."

Syssi grimaced. "What if nothing happens tonight? You can't stay up waiting for something that may or may not come."

He took her hand and kissed it. "We both know that there is no question whether it's going to happen; only when and where and what."

She nodded. "Let me know as soon as you hear anything."

"I will. Enjoy your soak."

With Syssi out of the room, the last of the façade he'd been keeping up for her sake had melted away. As he paced around his living room, Kian caught glimpses of himself every time he passed by the glass doors to the terrace, and the face staring back at him wasn't pretty, or even human. His fangs had punched down over his lower lip, and the swollen glands were distorting his features into something that looked savage, animalistic.

Time stretched into eternity, and when his phone finally

vibrated in his hand, Kian was almost relieved to get the bad news he'd been waiting for. But as he lifted it up to answer, it wasn't Onegus's face that was displayed on the screen, it was Bridget's.

A medical emergency? Highly unlikely. But then, what other reason did the doctor have to call him this late?

He tapped the green button to answer. "Yes, Bridget. What's going on?"

"You'd better come down here. I have an unconscious Doomer-attack victim I need to take care of, and you'll want to talk to the friend who brought him in."

"On my way."

20

ANDREW

*O*n his knees, pleasuring his woman, was exactly where Andrew wanted to be. But Nathalie's legs were trembling, and as much fun as holding her up with his hands under her sweet ass was, it was becoming difficult. Not for the first time, Andrew wondered how different it would be if he were immortal. Syssi had gotten stronger after her transition, and although he hadn't spoken with Michael about it, he was sure that the boy had gotten stronger too.

Even Vlad, with his spider arms, was most likely stronger than Andrew, and Jackson, well, the kid could probably finish him with one punch.

Ouch.

Transitioning was tempting, no doubt about it, but it was also scary as hell. Especially now that he had something to live for. Andrew wasn't a stranger to death. As a matter of fact, they were long time acquaintances, and he'd stared the fucker in the face many times before. He hadn't been afraid then because giving his life to save others was noble, and he'd been reconciled to the fact that one day his luck would run out.

But this was different.

To risk his life to gain something for himself felt frivolous to Andrew, even if that something was immortality. To borrow one of Kian's expressions, the Fates had been kind to him, keeping him alive when others in his unit hadn't been that lucky. He couldn't help the persistent thought that he'd been spared because of his willingness to sacrifice. But then, this line of thought was making him feel even guiltier for still breathing while his buddies were gone. Then again, it wasn't only his own immortality that was on the line. He had to consider that the love of his life had the same potential, and he was the one who should facilitate her transformation.

The irony of having these philosophical thoughts while his tongue was buried deep inside of Nathalie's cleft wasn't lost on him. Damn, he was a lousy lover. He'd better get his head back in the game before she noticed that his thoughts were miles away.

Redoubling his efforts, Andrew licked and sucked, holding on tight to Nathalie's ass while she gyrated her hips in sync with his tonguing. When her breath hitched, and she let out a guttural moan, he lifted her up and carried her to the bed, using the last of his strength to put her down gently and not let her drop.

Hopefully, she was too far gone to notice the quivering of his tired arm muscles. After all, a man had to preserve his damn pride, true?

"That was awesome," Nathalie rasped as she stretched her limbs, lying spread-eagled on her narrow bed.

Music to my ears. Andrew smirked. Even when his mind was distracted and he hadn't been focusing as he should, he'd given his woman a powerful orgasm.

"Scootch. Make room for me." He nudged her thigh with his knee.

"Nah, I'm not moving. You can cover me up with this incredibly handsome body of yours." She tapped her chest.

Okay, he could live with that. Andrew straddled Nathalie's legs, then lowered himself on top of her, bracing his forearms on both sides of her head.

Up close, her pleasure-suffused face was beyond beautiful and sexy as hell. And those pink, parted lips of hers were calling to him to take them. He dipped his head and kissed her, licking into her mouth with a tongue that still carried the taste of her juices. Nathalie moaned softly, her hips churning under him in invitation.

Andrew was tempted. In fact, his shaft had been throbbing painfully for far too long and denying it the pleasure of sinking into Nathalie's welcoming sheath was torturous. But he wanted to prolong her anticipation, driving her wild with need, so when he finally buried himself inside her, Nathalie's orgasm would catapult her into the stratosphere.

Andrew kept kissing her soft, fleshy lips and licking inside her mouth, his talented tongue dancing the mating dance with hers. Then he slid lower to pay homage to her perky little nipples, lavishing attention on each one until they were hard enough to poke a hole in a wall. But as he made a move to slide even lower, she caught his head and pulled him up by his hair.

"I want you inside me."

The lady knew what she wanted, when and how she wanted it, and he wasn't about to deny her. Whatever Nathalie wished for, Nathalie got, at least as far as it was in his power to oblige her wishes. Except, he was still going to push her a little, get her out of her comfort zone—because she loved it when he did that.

He positioned himself at her entry but didn't push. "Put me in," he instructed.

Nathalie reached between their bodies and took hold of his shaft, stroking it gently a few times before bearing down on it.

As he slowly sank into her wet heat, Andrew tried and failed to stifle a groan, but at least it came out somewhat muffled, and, hopefully, Fernando didn't hear a thing. Cupping Nathalie's cheeks, he held her gaze until he was fully seated inside her, and then he kissed her, deeply, passionately.

With her arms wrapped around him, Nathalie held on tight as she kissed him back, and for long moments Andrew didn't move inside her, enjoying the closeness, the connection, the joining of their bodies and their hearts. When he let go of her mouth, he touched his forehead to hers and whispered, "I love you, my Nathalie."

She brought her palm to his cheek, caressing it lightly. "I love you, my Andrew," she echoed, "But I need you to move."

And he did, unhurriedly, his thrusts shallow. Not only because anything more vigorous would've banged the headboard against the wall and they couldn't make noise, but because he wanted to prolong the pleasure as much as he could.

Except, if he had his sister's talent for predicting the future, he would've hurried up, because a moment later his phone went off with the ringtone he'd assigned to Kian, and he wished he hadn't taken his time. "Sorry, sweetheart, but I need to take it. They wouldn't call me this late if it weren't an emergency."

Her forehead wrinkled with worry. "Of course, go ahead."

Reluctantly, he abandoned the heaven of her wet embrace and rushed to retrieve the phone from the pocket of his pants.

"Yeah," he said.

"I need you to get here immediately. A female was captured by Doomers earlier tonight, and a male was savagely mauled."

Fuck, how the hell did that happen? Aren't immortal females supposed to be impossible to detect?

"I'm on my way." Andrew clicked the phone off and pulled on his pants without bothering to find his boxers.

"I have to go." When a quick glance produced only one sock, he decided to forgo those too and pushed his bare feet into his shoes.

"What happened?" Nathalie sat up in bed, clutching the comforter to her breasts.

He grabbed his shirt and shrugged it on while leaning to give her a quick kiss. "It's work related. I can't talk about it."

"Oh." She let out a relieved breath. "I thought something happened to someone in your family.

With a grimace, Andrew bent down to retrieve his jacket, electing not to respond and saving himself another unnecessary lie. Because in this case work and family were one and the same. He considered himself part of the clan—albeit not a fully-fledged member yet—and each of its members a relative.

21

SEBASTIAN

*A*s Sebastian maneuvered his Explorer into a tight parking spot in the club's lot, his cellphone went off. Damn, he hoped it wasn't the attorney canceling their assignation for tonight. After a miserable week of whipping and fucking inferior specimens, he was all juiced up for her. He was looking forward to a satisfying session with his favorite sub.

But glancing at the display, he was relieved to see that it wasn't the attorney or the club's coordinator, but one of his men. Except, why the hell was the idiot calling him? The standard protocol was for the men to direct any and all inquiries to either Robert or Tom, and if they in turn deemed it important, one of them would call Sebastian.

The breach of protocol was highly unusual.

For a moment, he considered ignoring the call and letting it go to voicemail. After all, he had a dungeon room reserved for the next ninety minutes, and he hated to cut it short even by a few. Whatever the guy needed could probably wait until after the session was over.

Or maybe not. In any case, he'd better find out or spend the whole time wondering about it instead of enjoying this long awaited session.

He shifted the gear to park, but left the engine running to answer the call. "This better be good, Rupert," he barked. It might have been his agitation, but Sebastian couldn't help the passing thought that the name the guy had chosen for himself was ridiculous. Was anyone else born in the second half of the twentieth century still named Rupert?

"This is better than good, boss. We have a first class surprise for you." There was some snorting in the background, and from the sound of it Rupert and his comrades were calling from inside a moving vehicle.

"Just tell me what it is. I don't have time for games."

"We've snatched an immortal female, and we have her here in the car with us. We are on our way back to base."

I'll be damned.

His assignation all but forgotten, Sebastian threw the gearshift into reverse, backed out of the spot, and did a fast K-turn, sending the vehicle into a controlled skid that had its premium tires squalling. The huge SUV tilted precariously for a split second before righting itself, and Sebastian stomped on the accelerator, flying into the street of the commercial park that was mercifully deserted at this time of night.

"How?" Turning right to head back to base, he floored the gas pedal.

"She and a male were outside the club we were sent to scope. They were smoking pot in the parking lot." Rupert's snort was accompanied by others in the background.

"Do you have both?" Getting on the freeway, Sebastian

forced himself to slow down to a lawful speed limit. The last thing he needed was to get pulled over by the cops for speeding.

"No, sir. There was a struggle, and the guy didn't make it. We left him there and took the female."

Morons.

Sebastian's grip on the steering wheel tightened. "Venom overdose?"

"Yes, sir. And there was not much left of his throat either. Sorry about that."

Well, he couldn't be too angry with the team that had brought him an immortal female. Hell, he couldn't believe they had actually done it. "Are you sure she is an immortal? It's not easy to tell."

"She fought like a wildcat, much stronger than a human female, and she is a soft and plump little thing—not some big muscular woman."

"Did you touch her?" He was going to kill any of them who'd dared. This one was his.

"No, sir. Only to subdue her and tranquilize her with venom."

"Good. Is she awake?"

"No, sir. She's still out."

Sebastian detected a note of worry in the guy's tone.

"Is she breathing?"

"Yes, sir."

"Then she is fine. How far away from base are you?"

"Another half an hour, sir."

"I'm on my way, but until I get there, lock her up in one of the rooms in the basement."

"Yes, sir."

He was about to click off when it occurred to him that the men expected to hear some praise, which they rightfully deserved. It was the first time since the cataclysm, as far as he knew, that an immortal female had been captured. "Excellent job, men. I'll see to it myself that you're all handsomely rewarded."

"Thank you, sir."

Sebastian ended the call and then dialed the club's coordinator. "Listen, something came up, and I can't make it tonight. Send my apologies to my partner and tell her that if she can find a substitute she is free to use the room I've reserved. I know you'll charge me for it anyway." He clicked off with a smile, feeling good about his magnanimous gesture. His attorney would be disappointed that he didn't show up, and as he had no problem with her playing with others, offering her the use of the room for free was his way of making it up to her.

Driving on the freeway that was still busy even at this late hour, Sebastian shook his head as he considered his good fortune. He still couldn't believe that there would be an immortal female waiting for him in his basement.

This was something every immortal male dreamed about and wished for. An immortal female represented a future, a chance of having immortal offspring, sons who would live as long as he did, sons he could train, sons he could impart his legacy to. The way Losham had done with him. In this, his uncle by blood and adoptive father was a superb example. If Sebastian did his job even half as well as his father had done, the sons he would raise would mature to be incredible men.

Frankly, though, this wasn't what had him excited.

Sebastian had never dreamed of becoming a father, or of having a mate. But he did crave having an indestructible toy, which was exactly what an immortal female was. No matter what he did to her, no matter how severely he would beat her, she would heal, and she would heal fast. There would be no residual damage, no scarring, and by the next day she would be as good as new and ready for another session.

22

KIAN

"Tell me again what happened, George, slowly this time," Kian said as patiently as he could. The guy was so distraught that he was barely coherent, and yet he'd adamantly refused to leave his friend's side and have this done in another room. Watching Bridget working on Ben, who was hanging onto life by a thread, sure as hell wasn't helping to calm George down.

With a practically nonexistent heartbeat, it was a wonder George had realized that Ben was still alive when he'd found him. Though Kian suspected that the guy hadn't known that at the time and had brought Ben to Bridget because he'd had no idea what else to do.

With a shaky hand, George brought the cup of water Kian had handed him to his mouth and took a sip. Some of it trickled from the corners of his mouth, and he wiped it with the sleeve of his shirt as he put the glass away. Sucking in a ragged breath, he looked at Kian with eyes that were red-rimmed and misted with tears. "I need to go to the bathroom for a minute," he said.

Poor kid, probably needed some time to collect himself, time Kian couldn't allow him while the safety of the whole clan was on the line. Still, a couple of minutes wouldn't make a difference.

"Go ahead, but don't delay."

Damn, he should've brought Syssi with him. It wasn't that he lacked compassion for the guy, it was just that providing comfort wasn't something Kian did well, while Syssi found it as natural as breathing. On the other hand, seeing the damage that had been done to Ben would probably freak her out.

That was why Kian hadn't told her where he was going, just that he needed to check on something. She'd given him a suspicious look, but he'd played it cool, and she seemed to buy his nonchalant attitude. But now that Ben's torn neck was no longer gruesomely displayed, but neatly wrapped with bandages, he could have her join them.

Kian pulled out his phone and texted Syssi. *If you are done with your bath, come down to Bridget's clinic. I need your help.*

Hopefully, his short message conveyed urgency without causing anxiety. Perhaps he should've worded it differently...Not that it would have helped. Syssi was going to be mad at him for not telling her right away as he had promised. Damn, he had no doubt that someone like the smooth-talking Onegus would've known how to say this in a way that would've sounded perfectly reasonable to her. Kian, on the other hand, tended to offend people with his gruff delivery, and a determined expression that was often mistaken for impatience or even anger.

With a curse, Kian ran his fingers through his hair.

There were big gaps in his education, the most glaring one being his deficient communication skills, the other being lack of emotional intelligence, or whatever they called the ability to provide solace and emotional support to another. In his defense, all this touchy-feely mumbo jumbo was the product of recent decades, while he was an ancient relic from a time where thinking like that would've gotten people killed.

But finding excuses for his shortcomings wasn't going to fix them. Problem was, at his advanced age, Kian doubted he had it in him to change or learn new skills. And really, as a leader, his job was to find people to perform tasks he was no good at instead of him trying to excel at everything. As hard as it was to admit, especially to someone with his enormous ego, it just wasn't possible. Onegus would've been a better choice to handle George's interrogation, but Kian had sent him to the crime scene to investigate. The only other Guardian available at the moment was Bhathian, whose grumpy attitude was the opposite of what was needed.

Kian's phone buzzed with Syssi's return message. *Getting dressed, be there in a minute.*

Regrettably, George came back at the same time Kian finished reading the text, which meant that until Syssi made it to the clinic, he would have to do his best with what little skills he had.

The guy glanced at his unconscious friend and sighed. With slumped shoulders, George shuffled to the chair he'd been sitting on before. Frankly, the sigh he'd let out had sounded more like a whimper, embarrassing for a grown man, and more so for an immortal who was training to become a Guardian. Obviously, the guy didn't have what it took.

Nevertheless, under the circumstances, he was doing his best.

Kian walked over to him and patted his shoulder awkwardly. "He is going to be okay, and he probably owes you his life."

George nodded, his back straightening a notch. "I guess you're right. But they took Carol, and I wasn't there to help her." He slumped again, dropping his head into his hands.

"Are you sure they've taken her? Maybe she escaped and is hiding?"

George shook his head. "I saw her purse on the ground. I didn't pick it up because I was desperate to save Ben. I tied my shirt around his neck to try and just keep everything together." He shuddered. "Fates, it looked as if his head was barely attached to what was left of his neck, and that at any moment that last piece would tear and he would be gone. The purse was the last thing on my mind as I carried him to the car while trying to keep his head immobile."

"How come you guys weren't together?"

George winced. "They went out to smoke, while I stayed inside. After more than twenty minutes passed and they didn't come back, I started to worry and went looking for them. When I couldn't find them, I checked to see if Carol's car was still there, thinking that maybe they'd ditched me. You know, played a nasty joke on me. Or perhaps they ran out of pot and went looking for more. I really started panicking when I found her Prius still parked at the lot. I started running around, hoping I'd find them hiding in some dark corner, sharing a joint. That's how I stumbled upon Ben. The block wall separating the parking lot from the house on the other side was casting shadows on the bushes growing next to it. I would've missed his body lying crumpled in those bushes if not for his white Converses. They reflected the little light coming from the floodlight attached to the back wall of the club."

A sob escaped George's throat, and he turned his face away. Kian patted his shoulder again. "You should get some rest. You can lie down on the cot in the other room and leave the door open. I don't think I have any more questions for you. If you happen to remember anything else, no matter how trivial, come find me in Bridget's office."

His face still turned the other way, George nodded.

Kian walked over to Bridget. "Let me know the moment Ben wakes up. And if you can do anything to hasten it, please do. I don't need to tell you what's at stake."

She regarded him with her smart eyes. "Are you going to order an evacuation?"

"I don't think I have a choice. I can't expect Carol to hold off for long."

"I need to stabilize him first."

"I know."

A gentle knock on the door announced Syssi, and Kian opened the way for her. She was trying to put on a brave face for him, but the strong scent of despair coming from her told him that Bhathian must've already updated her on what was going on.

"Is he going to make it?' she asked, her bottom lip quivering.

"Yes, he is. It's not easy to end the life of an immortal. As long as there is a tiniest of sparks, he'll live." Kian pulled

Syssi into a hug and squeezed tight, grateful that she was safe, that he was holding her, and that no one was going to take her away from him. Fates. Until now, he hadn't really internalized the shockingly devastating turn of events.

A female had been captured by Doomers.

A female he knew personally, a female whose face he would be seeing every time he closed his eyes until he freed her. Because he knew that he would move heaven and earth to get her out of the Doomers' clutches.

But first, he had to safeguard the rest of the clan, which meant relocating everyone residing in the keep, as well as anyone who had ever been in contact with Carol.

Luckily, he was a paranoid bastard and had a contingency plan for something exactly like this happening.

23

ANDREW

*A*s Andrew arrived at the keep, he had no idea where he was supposed to go. Kian hadn't told him where he was holding the meeting. Not wanting to bother the boss, he dialed Bhathian's number instead. An emergency meeting would no doubt include every Guardian available.

"Yeah," Bhathian answered.

"I'm already in the building, but I don't know where the meeting is held."

"Bridget's office."

"I'm on my way.

So the male had been brought in, and Bridget was taking care of him. This could be the only reason for having the meeting in her office.

Crap, he wasn't ready to face her yet. This was going to be awkward.

Fuck, what was he doing? Worrying about facing his ex-non-girlfriend while the whole clan was in turmoil? A female had been abducted by the fucking Doomers, and this time not by someone like Dalhu who had treated Amanda with the utmost respect, but by males who would do horrific things to her.

Getting face to face with Bridget would be fine. They were both adults, and they'd already said their piece to each other over the phone. This couldn't be much worse. Unless, she still had feelings for him...

Nah, the whole thing had been nothing more than two lonely people scratching each other's itch. Problem was, the scratching had been quite intense. It would be tough to talk to Bridget and not picture her naked with her face soft and relaxed in a post orgasmic bliss.

Fuck, get a hold of yourself, Spivak. You're a grown man who is in love with an amazing woman and is about to get married. You can be friends with an ex-lover and not imagine her naked just because you know how she looks without clothes. You're going to show her the utmost respect even if it kills you.

Thank God, Bridget wasn't in her office when he got there, and the small room was bursting at the seams with the four large men—Kian and three of the Guardians. If more were coming, they would have to move this meeting out to the hallway.

"Andrew." Kian waved him in. "I was just about to start the briefing. The victim is still unconscious, so all we have is George's report, which isn't much. Apparently, Carol and Ben went outside the club to smoke, and when they didn't return, George went out looking for them. He found Ben slumped in the alley behind the parking lot of the club, unconscious and with half of his throat torn out. All that was left of Carol was her purse, which he saw lying on the ground. I think it's a forgone conclusion that they were attacked by Doomers and that the fuckers took Carol."

"We need to evacuate," Yamanu said.

Bhathian crossed his arms over his chest and looked at Kian. "Question is to where and who needs to go?"

"For now, we get everyone through the tunnel to the other building, block off the access to the underground from here, and leave only the human security detail that has no idea the underground exists."

What the hell was Kian talking about? Andrew searched his memory for any mention of another location. "What other building?"

"The high rise across the street is ours as well. We can access it through a tunnel that goes under the road. We left the six top floors vacant just for a situation like this, and the apartments are furnished. We can have everybody out in a couple of hours."

"You want me to get on it, boss?" Bhathian asked.

"Yeah, you and Arwel. Unfortunately, the two of you are experienced in herding people out of their homes."

Yamanu pushed away from the counter he was leaning against. "I can thrall the security people to forget about all of us."

Kian nodded. "Wait until everyone is out before you do it."

"Naturally."

The three left, leaving him and his brother-in-law alone in Bridget's office.

"What do you want me to do?" Andrew asked. It seemed that Kian had summoned him and the Guardians not to brainstorm the situation but to assign tasks.

"A couple of things. First, I want you here when Ben wakes up. You've done this before and know what to ask. Then I want you to find the Doomers' fucking base. I'm going to call every male who has ever served as a Guardian —locals as well as those who live in Scotland—and even the few who reside with my mother in Alaska. I'm going to assemble an army and storm that motherfucking base of theirs as soon as you find it."

Damn, as if it were so easy. Andrew rubbed his neck.

As Kian walked over to him and put a hand on his shoulder, Andrew fought the instinct to back away. Kian's eyes were glowing with that eerie luminescence he got going whenever he was in a murderous state of mind, like the one he was in now, and his fangs were starting to show.

"I want you to go all out on this. In less than an hour, I'll have a bank account in your name ready, with a couple of million in it. Recruit as many people as you can. Spare no expense on informants. I don't care who you have to bribe, and I don't even care if the money goes to drug and arms dealers if they have information to sell. The only thing I care about is getting Carol out and eliminating the threat to my people. I want every fucking Doomer in this local unit dead. Hell, I want all of them wiped off the face of the earth, but for now I'll be satisfied with those who came here to hunt us."

Damn. When he'd been part of a rescue operation like this in the past, Andrew's job had been the actual retrieval. All the ground work of accumulating information had been done for him by people who were experts in doing just that. What Kian was tasking him with was to be the mastermind who orchestrated it all.

Flattering, that's for sure, and challenging, but could he pull it off?

Perhaps, if he had months instead of days, he could learn on the job. But Carol didn't have this kind of time, and the stakes were too high for him to use this as a learning experience. He had to bring in the best in the field, someone who had masterminded dozens of these kinds of operations.

Fuck, Andrew never thought a day would come when he would consider working with his fucking old boss again. Turner was a prick. Emotionless, demanding. A guy who'd never had one single good word to say to anyone. But he was brilliant, and the best strategist Andrew had ever met. Not that he had met that many. Nevertheless, as much as he hated the guy, he also admired him.

Turner had retired a year before Andrew, and he wondered whether the guy was still working in the same field or chilling on a tropical beach and enjoying his retirement. But knowing Turner, he'd probably joined some civilian operation and was making tons of dough, masterminding corporate espionage and takeovers. In Andrew's humble and unprofessional opinion, Turner was borderline sociopath, which meant the guy couldn't enjoy anything, let alone something like chilling on a beach.

Shaking his head, Andrew made the decision to seek his old boss out. God, he'd hoped never to see that SOB again, and now he was planning on recruiting him for this mission.

Kian eyed Andrew suspiciously. "Is there a problem? Am I asking too much of you? You need to tell me now."

"It is, but only because of the urgency. If I had more time, I could find the right people for the job, make a good plan, and eventually figure out how to coordinate everything. When I was involved with hostage retrieval, another department was in charge of gathering information, and yet another did the reconnaissance. My old boss, Turner, orchestrated the whole thing. He had done it so many times that he could do this sleepwalking. If I can get him to help us, there is no one better for this. He is perfect for the job. Turner retired a year before me, and I believe his contacts and informants are still active. Problem is, I have no idea how hard it will be to find him. But assuming I manage, there is the issue of telling him the truth about what we are dealing with. The bastard is good at keeping secrets, but I know you have a problem with involving humans."

Kian took a few moments to think it over, then shook his head. "I'm breaking all kinds of my own rules here, but I'm sick and tired of our old tactics. I don't want to cower and hide anymore, I don't want to wait anxiously for the Doomers to make their next move. This time, we bring the battle to them, and I don't care what it takes. Do it. Find that Turner guy and bring him here. Is he for sale?"

"I'm sure he is. And if not for the money, he'll do it for the fun of it. The guy was one hundred percent dedicated to the work. No other interests, no wife, no girlfriend, a complete loner. Turner lived the job. We used to joke that after being forced to retire, he probably jumped off the nearest bridge."

"Let's hope he didn't. We need him."

24

DALHU

"So, where are we moving to?" Dalhu asked Kian as he started wrapping Anandur's half done portrait in brown paper.

"Just across the street. But Carol doesn't know that we own it. In fact, we own half of the high rise buildings on this block, and I have vacant and furnished apartments in each of them."

"Smart. But what happens the next time your location is compromised? You can't keep evacuating your people like this. Where are you going to move them the next time?"

Instead of answering, Kian walked up to the bar, grimaced at the modest selection, and reached for the Chivas.

"Anyone want anything?"

"Can you fix me a gin and tonic?" Syssi joined him and wrapped her arm around his waist.

"Amanda? Anything for you?" Kian called.

From the moment she'd learned about the evacuation, Amanda had been busy packing her wardrobe, or rather supervising Onidu as he filled suitcase after suitcase with stuff she deemed absolutely necessary. Which was most of her closet.

"Gin and tonic sounds great!"

"Dalhu?"

"I'm good." He could drink later—after he was done packing the most important stuff, which were all of his creations. Not only were the paintings and drawings the only things of value he owned, but they all depicted clan members. In the event that the Doomers actually infiltrated the building, it would be a disaster if the portraits fell into their hands.

Kian handed Syssi her drink and the one he'd made for Amanda. She took the two tumblers and headed toward Amanda's closet.

Drink in hand, Kian walked over to Dalhu. "If I play this right, there won't be a next time."

"What's the plan?" Dalhu wondered if Kian trusted him enough to share.

"A war. I'm sick of running, and I'm not about to let them keep Carol. No one deserves the hell they'll put her through."

With only seven Guardians, one of them a female, Kian was deluding himself if he thought he could take on such a large contingent of Doomers. The Guardians were good, but not that good.

"You're somewhat short on warriors for that. But if you're going to do it, you can count me in." Dalhu didn't expect Kian to take him up on his offer, but he could hope. A good fight would release some of the pressure that had been building up inside him. His gym sessions with

Anandur were good for taking off the edge, but they were no substitute for the rush of battle.

Shockingly, Kian nodded. "I can definitely use you. You know them, their weaknesses, their strengths, their style of warfare. And as for the Guardians, I've already started calling all of those who have left the force. I haven't had much luck convincing them to come back yet. Those I've spoken to have gotten too comfortable in their civilian lives. But Carol's capture is a game changer. Any Guardian who refuses the call to save a female from Doomers will lose face."

"How many are there?"

"I have over a hundred and fifty names on the list. If I can get one third of them to come back, we are good."

Probably. The Guardians could take on a force twice as big as theirs, or even more, and come out on top.

"It will take time, Kian. Time Carol doesn't have."

The guy's face twisted into a grimace. "Tell me something I don't know."

"Regardless, you need to find a better solution for your keep."

"If you have some bright ideas, I'm open to suggestions."

"I hate to bring him up, but Navuh solved this problem beautifully. The Doomers don't know where the island is, and the human pilots are under powerful compulsion not to reveal the location. That way, if a Doomer is captured, he can't lead anyone back to base." Dalhu finished wrapping his fourth portrait and propped it against the two others he'd already put next to the front door.

Kian rubbed his neck. "Problem is, my people work in the city. How am I going to shuffle them to and from work every day? Windowless busses? Have them blindfolded and blast music in the transport, so they don't hear anything from the outside? It's much easier to do with a plane. Without visuals or a compass, it is nearly impossible to tell where it is going."

"Yeah, I guess you're right."

As Dalhu picked up another portrait to wrap, Amanda and Syssi entered the living room. He lifted his head to glance at his woman, prepared for the impact of her beauty that never failed to deliver a punch to his gut, a zap to his heart, and a hardening to his shaft. It hadn't diminished even an iota since the first time he'd seen her, and he was certain it never would.

"I have an idea," she said, bracing her elbow on her arm and swishing the ice cubes in her gin and tonic.

"About what?" Kian asked.

"How to solve the problem of the keep's location and the commute to work. It's not cheap, or easy, but it may work."

Kian chuckled. "As if any of your ideas are ever cheap, or easy."

"Ha, ha, ha." She rolled her eyes. "Remember the cabin Dalhu and I stayed in after he'd kidnapped me?"

"As if I could ever forget." Kian's face twisted in an angry scowl. Apparently, he still held a grudge over what had happened there. He was entitled, though. To protect Dalhu, Amanda had attacked her own brother, tearing out a chunk of Kian's hair while riding his back buck naked. Not a fond memory for the guy, that's for sure.

"Anyway, the location is perfect. With some grading work, the flat area can be significantly enlarged. The mountain it sits on isn't very steep. We can build a little city of bungalows, buy a few more helicopters, and shuttle whoever needs to get to work in the city to one of the rooftops we own."

Kian snorted. "And what? Have some thralled humans pilot the crafts? This is not something we do, Amanda."

"Of course not, silly. We can use the Odus—like Mother does."

Kian opened his mouth to say something, then closed it, then opened it again, frowned, and closed it again. "It might be doable. I'm just thinking aloud here, so you are all welcome to jump in and correct me, or offer better ideas. Let's say we build this base on the mountain. If we use cars to travel to and from the place, the extra traffic may attract attention, but the same is true if we use helicopters. Aircraft are monitored by humans, and unlike Annani and her people, who seldom leave her place, our people will need daily transport. On top of that, the place is too far away for ground transportation."

"How about a tunnel? Like on Passion Island? You land in one place, but then travel by car to another," Dalhu suggested.

Kian shook his head. "Too involved and time-consuming for daily commute."

"Could a decoy work?" Syssi asked.

"What do you mean?"

"I once saw a science fiction movie, where they had a huge camouflaged door leading into a side of a mountain, and the helicopters flew right in. We can have something like this, and build a fake landing pad and a helicopter hanger nearby as a decoy."

Kian raked his fingers through his hair. "It might work.

We can have William design and install something that will introduce a momentary interference, like a short glitch, to hide the fact that the helicopter landed in a different place. But the problem with this whole idea is the insane cost. On top of those we already have, for that kind of money I can build several luxurious high rise buildings in downtown Los Angeles, with connecting tunnels to the crypt and the underground structure. The buildings are designed in a way that access to the underground can be closed off or even eliminated with no one any the wiser."

"In that case, why not relocate everything to the underground?" Dalhu asked. "It will eliminate the need to pack up and move every time there is a breach in security. All you'll need to do is change the entry point."

Syssi shuddered. "I don't want to live without windows. It's okay for a few days, but not all of the time."

Amanda wrapped her arm around Syssi's shoulders. "Yeah, me neither. I love the idea of living in the mountains, with fresh air and beautiful views, but Kian is right; too complicated and too expensive."

"Wonders never cease. Are you agreeing with me? Do you have a fever?"

"Well, apart from the costs, how are we going to hide the massive building project? And what about the workers and suppliers? When we build in downtown Los Angeles, there is nothing peculiar about it, just another developer building for profit. But out there? Too many questions will be asked."

"If this was the only problem, it could be solved. I can bring a big construction crew from China or Mexico to do the work, and then thrall all of them before sending them back home. And as to passersby, I can have Brandon produce a movie *on location* as a cover-up."

"So the only problem is money?" Amanda asked. "We have plenty."

"No, it's not only the money. It's the whole thing. Here, we are in the center of the city. If I need Andrew, I call him, and he comes over, and if I want to buy my wife a present, I don't need to plan an expedition, I just hop in my car and go. We can go to restaurants, movies, and so on. Mountain air and nice views sound good for a vacation, not a permanent living arrangement."

Dalhu shrugged. "It works on Passion Island. No one is complaining about the living conditions there."

Kian shook his head. "That's because there are so many people, and only some of them are coming and going on missions. Besides, between the Doomers, the hookers, and the service personnel, not to mention the tourists, the population probably numbers in the tens of thousands—mortals and immortals. We have only a few hundred immortals, that's it. Something like this can't work for us."

Amanda sighed. "I wish there was a third alternative. Something in between these two extremes."

"You can think about it while you pack. The sooner we are all out of here the better. Syssi and I are already done, and I suggest you hurry up, Amanda. You don't need to pack your whole wardrobe."

"But what if the Doomers come in and destroy it?"

"Then you buy a new one. When was the last time you wore the same outfit twice?"

"Fine." Amanda huffed and stormed out of the room.

Kian glanced at the remaining portraits, then at those

that were already wrapped and ready to go. "Let me help you with these. It's taking you too long." He grabbed one of the canvases and headed toward the roll of brown paper.

"Thank you, I appreciate it," Dalhu helped him pull a large piece of paper and tore it off the roll.

"I'll go help Amanda," Syssi said, kissing her husband's cheek before heading toward the master closet.

If not for the dire circumstances, Dalhu could've enjoyed this. It almost felt like he was finally part of the family.

25

ANDREW

*A*lone in Bridget's office, Andrew paced around while waiting for Ben to wake the hell up, which could happen in the next couple of minutes, or the next day, or even longer. Trouble was, it was time he couldn't afford to waste.

If he had his laptop with him, he could dig into his old boss's file, or at least the parts his security clearance would allow to unlock. He had no doubt that the majority of Turner's file required the highest level of clearance, several degrees above Andrew's. Still, there was a slight chance that one of the old veterans, those who had served with Turner since the beginning of his career in the unit, had kept in touch with him over the years and would know where to find him.

Hopefully, the guy hadn't been such a fucking sociopath when he was younger and actually had made some friends.

Question was, whether Andrew's contact list included the phone numbers of the few old timers that had been still serving during his time. After being forced to retire, he hadn't called anyone other than Jack and Rodney, and he couldn't remember who he'd added to his phone's short list of contacts and who he had not.

Damn, as if he needed another reminder that his brain was aging along with his body. He used to have an impeccable memory.

With a curse, Andrew fished out his phone from the inside pocket of his jacket and started scrolling through the names.

The first one he recognized was Rafael's, or Rafi as they'd used to call him. But when he dialed the guy's number, all he got was the annoying notification that the number he had reached was no longer in service.

Damn.

The only other one on the list hadn't heard from Turner in more than ten years.

That left Andrew's buddies. He sent both of them a message. It was a long shot, but it was worth a try. Maybe they knew someone who knew someone who knew someone. It didn't hurt to cover all the bases.

With that done, Andrew couldn't think of anything else he could do while waiting, and decided it was time to grow a set and face Bridget. It had to be done sooner or later, and there was no better time than right now.

"Come in," she said when he knocked quietly on the door.

As he pushed it open, Andrew was impressed by the sophisticated equipment of the intensive care unit Bridget was keeping Ben in. Not that he knew anything about medical equipment, but he'd spent time in enough ICUs to recognize state of the art when he saw it.

"Hi, Bridget. How is your patient doing?"

"He'll live."

"With you as his doctor, I'm sure he will. But I need to know when to expect him to wake up. If it's in the next hour, I'll stay. Otherwise, my time can be better utilized doing other things."

She shrugged. "I know. And I wish I could give you a definite answer. But frankly, what do you expect to learn from him when he wakes up? With most of his throat missing, it will take Ben weeks of recovery until he'll be able to talk, and I doubt he'll be strong enough to write answers to your questions."

"Do you have a tablet here? Touching a finger to a screen doesn't require much effort if we hold it up for him."

"Yeah, I do."

"Good."

Bridget turned around, pretending to focus on the monitors tracking Ben's vitals whose output hadn't spiked or dropped even once.

Damn, this was awkward. What the hell was he supposed to say now?

That he was sorry? Maybe ask her about the guy she'd met at Julian's graduation?

She beat him to it. "This shouldn't be this awkward. I want us to be friends."

"I'd like that. But I can't help feeling guilty about ending it the way I did. You deserve better than a phone call."

Bridget tugged on her ponytail, readjusting the rubber band that held it secured at the top of her head. "You would've been right to feel like a heel if I wasn't guilty of even worse.

You called me before you made your move." She smiled with just one side of her mouth. "I was already halfway there. When Daniel started flirting with me, I didn't do anything to discourage him, even though I felt like a slut for actually encouraging him. It's just that the chemistry between us was off the charts. I couldn't resist. Hell, I didn't want to."

Phew, this was a huge relief. He should be just as gracious. "I should write this Daniel a thank-you note. If not for him, I would've felt like a scumbag. Because I had a similar reaction to Nathalie. There was no way I could've waited for you to come back before putting the moves on her."

"Is she your one?" Bridget pinned him with a set of smart blue eyes.

He nodded. "Without a doubt."

"Do you want to tell me about her?"

"Are you sure you're up to it? Maybe you should tell me about Daniel first."

The smile that spread over her lovely face was as good an indicator as anything she might have said about her feelings for the guy. "He is the head intern at the hospital where Julian is about to start his internship. He is thirty-one years old, about your height, but not as strongly built, and he is absolutely brilliant. I think I fell for his intellect first, or maybe it was his macabre sense of humor. Probably both. Not that the physical attraction wasn't enough, but I've been powerfully attracted to guys before." She blushed and looked down at her hands.

"I was to you." Her whisper sounded like an apology. "With Daniel, though, I felt an affinity. It's hard to describe, but it kind of felt like I'd known him forever and had finally found my way back home. Strange, right?"

She chuckled, an embarrassed high-pitched sound. "It's fascinating, the power our hormones have over our lives. We think we are in control, and that we are making our own decisions, but we are not. We are ruled by powerful chemicals that regulate our moods, influence who we think we are in love with. Free will is an illusion."

Andrew shook his head. "You can't really believe this. I'm sure hormones are part of it, but we are more than the chemical interactions in our brain. Our thoughts and beliefs might be colored by them, but we retain at least some control over our reactions."

"Or do we?"

She still wasn't convinced.

"You said it yourself. You were attracted to Daniel physically, but that wasn't what caused you to fall for him. You fell for his sense of humor and quick mind. I'm not a scientist, but I don't think humor and intellect produce pheromones."

"Ha, but the joy of laughing at a joke and having an intelligent conversation might."

Andrew raised his hands in surrender. "I give up. You're incorrigible."

"Just messing with you. I'm not completely convinced it's only chemical reactions either." Bridget winked. "But this is a discussion for philosophers. I want to hear all about your woman. I told you about mine, now it's your turn to tell me about yours."

Where should he start? Did Bridget know about Nathalie being Bhathian's daughter? Kian and Syssi knew, and Bhathian hadn't asked them to keep it a secret, but should he assume that they told everyone?

Andrew pulled out his phone. "Can you give me a moment? I need to send a quick text first."

"Sure…" Bridget's brows formed an arch.

Fully aware of how peculiar his behavior must've seemed to her, Andrew turned around and texted Bhathian, asking if he could tell Bridget. It took only a few seconds for the guy's short reply text to arrive.

It's fine.

Turning around, he slipped the phone back into the inside pocket of his jacket. "Sorry about that, but I had to ask Bhathian's permission first."

Her brows arched even higher. "Bhathian?"

"It's a long story, but Nathalie is Bhathian's daughter. Her mother had told him she was pregnant and then disappeared. He's been searching for her for years, not sure if he had a child or not. When he heard about my connections, he asked for my help. That's how I met her."

"Wow, what a story. Does she know?"

Andrew shook his head. "She doesn't even know her adoptive father is not her real one. And she thinks Bhathian is just a friend. But what's an even bigger story than Bhathian having a daughter is that we suspect her mother is an immortal. Unfortunately, the woman pulled another disappearing act, so we can't know for sure. Not until we find her."

"How is it possible?"

"We don't know. But going by Nathalie's account and a fairly recent picture, the woman hasn't aged even a little in thirty years."

"So Nathalie might be a Dormant?"

"Yes."

"Are you going to try to activate her?"

"I can't."

"I know that. But someone else can do it."

"Over my dead body."

Bridget laughed. "How did I know you were going to say that?"

Andrew grimaced. "I have no idea."

She patted his shoulder. "Right. So I guess you'll be attempting the transition after all."

"It seems so. But I want to find her mother first. I don't want to take the risk unless I'm convinced Nathalie is a Dormant."

"Does she know you're searching for her mother?"

"Bhathian and I offered to help find her, and Nathalie is under the impression that we are working for some secret government agency."

"I wonder what gave her that impression?" Bridget said mockingly.

Andrew tugged on his tie to loosen it. "I hate the fucking lies. But for now, I have no choice."

Bridget sighed. "Yeah, I know what you mean. Daniel thinks I'm Julian's sister. I'm going to have a tough time explaining things if he decides to come visit me in Los Angeles."

It occurred to him then that Bridget's guy lived thousands of miles away, which was probably a good thing. "I was under the impression that you guys didn't do relationships. So I assumed that after you said your goodbyes you thralled him to forget you."

"Usually yes. But females have a little more leeway. It's not like I need to thrall him each time we have sex." She chuckled. "Aside from my stamina, there is nothing that suggests I'm anything other than a human female. I really like Daniel. I want to see him again."

"Well, I guess it's okay given the distance. It's not like you guys are going to get together often enough for him to notice anything."

Andrew knew there was more to the story when Bridget began fidgeting with her stethoscope.

"Daniel is applying for positions in hospitals over here. And with his excellent record and a stellar recommendation from his chief of staff, he'll have no trouble finding one. I just don't know what I'll do once he moves here. It's difficult to keep the lies going even when he is on the other side of the continent."

"Tell me about it. I'm not even an immortal, and I'm forced to lie to the woman I love. With my job, I should be used to this, but keeping secrets that have to do with national security is easy. What I hate are the lies I have to tell Nathalie about my family. I had to come up with all kinds of contrived excuses as to why I haven't introduced her to my sister and her husband yet."

"Why didn't you? It's not like they have Immortal stamped on their foreheads. We interact with humans on a regular basis, and it's fine."

"I don't know. Syssi could pass for a human easily. After all, she was one until recently. But Kian is a different story. The dude is too good-looking for his own good."

Bridget laughed. "Are you jealous of your brother-in-law, Andrew?"

"I'm not. But I know Nathalie is going to gape at him like a fool. She will not be able to help it. And it's going to drive me crazy."

Bridget shook her head and patted his back. "You've got it bad, buddy."

"I know."

26

NATHALIE

"Good morning, Vlad." Nathalie opened the back door to let the guy in. She had gotten so used to him that most days his appearance no longer shocked her. But today, in addition to his usual all-black garb, the traces of black eyeliner around his eyes made his pale and gaunt face look more vampiric than ever.

"Good morning, Nathalie." He ducked his head as he entered, then closed the door behind him.

With a frown, she looked up at the top of his head. Had the boy grown a few inches since yesterday? Because as tall as he was, Vlad had never had a problem clearing the doorway before. But obviously, it was absurd, and the only reasonable explanation was that he was wearing heeled shoes. A glance at his feet confirmed her assumption. Vlad's black-leather boots reached midway to his calves, sported a row of metal buckles on their sides, and had platforms at least two inches high.

Good God, what was he thinking?

If any of the customers ventured into the kitchen and

saw this cross between Dracula and Frankenstein's monster, they would run away screaming.

Damn, how was she going to tell the kid to tone down his style without offending him? Maybe she should just let it go and hope no one peeked into the kitchen.

Oh, Nathalie, you are so sweet.

"Sage?"

"Did you say something?" Vlad asked while tying the apron's belt around his narrow midriff.

She waved a hand. "Just ignore me. Sometimes I talk to myself." Heck, if she could tolerate a vampire lookalike in her kitchen, Vlad could live with a boss who talked to herself.

He shrugged. "Just let me know when you're talking to me."

"No problem. I'm going upstairs for a few minutes. You're okay here by yourself?"

"You know I am."

"Fine." Yes she did, but out of courtesy, she had to ask.

Taking the stairs up to her apartment, she whispered, "Where were you? I didn't hear from you for days. I thought you were gone."

Gone where?

"How the hell should I know? To the great beyond? Heaven? Hell?"

I'm sorry I had you worried. It's difficult for me to estimate the passage of time. It's not the same as it is for the living.

"I wasn't worried. More like relieved."

Oh...

He sounded offended.

"Don't get me wrong. I like you, Sage. You seem like a

very nice guy. But hearing you in my head is not normal. I wish one day to be free of the voices. So every time a few days pass without intrusions, I get my hopes up."

I'm truly sorry.

Shit, Sage sounded as if he was on the verge of tears. "It's okay. It's not your fault. So what have you been up to?"

I was trying to figure out who I was before.

"Any luck?"

I must've done programming. I know how to do it. I can even ghost into a system and program it from the inside. I can influence electric pulses. If you want, I can type a message on your laptop's screen. But it has to be on.

Now he sounded excited, even proud. "Maybe later you can show me. But I have to get back to work."

I'll try to come back later today. But if I overshoot it will probably be tomorrow. And as to the kid, tell him he's got the rock star look nailed, but that it is not a look appropriate for a day job.

"You are good at this. You sure you were a programmer? Those guys' social skills are usually not that great."

I'm sure. Bye, Nathalie.

Sage was so nice and easygoing that she almost didn't mind his sporadic intrusions. After all, he always left when she asked him to, and his advice was actually useful.

When she returned to the kitchen, Nathalie leaned against the worktable where Vlad was busy cutting dough into little triangles and rolling them into croissants.

"Vlad, honey, I need to tell you something."

He paused, lifting his head to look at her with a worried expression on his face. "Did I do something wrong?"

"No, of course not. You're wonderful. And this outfit you are wearing is so cool, for a rock star, but not for a baker."

He glanced down at his boots. "I see."

"It's not just the boots. You have traces of makeup around your eyes. I know it's from last night's performance, but you need to take it off completely."

"I do?" He rubbed at his eyes. "I thought I got it all off."

She shook her head. "Go to the bathroom and see for yourself. You probably rubbed your eyes, and the little that was left got smeared all over. Happens to me every time I put eyeliner on."

Vlad rushed off and returned a few minutes later with an almost clean face. "I have a pair of sneakers in my car. I should go and put them on. The boots are cool, but they are not comfortable."

"Go, I'll finish this batch." Well, that went smoothly. *Thank you, Sage.*

You've never thanked me, even when I saved your little butt from getting in trouble.

Damn, she almost nicked her finger with the knife. What was it? The national ghost appreciation day or something?

"Tut, you bastard, you scared me. I thought you were gone for good."

First of all, I'm not a bastard. My parents were married when I was born, unfortunately, not happily. It was an arranged marriage. Not to say that all arranged marriages are doomed to fail, some work out beautifully, but I digress.

"Why are you still in my head?"

I wish I knew. Believe me, I want to go more than you want me gone. But it's like this single strand of hair tethers me to you, and it refuses to break. I think I'm supposed to teach you how to block the others before I'm allowed to leave.

She waved the hand holding the cutting knife as if he could see it. "Be my guest. I'd love to learn this trick."

Yeah, problem is, I'm not sure how you're supposed to do it. But I have a few suggestions that you may try.

Great, the blind leading the blind. "Shoot."

Imagine a door, one with heavy locks and a key that only you have. The next time Sage intrudes, imagine slamming the door in his face and locking it.

Nathalie winced. "That's terribly rude. Sage is nice. I'll feel awful about treating him like that."

Fine. I guess that's why you haven't been practicing blocking him like I've told you to do. If you like him so much, let him in on what you're trying to do. And if he is really so great, he'll help you figure it out.

"Oh yeah? How come you didn't offer yourself for me to practice on?"

You've got a point. Okay. I'm going to ghost out and then ghost back in. The moment you feel me coming, slam the door.

She frowned. "Most times I feel nothing until you start talking in my head. How am I supposed to slam the door when you're already inside?"

Good point.

"Can I imagine kicking you out with a giant boot to your ass?"

Whatever works, sweetheart. Let's try it.

Weird, now that she paid attention, she actually felt him ghosting out. So why hadn't she felt him ghosting in?

Focusing all of her attention on Tut's reentry, Nathalie tried to determine whether she could detect any peculiar sensation before he made his presence known by speaking to her inside her mind.

Well, I'm here. Kick me out.

She realized that there had been a slight pressure before he spoke, but to stop him would be like trying to close the door on a gust of wind—too late because it was already inside.

So all that was left was to try and boot him out. Or conversely, isolate him in a virtual soundproof booth. Nathalie closed her eyes and imagined that Tut was inside a special room in her brain, a glass isolation chamber with a trapdoor. She commanded the door to slide down shut, trapping him inside the chamber, then shrank the whole thing and put it on a shelf of an imaginary bookcase.

Waiting, she expected Tut's cackling laugh or snarky remark, but all she heard was silence.

No way. She couldn't have done it on her first try. "Say something!"

There was no response.

Ugh, having a ghost trapped in her imaginary isolation chamber, displayed like some trinket on her virtual bookcase, was even more freaky than hearing him talk to her. Nathalie closed her eyes and imagined the little glass box with a little shrunken Tut inside it expanding. When it was back to its original size, she commanded the trap door to lift. "Come on, Tut, get out and talk to me."

Don't ever do that again! The great Tut sounded shaky.

"So it worked?"

Yeah, it worked. But I don't think you want a bunch of trapped ghosts in your head. Even if you can keep them silent.

"What if I use this as a threat? I can tell uninvited intruders to either get out or stay trapped forever in a little glass box."

I'm positive that this would do the trick. It was the most terrifying experience of my existence—including the time I woke up dead.

"I'm sorry. I didn't know it would be so bad for you."

Oh, Nathalie. You are indeed way too nice.

God, even Tut's compliments sounded like insults. "Is it your way of saying that I'm a pushover?"

One last piece of advice in case I manage to finally get out of here for good. Stop putting everyone's welfare before your own. You come first. Everyone and everything else comes second.

"I don't think I can do it. But thanks for the advice."

Farewell, sweet Nathalie. Hope to never see you again.

"Same here."

27

CAROL

rap, what am I doing here?

As Carol opened her eyes, she was convinced that she had woken up in her old cell at the keep. Except, Ingrid must've done some decorating, because the little box of a room had pictures hanging on the walls, and Carol was lying on an actual bed with a headboard and footboard and not on a mattress on the floor.

Fates, she felt so spaced out. She must've really overdone it with the alcohol and the pot, and that was probably why she'd landed back in prison. Kian had warned her to watch it.

On second thought, they must've put her in a different cell, because there were two doors. Her old cell had only one. The bathroom area had been separated only by a partition. A quick glance confirmed that there was none here.

Which was worse. Because it meant that she was going to spend way more than a few days in the slammer this time.

But what had she done?

Had she been telling stories again?

Her memory was fuzzy, and she wasn't sure what had really happened and what had been a dream. There was a dim memory of being thrown over some guy's shoulder and carried away.

Boy, had she done more than pot?

It had been a while since she'd snorted, and even longer since she'd injected. Hopefully, she hadn't fallen off the wagon as the drunkards called it. But if she had, it must've been because someone had slipped it to her. She'd been good lately. Or as good as she could be.

Carol reached for the glass of water that someone had thoughtfully left for her on the nightstand and emptied it on a oner. Still thirsty, she looked around, hoping to find a pitcher or a bottle. There wasn't any in sight. Never mind, she could use the faucet in the bathroom. And anyway, now that she was thinking of water, she felt an urgent need to empty her bladder.

With her head spinning, it was a struggle to get vertical, and as she trudged toward the door leading to what she hoped was a bathroom, Carol was thankful for the small size of the room. Much easier to use the furniture and the walls for support when everything was in arm's reach.

Surprisingly, she found the bathroom kitted out for a female, with hairbrushes and a hair dryer, and an assortment of lotions and fragrances. There was even a fluffy white robe hanging on a hook, and on the floor below it, a pair of white terry slippers were still in their original packaging.

Nice. She didn't know they had cells dedicated to

females now. Or maybe it was all for her, since she was obviously going to spend a lot of time here.

With a sigh, she took care of business, then stepped into the shower. The water pressure wasn't as good as she remembered, which was the only downside of this new prison cell compared to her old one.

She spent a lot of time in the shower. After all, it wasn't as if she had anything else to do. When she was finally done, Carol used the dryer to dry her hair, which wasn't a complicated affair since she just waved it around her head and let her curls take shape naturally. Some lotion on her face and her hands, a little spritz of fragrance on her pulse points, and she felt like a new woman. There was no makeup, but then she had no one to get pretty for.

Lying in bed and watching TV, if there was one, or reading a book, was all she had to look forward to for the foreseeable future.

Pushing the door open, Carol frowned as an unfamiliar scent reached her nose. Was there a male in her room?

"Hello, darling. Did you have a pleasant time in the shower?"

A gasp escaped her throat, and she jumped back, slamming the bathroom door closed. Her heart pounding like a jackhammer, she backed away until her ass hit the wall.

The handle turned, and the male pushed the door open unhurriedly, smiling a blood-chilling smile. "Don't be afraid, little rabbit. I'm not going to hurt you. Yet. I just want to talk." He extended his arm in invitation.

There was nowhere to go, and instinctively she knew that making him wait was a really bad idea. Placing her shaking hand in his palm, she let the Doomer lead her back to the room.

Because yeah, this Dorothy was for sure not in Kansas anymore.

He had her sit on the bed while he took the only chair. "What's your name, darling?" he asked in a most pleasant tone that she didn't buy for a second.

"Carol." She managed a hoarse whisper.

"My poor darling, I see that you're parched. I'll call someone to bring you a drink of water. Would you care for something to eat? I'm afraid our culinary selection is limited at the moment, but I'm working on procuring a chef."

She shook her head. "I'm not hungry."

"Nonsense. You must eat, at least a little something." He pulled out his phone. "Tom, could you please bring a pitcher of water, a glass of orange juice, and some fruit and crackers for Carol?"

She heard the other guy respond with a 'coming right up.'

The weird thing was that the Doomer appeared genuine in his concern for her well-being. Except, it did nothing to assuage her fear of him. He wasn't a big male, no more than six feet tall, maybe even an inch or two shorter than that, and although trim and muscular, he wasn't buff. He had a handsome face and a pleasant voice, and yet he scared the crap out of her.

"By the way, I'm Sebastian, Sebastian Shar, but you can call me Master."

Carol swallowed. She wasn't a submissive. In fact, she had a very low tolerance for pain. But she'd played the game before with men who were more interested in dominating

I. T. LUCAS

than hurting her. As a courtesan, she had met her share of guys with deviant appetites, and she hadn't turned any away as long as they hadn't requested to tie her up. One on one and with nothing to restrain her, if things got out of hand, she could overpower a human male quite easily. Trouble was, this guy was an immortal male, a lot stronger than her, and she had a feeling he didn't play by the rules, nor was he interested in a mild game of domination.

There would be no safe words for her, no way out. Just pain.

A tear sliding down her cheek, she whispered. "Yes, Master."

"Smart girl. I see that we are going to get along splendidly."

28

SEBASTIAN

"Come in!" Sebastian called.

He wasn't surprised that Tom fulfilled his order so expeditiously. The guy probably couldn't wait to lay his eyes on the immortal female. Last night Tom hadn't been at the base when she'd been brought in, and Robert had been the lucky bastard who had made all the necessary arrangements for her.

As Tom came in with the tray, Carol raised a pair of pleading big blue eyes to the guy. Silly girl, there was no one here who would raise a finger to help her. She was completely at Sebastian's mercy.

Not that he had any.

Placing the tray on the nightstand, Tom leaned toward Carol, using the excuse to get close to the woman and take a sniff. The growl that started deep in Sebastian's throat had him hastily backing away.

"Would there be anything else, sir?"

Sir? Sebastian regarded Tom with a frown. Since when

had the insolent bastard become so courteous? Was he mocking him?

The pungent scents of fear and despair wafting off Carol masked Tom's more subtle one, but with a little effort, Sebastian managed to isolate it. The guy was scared.

Good. Fear would keep him from getting any smart ideas.

Carol belonged to Sebastian, exclusively.

"No, that will be all, Tom. You're excused."

"Yes, sir." Tom gave a slight bow and got out of the room as fast as his short legs could carry him.

Carol released a barely audible sigh and let her head drop. She hadn't touched anything on the tray, not even the water. The girl seemed frozen in her pose, barely breathing.

Obviously, she'd figured out Sebastian's intentions for her and was terrified. Which meant that even though she'd known the proper response, she wasn't a submissive. She had probably dabbled her dainty little feet in the game once or twice, and the little knowledge she had was more harmful than complete ignorance.

Sebastian realized that he needed to back off if he didn't want to break her. After all, it wasn't as if there was a chance in hell another immortal female would fall into his lap anytime in the near or far future. He was one lucky son of a bitch to snag this one.

Thank you, Mortdh.

He still toyed with the idea that Carol could be much more than an indestructible toy. He could get her pregnant, she could give him a son, an immortal whom he would raise and groom for greatness the same way Losham had done for him.

"Drink your juice, Carol."

She shook her head but didn't dare look up at him.

With a sigh, he got up and sat on the bed beside her. She scooted away, but he grabbed her chin, gently but firmly, and tilted her head, so she was forced to face him. Her big teary eyes and trembling lip had no effect on him, and it didn't matter to him if she was putting on a show or not.

"When I tell you to do something, I expect to be obeyed immediately. And by immediately I mean instantly. I will not tolerate even a split second delay. Is that clear?"

She nodded quickly, her little chin moving up and down as much as his fingers allowed, and her beautiful blonde curls bouncing enticingly around her elvish face.

The girl was not only adorable but seemed trainable. He smiled at her and gently cupped her cheek. "Now, was it so hard, darling? It's very simple. Obedience will be rewarded, and disobedience will be punished."

Carol seemed to relax a little.

Sebastian reached for the glass of juice and handed it to her. "I want to see you drink the whole thing. Take your time, I don't want you to choke on it, but I want this glass empty before you put it down."

She nodded.

"Tsk, tsk. I allowed a nod once, but I don't consider it a proper response."

She whispered, "Yes, Master."

"Much better. Now drink up."

29

ANDREW

"Rodney, my man, I owe you big time." Andrew scribbled the number Rodney had given him on a piece of paper. "How the hell did you find the old bastard?"

"Remember Chris?" Rodney asked.

"The new recruit? Sure, how could I forget a guy with a big tattoo of a naked woman on his back? He started training a few months before I left."

"Yup." Rodney chuckled. "Betty Boop but with no clothes. I remembered him mentioning that he went to a military academy with Turner's son."

"I'll be damned. Turner has a son? I didn't even know that the dude was married."

"He wasn't. Apparently, Turner knocked up the guy's mom during freshman year in college. I called him up; his name is Douglas by the way. He and his old man are not close, but he gets to meet Turner twice a year. His mom married another guy, but with Turner paying support all those years and then for the academy, she insisted that they stay in touch. Long story short, that's how I've gotten Turner's private number."

"Thanks, and I mean it, I owe you."

There was a moment of silence before Rodney replied. "How about you buy me a drink, and we call it even? We haven't gotten together in ages. What's up with that?"

Damn. Rodney was right. Ever since Andrew had gotten involved with the clan, he had neglected his friends. The last time he'd seen them had been on Amanda's rescue mission, which of course they remembered nothing of. As far as they were concerned, it had never happened. The hefty sum in their bank accounts had been explained as payment for a job so secret that they'd agreed to get hypnotized to forget. Pretty damn close to the truth. "You're absolutely right. How about Monday after work? We can call Jake."

"Why not tonight?"

"Sorry, I've already made other plans."

"You've got yourself a girlfriend, Spivak?"

"Yeah."

"About time. So have fun tonight with your girl, and we'll talk again on Monday."

"Good deal."

As he ended the call, Andrew stuffed the piece of paper with Turner's number in his pocket, collected his car keys and headed out. Most of the agents were already gone. People didn't do overtime on Friday unless it was absolutely necessary.

If not for Rodney's help, Andrew would've been one of the unlucky ones who had to stay behind, trying to dig out names he could hit for information. But now that he had Turner's number, he may be able to go home and take

Nathalie out as he'd planned before the shit had hit the fan with Carol's abduction. He still had the tickets.

The big question was whether Turner would accept the mission and take this thing off Andrew's shoulders. He'd call the guy from the car, on the burner phone he kept for instances like this. Not that he was doing anything illegal, but he preferred to keep his call to Turner private. The office was outfitted with surveillance cameras that were monitoring everything, and his cellphone was probably monitored as well. There was no reception in the underground structure, so he would have to drive out and park on the street or find a strip mall's parking lot somewhere nearby.

Five o'clock in the afternoon in downtown Los Angeles was the worst time to drive around, but at least there were plenty of parking spots in front of the nearest Starbucks.

As he turned off the ignition and reached for the burner phone, a sudden craving for a tall iced cappuccino had him out of the car and standing in line to order one. In the back of his mind, though, Andrew was well aware that this was nothing but stalling. Calling his old boss was a task he would've gladly delegated to someone else, and what's more, asking the bastard for a favor was something he had never imagined doing, outside of hell that is.

His ice-cold drink in hand, Andrew went back to his car... and just sat there.

Damn, why was he fretting about a bloody phone call? The condescending prick had no power over him, not anymore.

It had been such a relief when the guy had retired. It wasn't that Andrew could prove that Turner had done anything wrong. It was more about the potential. The bastard was an emotionless sociopath and therefore extremely dangerous. If he believed that sacrificing a team would achieve his objective, Andrew had no doubt the guy wouldn't even blink before sending them out on a suicide mission. In fact, he was convinced that Turner had done it on more than one occasion.

No soldier wanted his superior to deem him expendable. Not even an adrenaline junkie like Andrew.

On the other hand, he had to admit that Turner's brilliant mind had come up with strategies that had probably saved many more lives than his ice-cold heart had allowed to perish. But it was of little solace when some of those lost lives had belonged to Andrew's friends.

Besides, the condescending prick and his goddamned superiority complex had rubbed Andrew the wrong way. The fucker was indeed brilliant, but that didn't give him the right to treat everyone around him as if they were dimwits.

Anger was always a strong motivator for Andrew, and thinking about Turner's callous and condescending attitude had been enough to rile him up. He pulled out the piece of paper with Turner's number from one pocket, the phone from another, and punched in the numbers.

"Turner here, and who the hell are you?"

"Andrew Spivak, sir." Damn, Andrew wanted to bang his head against the steering wheel. Why the hell had he tagged on the honorific? Turner was no longer his commander. They were both civilians for fuck's sake.

"Spivak, how the hell did you get this number?"

Andrew rolled his eyes. Nothing had changed over the couple of years since he'd seen Turner. The guy was as *charming* as always. "It doesn't matter how. I need to know if you're interested in a civilian job that pays big money."

"I'm listening." Turner's tone had changed from angry to curious in a heartbeat.

"It's a short-term assignment, but it's urgent. Are you free to come on board right away?"

"For the right amount, I can be free by tomorrow. There is something I'm wrapping up, but it's at a stage that I can have someone else tie the loose ends if need be. How much are we talking about?"

"I can arrange a meeting for tomorrow morning, and you can name your price. A family member was taken by an enemy and the guy is willing to do and pay whatever it takes."

Turner snorted. "That's what you're calling me about? You can't handle something this simple on your own?"

Andrew gritted his teeth, striving for a measured tone. "It's way bigger than what I've just told you. But I can't tell you more until we meet face to face with the client."

"Fine. Where and when?"

He almost gave Turner the keep's address, when he thought better of it. If things didn't work out, Kian would thrall the guy. But if Turner inputted the address in some database it may later trigger a memory. After all, thralling didn't work as well on those with sharp minds. Besides, Kian had moved everyone to the other building, and he probably didn't want to conduct the meeting in the underground complex.

"Let's meet at the Starbucks on South Grand and from there drive together to the meeting place. Ten o'clock good for you?"

Turner chuckled. "Afraid I'll get lost on the way, Spivak?"

"Aw shucks, you've got me. With old age comes confusion and memory loss, I didn't want an old timer like you driving in circles."

That earned him a snort. "See you tomorrow, Spivak. Ten sharp. Starbucks."

"Yes, sir." Damn, old habits died hard.

Andrew returned the burner phone to the glove compartment, turned on the ignition, did a K-turn, pulled into the snail-pace traffic, and called Nathalie on his regular cellphone.

"Hi, sweetheart. Are you getting ready for tonight?"

She sighed. "Not yet. It's a madhouse in here. I don't think I'll be able to leave Jackson alone until we close."

Andrew had had Jackson make himself available to babysit Fernando every Friday so he could take Nathalie out. He'd kept the concert tickets a surprise, and until his talk with Turner he'd thought they would go to waste. But now that it seemed Turner was on board, Andrew could finally tell her about them.

"It's okay, the concert starts at eight, but the *Infected Mushroom* will probably not go up on stage until nine."

He heard Nathalie's shriek even though she was holding the phone away from her mouth. "Guys, Andrew got tickets for the Infected Mushroom, can you believe it?" She shrieked again then brought the phone again to her mouth. "How did you do it? They were sold out weeks ago."

"I have my mysterious ways. But I've got only two, so you shouldn't go advertising the fact to everyone. I'll get mobbed when I get there. Their fans are lunatics."

"That's not true."

"Says the lady who a moment ago shrieked like a possessed Valkyrie. Are the shop's windows still intact? Or should I stop by a glass repair store on the way?"

She laughed. "Don't worry, I'll sneak you in from the back so you won't get mobbed. And thank you. The Infected Mushroom is my favorite band."

"I know, that's why I pulled some strings to get these tickets."

"You're so sweet. But, Andrew, you hate their music. "

"I don't hate it. It's just that some of it sounds like burps. I'm not a big fan of concerts in general, they are too loud. But I bought us two pairs of quality earplugs. Just in case you want to protect your ears as well."

Damn, this sounded a lot like something his mother would've said.

Andrew sighed. Getting old was a bitch. He wondered if he would still feel this way when and if he transitioned. Probably not. Age-wise, Kian was ancient, but he talked and acted more or less the age he looked. Though not when he was talking business. Exuding the authority his job demanded, Kian seemed at least a decade older.

It would be fun watching him with Turner. Andrew would bet that his old boss couldn't intimidate Kian no matter how hard he tried. And he would try, no doubt about it.

Which reminded him that he still needed to call Kian and let him know about the meeting tomorrow morning.

"Yeah," Kian answered on the first ring.

"I'm meeting Turner tomorrow at ten at a Starbucks. Where do you want to meet him? Should I bring him to the keep, or the new place?"

"Let me give you an address of an office in one of the other buildings we own. I'd rather keep the new location secure."

"I'm driving. Can you text it to me?"

"I'll do it right now."

"Thanks."

30

KIAN

"*C*ome to bed." Syssi wrapped her arms around Kian's neck and pulled him down for a kiss.

For the first time, her soft curves and hungry lips didn't stir the beast inside him. He returned her kiss almost absentmindedly, his head a million miles away. Or more accurately, a little over five thousand, which was the distance between Los Angeles and Sari's keep in Scotland.

He pulled her hands away. "I have a few phone calls I need to make first. I'll join you later."

Damn, he should have said he was sorry, or told her that he loved her before turning down her sweet invitation. Was he ever going to learn? Kian expected to find a hurt expression as he glanced down at Syssi's beautiful face, but found a thoughtful and worried one instead.

"Are you going to call more of the retired Guardians?"

He sighed.

Unfortunately, almost all of the guys had chosen to remain in Scotland, and as inept as Kian was at charming people, he was even worse over the phone.

"I'm not having much luck. I've got two who said they would think about it, and only one who said he is coming on the next flight. I'm going to talk to Sari again and see if her results are better."

Syssi cupped his cheek. "I hope I'm not being presumptuous, offering you advice about dealing with people that you know so well, and I don't. But I think you're going about it all wrong."

"You're not being presumptuous, ever. You're my wife and my confidant. Who else is going to give me honest advice?"

Syssi chuckled. "Oh, I don't know... Amanda? Your mother? Sari?"

Yeah. He was surrounded by women who loved telling him what and how to do things. But in truth, Kian didn't mind. After all, he was only obligated to listen, and later decide if their advice was good or not, and whether to accept it or discard it.

"But I value yours the most." Kian meant it. Syssi seldom offered suggestions, but when she did, not only were they spot on, but he usually didn't think twice before implementing them.

"Okay. So here is the thing. I'm not surprised you're having trouble luring them back. You're asking these men to leave behind the life that they've built for themselves, and that they love. Instead, you should present it as an emergency situation for which their help is desperately needed, and once this crisis is over, they'll be free to return to their regular lives."

"But I want them to stay. Even after we get Carol back, I want to have a formidable force in place."

187

Syssi smirked and patted his cheek. "I know. But for now it is crucial to mobilize the men as quickly as possible. You don't have time to wait for them to reevaluate their lives and decide whether they are ready for a change or not. The old Guardians will find it very difficult to refuse a call to come save a female from Doomers, and once they are here and get a taste for the excitement and camaraderie, and whatever else men get out of serving together, some may elect to stay. As to the others, you can introduce a reserves program. They'll be called in for training now and then, and serve one month out of a year. Again, not an earth-shaking change, and, hopefully, one that they will find acceptable."

He picked her up and smashed her to him. "You're a genius, Syssi. This will work."

She kissed his cheek. "You've said it before, it's called teamwork."

As he looked into his wife's smiling eyes, Kian's heart swelled with love for her. She was such a blessing to him. "I'm so in love with you, sweet girl, that I can't imagine I could ever love you more, and yet I find that I do."

"Oh, you're such a romantic."

"Am not!"

"Yes, you are. Stop denying it." She wiggled out of his arms. "Go, make those phone calls already. I'm going to wait for you in bed." She winked before walking away, exaggerating the sashaying of her hips.

Fates, the woman had a sexy ass.

He forced himself to stick his itching palms into his pockets and head down the hallway to his makeshift office in the new apartment they'd moved to. It had been a while

DARK WARRIOR'S PROMISE

since he'd spanked her, and those swaying hips were her way to remind him that he'd been neglectful lately. It had been easier when they'd worked together—plenty of opportunities to find good excuses for playtime. But between their busy schedules and this latest crisis, he found it next to impossible to get into a playful mood.

With a sigh, Kian plopped down into his executive chair and picked up the receiver. It was mid-morning in Scotland, and Sari should be in her office.

"Kian, what's up? Any news about Carol?"

"No, still working on it. But I need those Guardians. Once we have the Doomers' location, I want to attack. Can't do it with six men. And no, I'm not taking Kri with us no matter how much she or you bitch about women's rights. I'm not going to risk another female falling into the Doomers' clutches." Damn, now he'd made himself furious.

"Calm down, Kian, I wasn't going to suggest that you do."

He sucked in a deep breath, then exhaled it forcefully. "Good."

Sari humphed. "I was hoping Syssi would manage to tame you. But I see that she hasn't. You still have a short fuse."

He snorted. "Oh, she tamed me alright. This is me tamed."

"If you say so. Okay, enough with the pleasantries, what do you need from me?"

Good old Sari—no nonsense and too busy for chitchat—just like him. "I told you. I need those Guardians. We have to stop pussyfooting around and get them on the plane by

189

tomorrow. Carol's abduction changes everything. It's no longer a long-term plan of building a larger force. I need as many Guardians as we can mobilize, and I need them here as soon as possible."

Sari sighed. "I'm not having any more luck than you, and I'm summoning each one of them for a private conference. They still shake their heads and say they will think about it and never come back to me."

"I was afraid of that. But Syssi had a great idea. We tell them that this is an emergency, and we need them to get Carol back. After that they can go home. We can't afford to let anyone off the hook, and I'm not above shaming them into it."

"Me neither. You want to split the list in half? That way we can do it faster."

"I have a better idea. Summon them all together at once for a mandatory meeting, and I'll talk to them via video conferencing."

"What time do you want them?"

"Let's say in an hour and a half? I'm going to prepare a rallying speech." He might not be a charmer, and heart-to-heart talks one on one were not his forte, but he was an experienced commander and knew how to address his warriors.

"No problem. Can you wait on the line for a few minutes? I'm going to shoot a quick email to my assistant. Now that it's only a summons for a meeting, I don't need to make the calls myself."

"I'm here."

Damn, he'd promised Syssi he would come to bed after

making the calls. But now that he had a speech to prepare and deliver, it wasn't going to happen. There was no way she would stay awake that long, and he would be an asshole if he asked her to. He'd have to make it up to her tomorrow morning.

"Okay, it's done. Beth is making the calls. The reason I asked you to wait is that I was wondering what are your plans for later, after this crisis is over. You'll be back to where you started at—no Guardian Force, and a keep that is easily compromised."

"I'm going to introduce a reserve program. A month of service every year and a few training sessions in between to keep everyone in shape. Hopefully, some will decide to stay. Besides, we are still working on training new Guardians. As for the keep, I don't know. And by the way, yours is not safer than mine. If one of your people gets captured, they can lead the enemy right to your front door. We've been safe as long as the Doomers didn't know where to start looking for us. You're still good; they have no idea where your keep is, but they know that mine is in Los Angeles. And now that they have Carol, the exact location is compromised. I had to move everyone into a new building. Thankfully, I have several in the area where I keep some of the floors vacant just for a situation like this. Otherwise, everyone would be staying at a hotel." He chuckled. "Who said that being paranoid is a bad thing?"

"What do you suggest we do? Not allow our people to come and go? We can't do that unless we abduct a bunch of humans and turn them into our sex slaves."

"Yeah, that is a problem. We've done a little brainstorming here, and we have a few ideas that are too crazy to mention, but I'm going to run them by William anyway. Maybe he can come up with something that is doable."

"You let me know when he does."

"I will."

31

ANDREW

*A*ndrew kissed Nathalie's warm cheek and carefully untangled their limbs to get out of bed without waking her. It had been late when they'd gotten home last night. She'd had the time of her life at the concert, jumping up and down and singing along with the rest of the teenagers. Or rather screaming. He'd had fun watching her. The music had been atrocious, and he was thankful for the earplugs, but nevertheless, the next time the Infected Mushroom were in town, he was going to purchase tickets no matter the cost. To see Nathalie so carefree and joyous he was willing to spend the money and tolerate the noise.

Besides, it wasn't all about altruism. She'd been full of excited energy when they had gotten home, and had found a most pleasurable way to release it. The blowjob she'd given him was one for the books. Then, of course, he'd repaid in kind, giving her multiple orgasms and keeping her up until three in the morning. The poor girl had fallen asleep exhausted, but with a big smile on her face.

Andrew smirked. *Job well done, Spivak, well done indeed.*

Making as little noise as possible, Andrew got dressed and then tiptoed out holding his shoes. He stopped for a moment outside Fernando's room, listening to the old man's snoring.

Good. Hopefully, he wouldn't be waking anytime soon.

Nathalie needed her sleep, and letting Fernando roam the place unsupervised was not a good idea. The guy was surprisingly sneaky, and God forbid he found a way to get out. He would get lost in no time and might fall prey to some punks. The old man didn't carry a wallet, or even wear a watch, and the punks might beat him up just because he had nothing they wanted. Not that there was much chance that these kind of scumbags would be awake so early on a Saturday morning.

Nevertheless, before leaving, Andrew made sure everything was locked up tight and the alarm was on.

The traffic was light on the way to the designated Starbucks, and he made it there more than half an hour before ten. Plenty of time to go in and fuel up on a grande double-shot cappuccino. He thought about getting an espresso for Turner but decided against it. It would be cold by the time his old boss arrived, and the bastard wouldn't be happy. With Turner, gestures of goodwill counted for nothing. He just didn't get the concept. All he cared about were results. An espresso with a less than perfect temperature would just piss him off.

Cup in one hand and a paper bag with the sandwich he'd ordered in the other, Andrew went back to his car to have his breakfast while waiting for the old bastard to arrive. Fifteen minutes later, a brand new black Cadillac pulled into the parking lot. Its license plates still displayed the dealership's logo, and the driver's shiny bald head belonged unmistakably to Turner.

The guy cut the engine and got out. He hadn't changed much in the past two years. Turner was still the same short and muscular bastard with a face of an angry bulldog.

He headed straight for Andrew's car. "Hello, Spivak," he said as he opened the passenger door and let himself in.

"It's good to see you, Turner," Andrew offered his hand, and the guy shook it. In a way, he wasn't lying. He was glad to drop Carol's case in Turner's lap so he could focus on finding Eva.

"You too, Spivak."

"So, what have you been up to?" Andrew turned the ignition on and pulled out of the parking lot.

"Oh, a little bit of this, a little bit of that."

"Independent work?"

"Yeah. I didn't like what the guys upstairs had to offer."

"Why? It's not like you were giving up active duty, like me. Whatever they offered you was probably not all that much different from what you were doing before."

Turner nodded. "True, but the money was better outside. For a change, I wanted to get compensated according to my abilities, not some standard pay package dictated by my rank."

"And did you get it?"

"I'm working on it. You said this guy we are going to see will pay whatever I ask for."

Damn, had he actually said that? "What I meant was that he was looking for the best and was willing to pay accordingly. It still has to be reasonable. He is a savvy businessman."

"Of course. But I know what I'm worth."

"I'm not in a position to negotiate for him. I have no financial stake in this. I'm doing it purely as a favor. For both of you." And for himself, but Turner didn't need to know that.

Turner cast him a calculating glance but said nothing.

The address Kian had given Andrew was located one street over from the keep. It was a fancy high rise office building with a valet service, which Andrew decided to use.

The front desk was just that, not a security station, and no one stopped Turner and him as they headed for the elevators. They got out on the fifth floor and walked down the wide corridor until they reached suite number five hundred and four. There was no name plaque on the double doors, just the number, and as Andrew knocked before pushing it open, he wasn't sure what and who was waiting for them inside.

The front room was kitted out as a reception area, and Andrew was surprised to find Shai sitting behind a desk with a computer and a big stack of files. This was either an elaborate setup to impress Turner or Kian's new temporary office.

"Go right in. He is waiting for you." Shai waved a hand to one of the two inner doors.

"Thank you," Andrew said and led the way.

Turner hadn't said a thing since they'd arrived at the building, but his eyes were busy watching and recording everything.

Kian wasn't alone in the big executive office. Brundar and Bhathian were with him, and the three were sitting around an oblong conference table that took most of the floor space. As they rose up to greet him and Turner, his old boss didn't bat an eyelid at the three imposing men towering over him, even though each topped him by almost a full head.

Kian offered his hand. "Mr. Turner, I presume?"

Turner clasped the guy's big hand and smiled, but there was no warmth in it. Its purpose was to show that he was in no way intimidated by Kian and his bodyguards. "In the flesh. And you are?"

"Kian."

"Kian what?"

"Just Kian. Please, take a seat." He pointed to one of the chairs surrounding the table.

Turner sat down and looked at the other men. "Aren't you going to introduce me to your associates?"

Kian took his place at the head of the table. "My bad. This is Bhathian, and that is Brundar." Each nodded when Kian said his name.

"Scots?"

"Aye," Bhathian let his accent revert to its original brogue.

Brundar inclined his head in a nod.

"What a coincidence, I'm half a Scot on my mother's side."

Turner rubbed his hands together, and the first genuine smile spread across his face. "So, boys, what are we dealing with here." As always, the guy was all business.

Kian cast Andrew a quick glance as if asking him if it was okay to confide in Turner, but this wasn't for Andrew to decide. Kian was on his own. He shrugged.

"First, Mr. Turner, there are some rules we need to agree on."

"Shoot."

"Whatever my associates and I tell you, stays between us. The information we are sharing with you must be held in the utmost confidentiality. My attorney prepared this, and I would like you to read it and sign it before we begin." He pushed a legal-sized piece of paper toward Turner.

Turner smirked as he scanned the thing, which took him only a couple of seconds. And yet, Andrew had no doubt the guy had read every word. He pulled out a pen from his light jacket's inner pocket and scribbled his signature on the dotted line.

Pushing the thing across the table, he looked at Kian. "If I didn't know how to keep secrets, I wouldn't have been as successful as I am in this field. Heck, I would probably be dead. That's the number one rule in my line of work. Whatever I know goes with me to the grave. I tell the people who work for me only what they need to know, and I make sure that no one person needs to know too much. I can provide references if you want proof."

Kian looked pointedly at Andrew and lifted a brow.

Turner was boasting a little to impress Kian, but he wasn't lying. Problem was, one never knew with sociopaths. The lack of emotions made them the world's best liars, and Andrew wasn't sure his gift worked on them. On the other hand, he had no proof that Turner was indeed a sociopath. It was just his unprofessional and totally biased opinion.

Andrew nodded. Confirming that Turner hadn't been lying.

"Okay, so this is the situation. We are immortal and so are our enemies—" Kian dove right in without preamble.

Andrew watched Turner, waiting for an incredulous brow lift, or a smirk. He'd even been prepared to intervene in case the guy got up and told them to stop wasting his time. But Turner's face revealed nothing. Damn, he was good. If the guy ever got tired from the cloak and dagger game, he could play poker professionally and make a fortune.

"Since the Doomers' patriarch dropped that nuclear bomb that eliminated our ancestors, including him, his successor and disciples have been pursuing two objectives. To kill us off, and to destroy any progress we help humanity achieve. Almost every dark age, and there were many aside from those you learn about, was instigated by them. Problem is, they outnumber us by many multiples—"

As Kian continued to tell him the abbreviated version of the clan's history and the part they had played in shaping human civilization, Turner's expression didn't change throughout the bizarre tale. And when Kian was done, Turner nodded instead of walking out like most people would have done in his place.

But Turner wasn't most people.

"I've always believed that there were some mysterious forces at play. Things just didn't add up. And major events in history couldn't have happened for the reasons I've read about in books, but I couldn't deduce a better explanation. I'm an atheist, so the God and Devil thing didn't do it for me. The missing pieces of that puzzle were driving me crazy. Thank you for telling me what they were."

In the silence that followed, Kian's amazed expression

echoed Andrew's. "I didn't expect you to just accept my tale so easily. I was prepared to make a demonstration."

Turner chuckled and waved his hand. "By all means, I would love to see what you can do."

Kian turned to his men. "Brundar, please show our guest one of your tricks."

Brundar shrugged and snapped his fingers. Immediately, the three immortals vanished. Then, with another finger snap, he brought them back.

Turner clapped his hands. "That was fantastic. Is the finger snapping necessary? Or is it just for show?"

"What do you think?" Brundar asked.

"I think you don't need it."

Brundar nodded. "You're right."

"Impressive." Turner looked at Kian. "Back to the business at hand. Let's recap what we know and what we don't."

"Would you like to write it down?" Kian suggested.

Turner smiled and pointed to his head. "It's all up here. I just want to make sure you didn't forget to tell me anything."

Smug bastard. Still acting all superior.

But Kian didn't seem to notice, or maybe he just didn't mind. "Good idea." He motioned for Turner to begin.

When all the details had been rehashed, Turner pushed to his feet, and the rest of them followed. He offered Kian his hand. "I have all I need for now. How do I contact you?"

"Through Andrew."

Interesting, so Kian still didn't trust Turner. Or maybe he was just being cautious. As it was, Turner was walking away with nothing but an unbelievable tale he had no way to prove. Having an address and contact information was more tangible.

"Good deal. I'll start working on it right away. I'll contact you as soon as I have anything. I expect to have it wrapped up in a few days."

"We didn't discuss your pay."

"I'm a reasonable man. I'll provide you with a detailed list of my expenses which, of course, I expect to be reimbursed for. And once I find your enemy's hideout, and you verify the information, I want a quarter of a million on top of that. But if you want me to plan and coordinate the attack and rescue, then the price doubles."

Kian nodded and shook Turner's hand. "It's a deal. Would you like to put it in writing?"

Turner snorted. "Contracts are worthless in our business. Trust and reputation are everything. Besides, if you fail to pay my fee, I'll find a way to collect it." He winked.

32

NATHALIE

*A*ndrew was gone when Nathalie woke up, but the space where he'd been sleeping snuggled up to her was still warm, and his scent lingered on his pillow.

His pillow. In her bed. Nice.

Lifting it, she brought it to her face and took a good sniff. The effect was immediate—a feeling of languid contentment. She wondered if Andrew's trace scent carried pheromones. It made sense, though; otherwise, her physical response to an inanimate object was hard to explain. Or perhaps it was as simple as his smell reminding her of how much she loved her man.

Last night, he'd pleasured her for hours, and even though she was paying the price this morning, it had been well worth it.

Unfortunately, she couldn't go back to sleep, or spend half the morning thinking about how wonderful Andrew was. It was time to get up and see about Papi's breakfast. Hopefully, he was still in bed and hadn't tried to fend for himself. The man who'd run a busy café for most of his adult life was now a disaster in the kitchen. The muscle memory was still there, so he could prepare dough and make cookies and breads same as he had done for years. Problem was that he would forget the things in the oven and burn them to a crisp, or set the kitchen on fire by forgetting his omelet on the stove.

Just thinking about all the possible disasters her father could cause had her out of bed in a flash. Wrapping a robe around her, Nathalie opened her door and sniffed. Thank God. The hallway didn't smell of burned food.

Her weekend morning routine was the same as every other day, and Nathalie showered and got dressed quickly. When she was done, she went looking for her father, finding him sitting in the kitchen with an empty cereal bowl in front of him.

"Good morning, Papi." She leaned and kissed his cheek.

"Good morning to you too, sleepyhead." He tugged playfully on the bottom of her braid, the same way he'd used to do when she was a little girl.

"Would you like me to make you an omelet and some toast?" she asked.

"You know I do. Your omelets are delicious. You should make one for Andrew too."

Nathalie felt herself blush. "I don't know when he's coming. I'll make him one when he gets here."

Papi tilted his face up toward the ceiling but then shrugged. "I thought he stayed the night, but I must've been mistaken."

Avoiding his questioning eyes, she turned around and opened the fridge. "How many eggs do you want in your omelet?"

"Three will do."

With her back still turned to her father, Nathalie got busy chopping an onion and a red bell pepper for the filling. Hopefully, he'd drop the subject.

Shit, she should just come out and say it, and if her father threw a tantrum, so be it. When she was young, he would often trap her into admitting all kinds of wrongdoing by calmly implying that he'd already known about it, and then admonish her anyway. But she was a grown woman, and shouldn't fear her father's chiding.

The vegetables sizzling in the skillet must've masked the sound of the back door opening, and Andrew's hand on the small of her back startled her. "I didn't hear you come in."

He leaned and planted a soft kiss on her cheek. "Good morning, beautiful. It smells amazing in here. What are you making?"

"An omelet. Take a seat. I'll make you one too."

"Can I help?"

She chuckled. "No, not really."

Andrew grabbed the only other stool and sat down next to Fernando. "Good morning, sir."

"Good morning, young man. Would you like a section of my newspaper?" He lifted the carefully folded sections he was done with.

"Sure, thank you."

Andrew pretended to flip through the pages until Fernando got up, holding the few sections he hadn't read yet under his arm, and headed for the downstairs bathroom.

"How did your meeting go?" she asked.

"Very well. The powers that be dropped a big project in my lap that I didn't feel I was qualified for. So I contacted an old colleague who happens to be an expert in that particular field. I arranged a meeting, and, thankfully, it was agreed that he would be taking over for me. Which is great news, because this project is so big and complicated that it would've taken over my life for the foreseeable future. I would've hated not being able to see you every evening. Besides, I want to continue searching for your mother. That's my top priority right now."

Nathalie dropped the new batch of chopped vegetables into the frying pan and turned to face Andrew. "Why?"

"Why what?"

"Why is finding my mother top priority for you?"

She saw his Adam's apple bob as he swallowed, and for a fleeting moment an odd expression settled over his face. Nathalie wished she was better at reading facial cues because Andrew's didn't make sense. There was guilt, and longing, and hope. Strong feelings for a woman he'd never met before.

And just like that all of her suspicions came rushing back.

"Because it's important to you, of course," he said, looking her straight in the eyes as he lied. He was good, appearing so sincere and loving, but she knew he wasn't telling her the truth. Not all of it anyway.

The smell of burning vegetables forced her to release her gaze, and she quickly turned around to kill the burner, then turned back and stared him down. "What's going on, Andrew? Why are you so desperate to find my mother? A total stranger to you?" She pointed the spatula at him. "And don't you dare lie to me. I know there is more to it than helping me. There is something you need from her. Does it have to do with her work for the government? Some secrets you need to uncover?" She narrowed her eyes. "Or maybe secrets you want to make sure stay buried?"

"Whoa, whoa." Andrew raised both palms in the air. "You've got some imagination on you, girl. I swear to God that I'm not after any government secrets. This is purely personal."

"Personal how? And don't tell me it's all about me."

"But it is! I have to find her for your sake."

"You're driving me nuts, Andrew. I'm going to swat you over the head with this spatula if you don't start talking."

Andrew dropped his head and rubbed the back of his neck. "I can't tell you what it is exactly, not until I find her. But I can generalize. It has to do with genetics. Something she might have and had transferred to you."

"Oh, my God! What is it? Am I sick? Tell me the truth!"

Andrew got up and reached for her, pulling her into his arms. "You're not sick. But you might be very special." He chuckled. "Not that you're not special to me as you are, but you might be a rare possessor of a genetic mutation. It's not dangerous, and it's not life-threatening, on the contrary. But for reasons I'm not free to disclose, I'm not allowed to tell you unless I'm positive that you are indeed a carrier. And the only way to find out is to find your mother."

Damn, damn, damn. He sounded so sincere that she was inclined to believe him. But what did it mean? For some reason, she remembered how accepting he'd been when she'd told him about the voices. "Does it have anything to do with my ghosts?"

"In a way, yes. Special abilities are one of the indicators, but they are not proof positive."

"Special abilities or mental disabilities? Tell me the truth, Andrew." Maybe it was this rare genetic mutation that was causing her hallucinations?

"Definitely special abilities."

This was so frustrating. She needed to know more, but he was feeding her crumbs that were just whetting her appetite for more. "Does it have anything to do with the government?"

He shook his head. "No."

"So who is not allowing you to talk about it?"

"I can't tell you."

She pushed him away and punched his shoulder. "This is not going to work, Andrew. I love you, but I can't stand the secrets and the lies. Why haven't I met your sister yet? What are you hiding?"

"Fuck, Nathalie, this is the worst time possible for this. Syssi and her husband are going through something difficult right now, and I'll feel like a complete asshole if I demand that they drop everything and come meet you now."

Nathalie crossed her arms over her chest. "What happened?"

"Their building was compromised and they had to move."

"You're not making any sense. What does a compromised building mean? Water damage? Fire? Vermin? What?"

"Security. Kian's family has enemies, and it is crucial that their location is kept secret. Once it's compromised, it's no longer safe."

This was just great. Worst case scenario—Andrew's sister was married to the mob; best case scenario—Kian and his family were political refugees from somewhere. But whatever the case, Andrew was not going to tell her. He would just come up with another lame excuse.

"I'm sure they can take a break from whatever they are doing and meet us for dinner at a restaurant. They need to eat sometime. Right? So why not with us. We can pick a place that is close to where they are staying, and I'll ask Jackson to stay with my father."

"I'll see what I can do."

"You'd better…"

33

ANANDUR

I'm not going to clean another fucking thing for as long as I live.

Anandur dropped the scrubbing brush inside his bucket. The yacht he'd been cleaning this afternoon hadn't been washed in Fates knew how long, and he'd been going back and forth between the deck and the nearest sink to empty his bucket and get fresh sudsy water. It would've been so easy to just dump the contents overboard, but he had an audience.

He always had a fucking audience. Normally, he wouldn't have minded the females watching him, lounging on the decks of their respective yachts with drinks in hand and leering expressions on their faces. He liked to put on a good show. But this was not the time for this.

He'd been pussyfooting around Lana, being all noble and shit, and that's why he was still stuck doing this fucking pretend job while his time could've been better spent looking for Carol.

Trouble was, no one even knew where to start.

Good thing that Andrew's old boss from Special Ops, a guy named Turner, had taken over the investigation. Apparently, he had an extensive network of informants, snoops, and snitches. It was only a matter of time until information would start pouring in. For what Kian was willing to pay, the bloody snitches would clamor to deliver whatever they could.

He'd better wrap up this investigation quickly.

Kian was recruiting every Guardian who had ever served, and Anandur would be damned if he allowed the fun and games to start without him because he was stuck washing decks. Hell would freeze over before he would let an opportunity like this pass him by.

For the first time in the clan's history, they were going on the offensive. Storming a Doomers' stronghold.

If Lana didn't start talking tonight, he was going to thrall the hell out of her, and fuck the consequences. He could no longer afford to play nice.

Frustrated, Anandur dumped the contents of his bucket, flooding the top deck with soapy water, and grabbed a broom. As he put the thing to good use, he was dimly aware that he was working at an inhuman speed, and the gasps coming from the neighboring yachts confirmed it. But he was so done with this nonsense. After this, he was going to pitch the damn bucket into the nearest dumpster and never scrub anything again.

Catching sight of Lana heading his way, Anandur bowed to his admiring audience. The sounds of their enthusiastic clapping and whistling followed him as he jumped off to intercept her.

"What this?" She waved a hand toward the females.

"My audience of lusty wenches."

"He is wiz me!" She showed them her fist.

Anandur pulled her in for a scorching kiss that brought another round of catcalls and claps. "Baby, I'm all yours."

She tried to look dismissive, but he knew she liked him saying it, even though they both knew it for the lie it was.

"Come, I make dinner."

He wrapped an arm around her shoulders. "You're spoiling me, darling. What did you make?"

"Your favorite. Steak."

"Just one?"

"Five."

"That's my girl."

As they got closer to the yacht Lana was looking after, the smell of grilled meat was mouthwatering, and Anandur's stomach responded with a loud growl.

Lana patted his midsection. "Good, you hungry."

For some reason, the woman loved feeding him and delighted in watching him consume inordinate amounts of food. The more he ate, the bigger was her smile. Which was saying something, since the Russian seldom smiled. Not because she was unhappy, necessarily, but because she considered it a perceived weakness. An angry face was a tough face, and the message it sent was 'I'm not someone you want to mess with.'

As they sat down to eat the dinner she'd prepared, Lana poured them each vodka—to help the food go down. Anandur didn't disappoint, devouring all five steaks and guzzling most of the vodka. Lana had only two, but she heaped her plate with mashed potatoes, and as the level in the bottle dropped to dangerous levels, she opened another one.

"Thank you, baby, this was an excellent meal." Anandur popped the button on his shorts, giving his expanded stomach some room. The afternoon spent in the sun and the food were taking their toll, and he felt his eyelids droop.

Bad idea.

As soon as he did, Carol's face appeared behind his closed lids, and the wave of guilt that washed over him twisted his face into an ugly grimace.

"What's wrong?" He heard Lana's worried tone. "The food not good? You want more vodka? It's good for the stomach."

Anandur forced his eyes opened. "No, baby, it's not the food."

"So what is it?"

Eh, what the hell, he might as well tell her. "My cousin was kidnapped by some thugs from a parking lot of a club. I fear for her, but I don't know what to do or where to look for her. It's just eating me from the inside, this feeling of helplessness. And here I am, enjoying a great dinner with a great girl while my cousin is suffering at their hands. Or maybe even dead."

Damn, his venom glands were swelling, and his fangs were probably showing. With Lana watching, he shouldn't have allowed himself to think about Carol in the hands of Doomers. It would be best if he kept his mouth closed.

"You go to police?"

"Yes." Naturally, they hadn't, but explaining why would have complicated things. He didn't want to go into lengthy and elaborate lies. The short answer was better.

She harrumphed. "Police not good for this."

"I know. But who is?"

"Is she pretty? Your cousin?"

"Yes. Very."

"You need to find a Vor and ask help."

"Who or what is Vor?"

"Vor is a boss, criminal big boss. They know more what's going on than police. But you owe him if he help you."

"Oh, like a mafia boss?"

"Yes. Big, big criminal."

"Do you know someone like that?"

She shrugged. "Maybe I ask a friend. Maybe a friend of a friend know."

There was an opening here he could use to get more information out of her. This hadn't been his intention when he'd told Lana about Carol, simply because he hadn't thought one had anything to do with the other. There was no connection between Alex's nefarious activities and Carol's abduction. After all, Alex was kidnapping women to sell for sex slavery, and the Doomers catching Carol was just a stroke of really bad luck…

But wait a minute, there was a connection; the local unit who'd arrived to hunt for immortal males wasn't here to acquire women, but their headquarters was. It was entirely possible that the Doomers were using scumbags like Alex to do the dirty work for them—to procure new stocks of young females for their island.

He could use Carol's case to lure Lana into talking about it. "The mafia is not interested in random abductions perpetrated by rapists. They will know something only if the thugs that took her are sex traders who will try to sell her."

Lana looked into her vodka glass and swished the liquid in slow circles. "You said she is pretty. If she has red hair like you and white skin, they can sell her for lot of money."

"How would you know about this kind of trade?"

She shrugged. "It's not secret. Everyone know about it. I read in newspaper."

Anandur didn't need Andrew's lie-detector skills to know that she was lying. For an accomplice in one of the most heinous categories of crimes, Lana was a lousy liar.

"What did they say in the newspaper?" he asked, hoping to get her to talk some more under the pretense of reading about it in an article.

"They say girls are stolen from the streets and sold for sex. They take the easy ones. Girls who run away from home, girls that use drugs and are selling sex to get money for the drugs. Girls that no one will miss and report their disappearance to the police."

Anandur didn't need to pretend his outrage. "This is despicable. What kind of scum does things like that?"

Lana winced. "People do very bad things for money."

"Money is not everything."

"When you don't have it, sometimes it is."

Given the sheen of tears in her pale blue eyes, Lana wasn't indifferent to the fate of the women Alex was smuggling. In fact, it seemed that under the thin veneer of toughness, Lana felt guilty.

He took her hand and gave it a light squeeze. "Do you want to talk about it? Carrying it all inside is corrosive. You can share your burden with me."

She looked away and pulled her hand out of his grasp. "I don't know what you talk about. I'm just sad for the girls."

It was time to stop playing and get serious. He wasn't good at thralling. Hell, he absolutely sucked at it. The slightest resistance could block him. But Lana was in a vulnerable state, and her defenses were down. He could tell she wanted to unburden herself of the guilt she was carrying. All she needed was a little push—something even his weak thrall could accomplish.

"I know, baby, it is tragic. You can tell me everything, your secrets are safe with me."

ANDREW

"*I*'m going to get us a movie. Anything in particular that you're in the mood for?" Andrew asked as he parked the car.

They had taken Fernando on a little trip down to Santa Monica Pier and a long walk on the beach, then stopped for ice cream on their way home. Exhausted by the long day in the sun, Fernando had fallen asleep in the car and was snoring loudly.

"Whatever you bring is fine with me." Nathalie got out and opened the back door. "Papi, we are home. Time to wake up." She nudged his shoulder.

The snoring stopped with a snort. "I wasn't sleeping."

Nathalie laughed. "Of course not. You always snore while wide awake. Come on, let's go." She helped him get out of the car, her hand gripping his arm as he swayed— dangerously close to stumbling. Andrew wished it was the sleepiness that was affecting Fernando's balance, but Nathalie had explained that this was just another manifestation of her father's dementia. It wasn't bad, not yet, but the

216

doctor's advice was to get Fernando a walking cane as soon as it got worse. At his age, a fall could be extremely dangerous. Old bones just didn't mend as well.

Andrew grimaced. He should remember this the next time he decided to play warrior.

"Don't take long." Nathalie waved as she opened the shop's door.

Renting a movie was just the excuse he'd needed to get some private time and call Syssi about that damned dinner get-together Nathalie was demanding. Fuck, she couldn't have picked a worse time for this. The last thing Syssi and Kian had the time or energy for was a meeting with their future sister-in-law.

Man, he still couldn't believe that he'd found the one, and that she agreed to marry him. But with the long engagement Nathalie wanted, there was always a chance she'd change her mind.

Especially if he didn't make this damn call.

"Hi, Andrew." Syssi answered her cellphone on the first ring.

"Hi, yourself. How is the new place?"

"Oh, it's fine. Not as luxurious as the penthouse, that's for sure, but I'll take safety over luxury any day and twice on Sunday."

"Amen to that. Listen, I know that this is probably the worst possible time for something like this, but Nathalie is giving me grief for not introducing her to my family yet and wants to meet you guys for dinner."

"She is absolutely right. And we would love to. How about tonight?"

"Are you sure? You should check with Kian."

"Here, talk to him yourself. I'm sure he's just as thrilled to finally meet Nathalie as I am."

Maybe so, but Andrew was sure that there was a shitload of things Kian had to attend to, most of which took precedence over meeting Andrew's fiancée.

"We can do dinner tonight. A quick one." Kian's no-nonsense attitude was a relief.

"Thanks, man. It means a lot to me. With all the shit you're dealing with, I know it's not easy to drop everything just to make my fiancée happy."

Kian chuckled. "Nonsense, family comes first. And anyway, I've taken care of everything I could for now, so this is actually a good time. As soon as Turner delivers, shit is going to hit the fan, and well… Fates know when we'll have time for anything fun again."

"Makes sense. Where and when?"

"It's five now, and I'm sure Syssi needs time to get ready, so let's aim for eight. And as to where? There is only one place I deem safe enough at the moment— By Invitation Only. I'll text you the address."

"Isn't this the fancy-schmancy restaurant where you proposed to Syssi?"

"It is."

"I thought you had to be a billionaire to get in."

Kian chuckled. "Or the brother-in-law of one of the owners."

"I hope Nathalie will not freak out when she sees the place."

"If she has anything of her father in her, she'll be fine as long as the food is good. And it is."

"About that. Remind Syssi that Nathalie still doesn't

know anything about Bhathian being her father or any of the other stuff. She's aware that he is a relative of yours and so is Jackson. But that's it."

"Don't worry so much. See you later."

Yeah, as if he could. With a brother-in-law that looked like a statue of a Greek god, Andrew was worried about more than a simple slip of a tongue. He clicked off the call and started looking for a convenient place to make a U-turn. After all, he and Nathalie wouldn't be watching a movie tonight.

She was in the kitchen when he got in, making sandwiches for their dinner.

"Guess what." He circled her tiny waist with his hands.

She smiled. "What?"

Andrew pulled her into his arms. "I've talked to Syssi and Kian, and we are meeting them tonight for dinner at a fancy restaurant called By Invitation Only. It's a members-only place, and the food is supposed to be amazing."

"Oh, my God! Tonight? Why so soon? I have nothing to wear!" Nathalie dropped her apron on the work table in the kitchen and ran upstairs as if the place was on fire.

This hadn't been the response he'd been expecting. Go figure. He'd arranged exactly what she'd asked him to, and instead of being happy about it she was having an anxiety attack.

Were all women this confusing?

How the hell was a guy supposed to know how to please them if they themselves were so conflicted about what they wanted?

With a sigh, Andrew finished making the sandwiches Nathalie had started and then loaded them on a platter.

After all, Fernando still needed to eat, and Jackson, who was coming to watch him, would want some too. God knew the kid had a healthy appetite.

"Andrew!" Nathalie hollered from the top of the stairs. "You don't have anything to wear either! Go home and change!"

She had a point. By Invitation Only was not a place he could show up wearing jeans and a T-shirt, not to mention sneakers that were covered in sand. Damn, did he even own a suit fancy enough for that place?

Probably not, and wearing the tux from Syssi's wedding wasn't going to cut it either. Suddenly, Nathalie's panic started to make sense to him.

Andrew glanced at his watch. It was only twenty minutes past five. Could they make a quick run to the nearest Macy's and get some decent clothes?

With a new idea brewing in his head, Andrew headed for Nathalie's room. He took the stairs two at a time, and what he saw when he got there cemented his idea. Looking like a woman possessed, Nathalie stood in front of the mirrored closet doors, wearing only her bra and her panties. But there was barely anything left hanging inside. Most of her clothes were strewn about the floor.

For a moment, he got distracted by her mouthwatering backside, but all carnal thoughts were forgotten when she turned to him with tears in her eyes.

"I can't go. Call and cancel. Tell your sister that I came down with a cold or something."

When he pulled her into his arms, she was stiff as a broom, but eventually, she slumped into him. "I'm so sorry. But I just can't. Not to a place like that," she murmured.

He stroked her shiny hair. "I have an idea. We shower, you put on your makeup and do your hair, we drive to the nearest Macy's, get clothes and shoes and whatever else we need, and looking great in our new stuff we drive to that fancy restaurant. But we need to hurry."

"What about my father? We can't leave him alone, and Jackson will not get here before seven."

"I'll call him and ask him to come over right now."

Nathalie stretched on her tiptoes and kissed Andrew's lips before looking up at him with a pair of smiling eyes. "Did I tell you lately how much I love you?"

NATHALIE

"*S*top fretting. You look beautiful," Andrew said as Nathalie checked herself out in yet another mirror—one of the many they passed by on their way out of Macy's.

She couldn't help it. It had been ages since she'd worn anything that wasn't either jean color or black, and it was startling to catch her reflection in the red dress Andrew had chosen for her. She would've never even looked at it if it hadn't been for him, and not only because of the bright color. The dress clung to her curves, and the narrow belt that came with it emphasized her small waist, which was good, but it also made her big butt look positively enormous, which was really bad. And yet, Andrew had insisted that her big ass was beautiful, firm and shapely, and that it was a crime to hide something as sexy as that under too much fabric.

A pair of elegant, low-heeled black pumps completed the outfit. After showering, she hadn't had time to blow out her hair and had left it loose to air dry. The bottoms curled up a little and looked as if she had spent hours at a salon to achieve the effect. A little bit of eyeliner and mascara brought out her eyes, and she hadn't bothered with anything else. As it was, the red dress contrasting with her dark, almost black hair already felt like too much color.

Andrew looked dashing in his new charcoal suit and a cream colored dress shirt. The tie they'd selected was silk, burgundy with a charcoal pattern on it, and he'd even splurged on a fancy cologne for himself and a perfume by the same designer for her. It was so nice of him to pay for all of this stuff. Andrew wasn't rich, and from what she'd gleaned he was getting a decent salary that allowed for a comfortable living but not for frivolous splurging. Nathalie wasn't a big spender either, and not only because she never had the money to waste on luxuries. She certainly didn't expect Andrew to shower her with gifts. But it was nice to know that her future husband wasn't stingy.

She smiled at him. "I'm not fretting, just trying to get used to all this color. I haven't worn red since I was a little girl."

He opened the door for her, and they exited into the parking lot. "That's a shame. Red looks good on you."

For some reason, he sounded strange as he said it, and she cast him a sidelong glance. There was no reason for him to lie to her about it. After all, he could've chosen the same dress in a different color for her. But something about the color bothered him.

Whatever. She wasn't going to ask. There should be no secrets between them, but that didn't mean that they had to share every little thought. Some privacy and some mystery weren't necessarily a bad thing for a healthy relationship.

Nathalie hadn't shared with Andrew her latest ghostly communications, and it was fine. Unless it concerned him, she didn't feel the need to tell him about it every time it happened.

"Is there anything I should know about your sister and her husband?" she asked as the GPS indicated that they were nearing their destination. "Touchy subjects I should avoid? Like religion, politics, money?"

Andrew chuckled. "Those are better left alone no matter who you talk to. But Syssi and Kian are chill. Feel free to talk about whatever you want."

That was good to know. Her social skills were honed by years of dealing with customers, but it wasn't the same as spending a whole evening with people she didn't know. People she needed to impress so they would deem her worthy of Andrew.

Oh, God. What if they didn't?

She was a baker who didn't have a college degree, and her reading was limited to romance novels. So unless Andrew's sister was into those too, they would have little to talk about. Damn, she should've read today's newspaper to brush up on current affairs. If they started discussing topics that she had no clue about, she'd look like an idiot.

Damn it. Why the hell had she pestered Andrew about meeting his sister before thinking to prepare herself better?

Nathalie sighed, letting herself slide low in her seat.

Andrew put a hand on her knee. "What's the matter?"

"I'm a little nervous. What if they don't like me?"

"Don't be silly, they are going to love you."

"What if they think I'm dumb? What if we have nothing to talk about?"

"Don't worry. If you run out of topics, I'll cover for you. I have an arsenal of stories about Syssi's shenanigans as a little girl that would keep everyone entertained for hours."

God, she felt so lucky to have an incredible man like Andrew. A man who she knew would always have her back.

Nathalie grasped his hand and gave it a squeeze. "I love you so much."

"Ditto."

As Andrew turned into a parking lot and pulled up to the valet sign, Nathalie glanced around, but didn't see anything that indicated that there was a restaurant anywhere, or any other place that was open for business at this time for that matter. The house to the right had a sign that proclaimed it to be a dental office, and the one to the left said Dr. Chen, Chiropractor.

Two uniformed guys opened her and Andrew's doors at the same time. One took the keys and scribbled Andrew's name on a tag he attached to them; the other one said, "Welcome to By Invitation Only. Please, follow me."

He led them to the rear of the parking lot and punched a code into a keypad that was attached to a narrow iron gate in the tall block wall. A lush garden greeted them on the other side, and as they followed the valet down a stone walkway that wound between neatly trimmed mature trees, bushes, and flowerbeds, Nathalie had a feeling that she'd stepped into a different dimension.

The only illumination came from tiny LEDs embedded

in the narrow walkway. But as they wended deeper into the garden, she saw more and more outdoor lights, bathing the greenery in a lambent light. They passed a few sitting areas with comfortable looking lounge furniture, but nobody was sitting in any of them.

Holding onto Andrew's hand, Nathalie wondered how much further they were going to have to walk. The path seemed to go on and on. She leaned into Andrew and whispered, "I'm glad I chose these shoes. I would've been miserable walking this far in high heels."

"Why are you whispering?"

She chuckled. "I don't know. It kind of looks like an enchanted forest, and I don't want to spook the magical creatures."

He wrapped his arm around her shoulders. "The only magic here is lots and lots of money."

The valet turned back with a smile. "We are almost there. Follow me and watch your step."

As they approached a stone staircase leading down a pretty steep slope, Nathalie was relieved to see a courtyard at the bottom that was set up with tables and chairs, some of which were occupied. Behind it was a one-story building that housed the restaurant.

"Aren't you required to have wheelchair access?" she asked the valet.

"Oh, but we do, Madame. Over there we have a lift." He pointed.

It was hard to see in the dark, but a few feet away there was something that looked like an ornate iron cage resembling an old fashioned elevator.

"Would you like to use it?" Andrew asked, glancing at her shoes.

"No, I'm fine. Just hold my hand as we go down these steps."

"My pleasure."

His arm was strong and steady as she leaned on it for support. Her heels were short but spiky, and if one caught in the grooves between the stones the stairs were paved with, she could twist her ankle and tumble all the way down.

This wasn't a good design for a fancy place like this, but she had to admit that it was beautiful and very private.

"If this is just the approach, I can't imagine what the inside of the restaurant is like," she whispered to Andrew.

"My thoughts exactly."

As the valet pushed the double doors open, a hostess with long legs and a perfect set of teeth welcomed them. "Ms. Vega, Mr. Spivak, welcome to By Invitation Only. Please, follow me."

Nice. It seemed that guests of this place were chaperoned from the moment they exited their vehicles until they returned to them. And the hostess was waiting for them because the other valet must've informed her that they had arrived and were on their way.

The interior was dimly illuminated, and soft music was playing in the background. But Nathalie was surprised to find the place not as large or as ostentatiously decorated as she'd been expecting.

Along the walls, a few semi-circled alcoves provided a more intimate seating, and the various sized round tables that took up most of the floor were generously spaced from each other. With the music playing in the background, hushed conversations could remain private while everyone still got to be seen.

Nathalie gasped as she recognized a famous movie star, digging her fingers into Andrew's arm while fighting the urge to run up to him and ask for his autograph. The guy was gorgeous on screen, but he was even better in person. Not surprisingly, the woman sitting at the table with him could have put the whole lineup of Victoria's Secret models to shame.

"Come on, stop staring." Andrew tugged on her hand, and she realized that the hostess was waiting for them a few feet away in front of one of the alcoves. It was more secluded than the others, tucked into a corner of walls, and the little candles that were glowing from each one of the other tables were extinguished.

Nathalie couldn't see the people sitting inside and wondered if it was intentional. But Andrew hadn't said anything about Syssi or her husband being famous, so there was no reason for them to hide in a shadowed corner.

Or was there…

Perhaps Andrew had been stalling the introduction for a reason. But she couldn't imagine what it might be.

As they caught up to the hostess, a tall man pushed to his feet and stepped out of the alcove… rendering Nathalie speechless.

The movie star had nothing on Syssi's husband. No wonder she was hiding him in a dark corner. Every woman in this place would've been drooling all over him if Syssi had allowed them to see him.

"Nathalie, it's a pleasure to finally meet you. I've heard so much about you." He offered his hand and after a moment she took it, only to get pulled into a chest that was made from granite. He was surprisingly gentle for a man this big, and she realized that he was being careful with her.

She heard a feminine giggle coming from behind Kian's back. "Kian, let go of Nathalie before Andrew explodes."

He released her immediately and stepped aside to let his wife come forward. Syssi's smile was genuine and friendly as she embraced Nathalie, and her body soft. But under the softness there was strength. Syssi must've been working out, a lot.

"Come, let's sit. I took the liberty of ordering appetizers for us. I'm starving. But, of course, you can order your own." Syssi slid into the booth, pulling Nathalie by the hand to sit next to her and leaving the guys no choice but to sit across from them. "The food here is amazing. Gerard is a genius, and he is also Kian's cousin. He catered our wedding, by the way. Well, part catered, because it was such a rush job that he couldn't do the whole thing. But he gave us the recipes to prepare the rest, and our household staff handled it beautifully. They are partners, Kian and Gerard, but Kian is a silent one. He just put the money up for this place. Everything else is Gerard. He'll probably come over later and introduce himself."

Nathalie smiled, feeling her shoulders relax. Evidently, she'd worried for nothing. Syssi was taking over the conversation, which was perfect. All Nathalie had to do was listen and nod.

"Oh, my. I don't know what happened to me. I'm usually not so chatty. It's just that I'm so excited to finally meet you,

Nathalie." Syssi leaned into her and whispered in her ear, "You have no idea how worried I was about my picky brother. I was afraid he would remain a life-long bachelor. Can you imagine? It would've been such a loss. He is going to make a wonderful father. Ask me how I know." She nudged Nathalie's arm.

Nathalie barely stifled a chuckle. "Okay. How do you know?"

"Because he practically raised me. Our parents had Andrew and then for many years our mom couldn't conceive. So when I came along, and a year later Jacob, Andrew was already a teenager. He did a good job, and it's a big endorsement considering that it's coming from me."

All of this was news to her. Andrew had never talked about raising his siblings. Heck, she didn't even know that he had a brother. The only one he ever mentioned was Syssi. "Andrew is so tight-lipped. I didn't know any of this." She glanced at Andrew, who was watching her conversation with Syssi with an amused smile on his face. "How come you didn't tell me you have a brother?"

His smile melted away. "Had. I had a brother. Jacob was killed in a motorcycle accident."

Damn. Way to go ruining Andrew's mood. But how was she supposed to know?

Nathalie felt Syssi's hand on hers. "It happened a long time ago. It's hard for me to talk about it, so I'm sure it's hard for Andrew too. Let's talk about happier subjects." She smirked. "Like when are you two going to get married? I'm a pro after planning our wedding, and I'm offering my services. Because let me tell you, it is way more complicated than it seems. And the dress, oh my, wait until Kian's sister introduces you to her friend Joann. She has connections in all the big designer houses. Thanks to her my wedding dress was not only beautiful, but it was made in under two weeks. Can you believe it? Two weeks! Hold on, let me get my phone and show you some pictures—"

SEBASTIAN

"*P*lease," Carol pleaded weakly.

She should've known by now that her pleas were not going to stop what Sebastian was doing to her. But she probably couldn't help it, which was fine by him.

He loved the sounds she was making. The screams, the begging, the sobbing, these were all music to his ears. The only thing he didn't allow was cursing, which she'd indulged in before learning the cost of such disrespect.

In a way, he was hoping she would slip and call him vile names again.

Too accustomed to fragile humans, he'd stopped choking her when she'd turned blue, letting go of her before she passed out. Only later, he'd realized his mistake. She couldn't die. He could choke her literally to death, and she'd resurrect. Save for decapitating her or cutting out her heart he couldn't kill her even if he tried. And how awesome was that? Next time he wasn't going to stop until he choked the life out of her. Temporarily that is.

Somewhere in the back of his mind, he pitied her... a little. After all, he wasn't completely heartless. Carol wasn't a masochist, not even a submissive, and derived no pleasure whatsoever from the torture he was inflicting on her.

But he was a master at this; he would mold her into whatever he wanted her to be.

As much as she hated herself for it, blaming it on her traitorous body, Carol was always wet when he entered her. But it wasn't her body that was betraying her, it was her mind.

The mind he played so masterfully.

After a session, he tended to her, cuddled her, told her she was a good girl, and it was impossible for her to resist the comfort he was offering because she had no one else to turn to.

Sebastian was having the time of his life, but not everyone in his abode was enjoying this. The other girls were terrified, except for Letty of course, who had gladly stepped aside to make room for his new whipping toy. Even some of his men were giving him the stink eye. Most didn't give a damn about what he was doing to the female, but some couldn't stomach it. He'd never gone that far with Letty.

His basement playroom needed soundproofing, but until this was done, he had a convenient excuse no one could argue with. After all, the female had to be tortured for information.

They didn't need to know that he'd already done that. Not that she had anything of any value to divulge. She had no idea where the headquarters were, she had never been invited. And when he'd asked her about Guardians, it was obvious she had no idea what he was talking about. Carol was a beautiful female, but she was dumb as a brick, a drunkard, and a pothead.

There was, naturally, a chance that she'd been lying, but he doubted it.

It was true that the stench of fear and pungent aroma of despair had been so overpowering that there was no way he could've scented any of Carol's other emotions. And lying produced a very subtle one. But she was a soft little female, enduring pain that would've made tough guys sing.

His problem was that the excuse he'd given his men had a very short expiration date. They wouldn't tolerate this for much longer, and Sebastian didn't want to lose their loyalty over this. Mortdh knew how long and how carefully he'd cultivated this bunch of warriors. But the funny thing about people was, mortals and immortals alike, that what they couldn't hear or see they could pretend wasn't happening even when they knew for a fact that it was.

He was counting on this phenomenon to solve his problem.

The room he had designated for his own use had already undergone a few modifications. First, he'd had to reinforce the restraints. The female was much stronger than the average human. The second thing he had done was to remove the carpet. After Carol's first whipping, the thing had gotten so soaked with her blood that it had been beyond salvaging. The concrete floor was much easier to hose down. The third thing he'd done was to install the big wooden X Carol was now strapped to.

Admiring his work, he deemed the pattern he'd painted on her slender back and her pert ass complete, and moved his strikes to the back of her thighs. The deep welts were bleeding profusely, and Carol was so exhausted she'd stopped screaming several strikes ago. The only reason she was still up and perfectly positioned for the whipping was the ingenious contraption she was secured to. Her wrists and her ankles were each chained to one of the X's arms, while a strong leather harness kept her middle tied to the center of the X. She had zero wiggle room.

He was so hard he could drill holes in that X with his shaft. But he couldn't fuck her yet.

First, he had to complete the design he was drawing with his whip on her flesh, then he needed to take her down, lay her on her stomach and tend to her wounds until the skin mended and the bleeding stopped.

He found it fascinating to watch her heal. In less than an hour, the skin wounds would close, and by tomorrow there would be no sign of the whipping she'd taken.

A new and unblemished canvas for him to paint on again.

37

ANDREW

*W*histling as he walked into the office on Monday morning, Andrew earned himself a couple of raised brows. People weren't used to seeing him so joyful. He was more of a somber guy. But after a great weekend with Nathalie, he was in a good mood today.

Except, he couldn't shake the feeling of guilt casting shadows on his happiness like a dark, stormy cloud. He shouldn't be happy when poor Carol was suffering at the hands of Doomers.

But the thing was, he didn't know Carol, had never met her, and although he tried to feel more for her, to him she was just another case of misfortune. Of random cruelty. One of the many faceless victims he couldn't help no matter how much he wanted to.

In fact, he shouldn't feel guilty at all. He'd handed the job to Turner, putting aside his deep antipathy towards the man, not to mention his own pride, in order to increase her chances of being found. Turner was a much better choice for this particular job, mainly because of his network of snitches.

The brilliance was just a bonus.

And a pain in the ass.

That arrogant son of a bitch had always grated on Andrew's nerves. Andrew didn't begrudge the guy his brilliance, but he hated the way Turner liked to rub everyone's noses in it.

Damn, just thinking about the bastard had soured Andrew's good mood. But all he had to do to get it back was to remember Saturday night's get together with Syssi and Kian.

Throughout the evening, Syssi had chatted up a storm with Nathalie, while he and Kian had spent most of it just listening to the girls talk. And eating of course. Kian's cousin was a culinary genius. Andrew had sampled some of the appetizers the guy had made for Syssi's wedding, but those little tidbits of tasty couldn't compare to the five-course dinner he'd had last night. None of it tasted like anything he'd ever put in his mouth before. Naturally, Kian had taken care of the bill, not allowing Andrew even a peek, but he had no doubt that the amount had been astronomical. Perhaps not for Kian, the guy could probably eat at a place like that every day. But it was out of reach for someone of Andrew's means, even for a once a month visit.

When it had gotten late, pulling the girls apart had been no easy feat, and after exchanging phone numbers, the two had parted with hugs and kisses like the best of friends.

Kian wasn't a fool, and he'd wisely refrained from sharing his opinion about Nathalie with Andrew. But Andrew had had no trouble deciphering the guy's brief look over. The bastard was lucky that the looks he'd been casting Syssi, all throughout dinner, had been so full of love and lust that by comparison, the one he'd given Nathalie had been purely platonic.

"Morning, Spivak. You're in a good mood today. What happened, you got laid last night?" Andrew heard Tim's mocking tone from across the room.

Damn, he'd been so preoccupied with his inner musings that he hadn't noticed the extra desk that had been added to the place, or that fucking Tim had been sitting behind it.

"What the hell are you doing here?"

"The boss said I can park it here until they clean up the mess in my cubicle."

"What mess?"

Tim winced. "Some idiot pissed on the carpet."

Andrew chuckled. "Appropriate, I would say. You piss off people all of the time, and for once someone pissed back."

"Yeah, yeah. Blow me."

"You're not my type."

Andrew parked his ass in his chair and turned on his computer. It was good that Tim's desk was on the other side of the room. He had a shitload of work to do, and Tim liked to talk. For some inexplicable reason, Andrew was one of the few people the guy considered a friend. A dubious honor that meant that he wouldn't let him be. But Andrew had no time for that. Aside from his regular assignments, he had some private business to attend to. Eva's case was gnawing a hole in his gut, and he couldn't wait to sink his teeth into it.

Especially since he'd finally thought of a way to get into those fucking Swiss bank accounts. He needed a hacker.

One or more of the other departments in this building was for sure employing these types, but he didn't know which and wasn't sure who to ask. It wasn't as if the fact that the government was using hackers was made official. There were no offices with plaques that said 'So and So, Hacker.'

Hell, perhaps he could take advantage of the situation and start his inquiry with Tim. The guy was the only forensic artist on premises and had done work for many of the departments. He might know somebody who knew a hacker.

"Hey, Tim, you got a moment?"

"For you, always. But it comes at a price."

"How about coffee in the break room?"

"You're a stingy date, but fine. Go ahead, I'll join you when I'm done with this sketch. Two minutes tops."

It took him five.

"Here, I made it special for you." Andrew handed him the paper cup.

"I'm touched. So what do you need?"

"A hacker."

"What for?"

"I need someone who can follow money that is funneled through a Swiss bank account."

Tim took a sip of his coffee, then flipped open a donut box someone had left behind. The thing was empty save for a few leftover sprinkles. Tim grimaced and opened the fridge, searching for something edible he could pilfer. "You need a good one."

"You know someone?"

Tim smirked, pulling out a half-empty jar of salsa and an In-N-Out cardboard container with a few leftover fries. "I do, but he is hard to get to."

"How so?"

Dipping a fry in the salsa, Tim stuffed it in his mouth and chewed. "There is this kid, a fucking world class hacker, working for our cyber security department. When he was fifteen, he hacked into some top secret shit at the Pentagon and got caught. The kid was too young to be put under lock and key, but also too dangerous to be allowed to do more harm. So they put him under house arrest with twenty-four-seven supervision. The kid isn't allowed to take a piss without his handler's approval. But there is no other way. Supposedly, no monitoring equipment is safe from his hacking. He can break into anything."

"How do I get to him?"

"I've told you. He works for cyber security on the fifth floor."

"Does he still have a handler?"

"Yup. That's how I know him. I'm friends with one of them. There are several who are assigned to the boy genius, and they take turns."

"That must be tough for a kid. How old is he now?"

"I guess seventeen or eighteen. I'm not sure. Last I saw of him was before Christmas last year. Do you want to go up during lunch break? I'll introduce you."

It all sounded good, except how the hell was this kid supposed to do any private work if he was living under a microscope? And even if he could, why would he take a risk for a stranger?

But it wouldn't hurt to talk to him. Andrew could try to tempt the kid with money, and if this didn't work, he could ask him to recommend someone else. As far as he knew, the underground community of the cyber world was interconnected, and hackers knew of other hackers.

38

NATHALIE

"*I* met your cousin and his wife, Andrew's sister, on Saturday," Nathalie told Jackson as soon as the morning rush was over and they had a moment to breathe.

"Oh, yeah?" He didn't seem surprised.

"Yeah." She tried to stare him down, which was difficult since he was way taller than her. Had he been that tall when he'd started working for her? He seemed to be the same height as Andrew now, and Andrew was over six feet tall.

"How did it go?" Jackson's face revealed slight nervousness.

"Very well."

"I'm glad." He seemed relieved. So this was more about the impression his cousin and Syssi had left on her than anything else. Such a good kid—he was worried about her getting along with Andrew's sister and her husband.

"It was great. Syssi is a sweetheart, one of the nicest people I've ever met, and the food at that restaurant was out of this world. I've never eaten anything so fancy or so tasty.

Syssi said that Gerard catered part of her and Kian's wedding so you must know how good it is."

Jackson snorted. "To tell you the truth, I didn't get to eat much at the reception."

"Too busy chasing girls?"

"I wish, but no. Me and my friends snagged a few bottles of alcohol and drank them in hiding. When we were done, they were collecting the dirty dishes."

"I bet you guys got in trouble for that."

"Yeah, we did. And I can't even say that it was worth it. Hangovers are a bitch."

"Well, at least you've learned your lesson."

"I certainly did." Jackson tugged on the bottom of his T-shirt and adjusted the apron he was wearing over it. "What did you think of Kian?" Again, he sounded a bit anxious.

"Besides being the most handsome man I've ever seen?"

Jackson smirked. "He is? I thought that was me."

She punched his bicep. "You're still a boy. But when you're all grown up, don't go asking the mirror who is the most handsome of them all because it might choose you and give Kian ideas. The guy is scary."

Jackson's teasing and smug expression evaporated, replaced by an offended one. In fact, she'd never seen him as angry as he looked now, and as he glared at her, she took a step back. This handsome, pleasant young man wasn't as harmless as he pretended to be. And even though she knew she was perfectly safe with Jackson, that dangerous quality that she'd sensed in him from the start frightened her.

"So that's what you think of him? That he is like that wicked queen in Snow White? You're so wrong. Kian is a tough and strong leader, but he is fair, and he works his butt off for the family." Jackson seemed to notice that she was backing away from him and took a deep breath, then continued in a much calmer tone. "You just need to get to know him better; that's all."

"I'm sure you're right. It's just that he didn't say much during dinner, and he seemed kind of brooding. On a positive note, though, for a guy that looks like a god, he is surprisingly not full of himself, and he gazes at his wife as if he can't wait to get her alone and have his way with her. Which is kind of sweet. He didn't look at any of the other women in the restaurant. And I can tell you, without exaggerating, that there were more than one or two who made all of the Victoria's Secret models look ordinary."

That brought back the smile to Jackson's face. "Damn, I wish I could go there."

She patted his arm. "I don't think you can afford it."

"One day I will." He shrugged, then added with a wink, "When I'm heading Nathalie's baked goods empire."

Nathalie made a face and waved a dismissive hand at him. The boy was such a dreamer. Her chances of heading a baked goods empire were the same as Jackson's band getting to perform at the Staples Center. Non-existent.

39

ANDREW

"Hey, Volaski, can we go talk to your boy genius?" Tim asked the agent sitting behind a desk, which was practically glued to the glass wall separating the hacker's lair from the larger one they were standing in. By the looks of it, this was the handler. His guard station looked like any of the other work tables in the room, but unlike the others, it was clear of anything aside from a mug of coffee and Volaski's phone.

As Andrew peered through the glass partition into the hacker's domain, all he could see was the back of an executive chair and an array of monitors that looked like NASA's ground control center.

"You mean the royal pain in the ass? Go ahead, be my guest," Volaski said, waving a hand toward the glass door… in the glass wall…

Poor kid, he was watched like a monkey in a zoo.

"Do you need to buzz us in?"

"It's open. The boss loosened the security on our primadonna. He is free to go anywhere he wants as long as he doesn't leave the building."

"And when he goes home?"

Volaski shook his head. "As soon as Roni turned eighteen, which was three weeks ago, he moved out of his parents' house. Now he lives here."

"You're shitting me. I didn't know we have residential apartments."

"We do now. The seventh floor had some unused space, and they converted one of the larger offices into a studio apartment for his royal highness. Anything to keep him happy and working overtime. I'm telling you, pretty soon the whole place will get overrun by pimply kids with nimble fingers, and we will become obsolete. This is just the start. Mark my words, in a couple of years, this place will look like Google. With a barista serving cappuccinos and a sushi bar—anything to keep the geeks from going home."

Tim snorted. "Are you done?"

"Yeah, sorry about the rant. But that's the future, my friends. You just wait and see. I know what I'm talking about." Volaski waved a hand toward the glass door. "Just go."

As Tim pushed the door open, the big leather chair took a spin, bringing its occupant to face them. The infamous, almighty hacker, was indeed a pimply, scrawny teenager, sitting in a chair built for a much larger occupant. But Roni's confident smirk made one thing clear. The guy's size might have been on the scrawny side, but his ego sure wasn't.

"Roni, my man. How've you been?" Tim high-fived the guy.

Roni remained seated, his flip-flop clad feet resting on the chair's spider legs. "As well as can be expected for a prisoner." The deep baritone coming from that narrow chest was surprising. Without seeing the speaker, Andrew would've imagined a big fat guy, and definitely older.

"I heard that they are giving you some breathing room now."

"Not voluntarily. It happened only after some threats and promises were exchanged with the boss and then his bosses."

"I'm glad it all worked out for you."

Roni glanced around his glass cage. "Yeah, I'm so fucking happy. Who's your friend, Tim?"

"This is Andrew. He works in the anti-terrorism department."

"Nice to meet you, Roni." Andrew offered his hand as Tim introduced him, and the kid shook it with a hand that felt as delicate as a girl's.

"You too. What can I do for you, Andrew?"

All working spaces in the building were bugged, and this room probably doubly so. Which wouldn't have been a problem if what Andrew was asking for had to do with the file he was working on, not his private investigation. But whoever was monitoring the recordings wouldn't know that for a fact. Careful wording could make his request seem legit.

"There is a money trail I'm investigating that stops in Switzerland. I need someone who can pick up its scent, sniff it behind their protective walls, and find where it goes from there."

"What's in it for me?" the kid asked straight out.

No wonder he and Tim got along. "Isn't it your job?"

"Nope, I work for cyber security, and if I have time after I'm done with what my department tasks me with, I can take a look at it. But with my workload, it could be weeks before I can get to it, if ever. So if you want it done, it will take an expediting fee."

"Name it."

The smile on the kid's face looked like something he had not practiced in a while. "Let's start with a game of poker. I'm going out of my mind with boredom up in my fabulous, technology free apartment. I need someone to play with. If you win, I'll owe you a favor. If you lose, you'll owe me one. How about that?"

"Are you any good?" Andrew lifted a brow.

"No, not really. I'm still learning."

Yeah right. Roni's eyes shone with intelligence, and Andrew had no doubt that the kid's thought process was about ten times faster than his own. Roni knew he was going to win, and what's more he knew that Andrew was on to him.

"Fine, one game. When?"

Roni pushed his glasses up his nose and leaned toward one of the monitors to check the time. "I haven't had lunch yet, did you?"

"No. This is my lunch break."

Roni pushed up to his feet. "Perfect, then we can have something to eat at my place while we play. I can even make you coffee."

"Am I invited too? Tim asked.

"Sure, follow me."

Roni stopped by Volaski's desk and lifted his arms. "Do

it fast, I'm taking my friends up to my place for lunch and a game of poker."

When Volaski pushed away from his desk, got up, and patted Roni down, Andrew understood what this was about.

"You're good to go." Volaski dropped back in his chair.

As they walked out into the corridor and stopped by the elevators, Andrew glanced at Roni. "Does he do it every time you leave?"

"That's the only way they agreed to leave my apartment bug free." He shrugged his narrow shoulders. "Even I can't imagine a way to smuggle equipment from the office to my place in my pockets." He patted his baggy jeans. "They are just paranoid. And stupid." He said the last words loudly and looked up at the surveillance cameras.

"Why would I try anything when I'm on probation?" he said as they stepped into the elevator. "I'm not an idiot. I don't want to go to a real jail. This is bad enough."

Tim snorted. "You're never going to be thrown in jail. You're too valuable, and you know it."

Roni shrugged. "I'm not the only hacker or even the best. There is probably a snotty twelve-year-old somewhere who can do what I do and better. These kids are getting younger and younger."

And that was coming from the mouth of an eighteen-year-old.

The door to his studio was unlocked, which made sense. No one who didn't belong could get inside this building. Roni's apartment was safer than if he was rooming in a bank vault.

On the inside, it looked like a college dorm and smelled

just as bad. The small sink in what passed for a kitchen was overflowing with dirty dishes, and dirty clothes and socks were everywhere. In fact, it was impossible to make a step and touch down on a clear patch of carpet.

"What happened? The cleaning crew skipped your place?" Andrew asked.

"I don't let them in. They will just snoop around my stuff."

Tim chuckled. "Newsflash, you have nothing to hide here. And they can snoop as much as they want while you're working."

"They don't."

"Don't be naive, kid."

"Trust me, I'm not. I'd know if they did."

Andrew cleared a spot on the couch by throwing a bunch of stinky clothes on the floor. This was such an unpleasant flashback to his time in college. His roommates had been just as bad. And since he couldn't stand it, Andrew had ended up acting as their maid.

As Roni turned on a sound system, the music was mercifully tolerable. He pulled three beers out of his fridge and a big bag of nachos from one of the cabinets.

He handed Andrew and Tim their beers and snapped the bag of nachos open. "Lunch."

"They let you drink beer?"

"One of the perks I negotiated." Roni threw the rest of the stuff covering the couch on the floor and sat next to Andrew.

"Where are the cards, kid?"

Roni took a swig from the beer, then pinned Andrew with a pair of smart eyes. "Neither of you have a sporting chance against me. I have an eidetic memory and make calculations in my head faster than the machine."

Great, another jerk who was too full of himself. Except, in Roni's case, Andrew knew it wasn't empty boasting. He was just saying it as it was.

"The game was obviously a ruse. What do you really want?"

"I want to get laid." The kid dropped the bomb.

Andrew scooted away. "I don't swing that way, buddy, and neither does Tim. At least as far as I know. You approached the wrong guys."

Roni rolled his eyes. "With a girl! I want you to bring me a girl. Someone around my age, and pretty. Not some old hag."

Damn, talk about mission impossible.

"And how am I supposed to arrange that?"

First of all, he wasn't a pimp. But even if he miraculously found a girl who volunteered to help Roni change his status from virgin to gotten laid, how would Andrew manage to smuggle her into the highly secure building?

"That's your problem, dude. But I can promise you that if you do, I'll find that money trail for you even if it leads straight to hell. There is no firewall I can't get through. There is always a flaw in the system. Perfection doesn't exist."

"You sure there is nothing else you need? Cuban cigars? A rare whiskey?"

"Nope."

"A cushy bank account? I can pay you well."

Roni looked at Andrew with the same infuriatingly

condescending look as Turner. "And what would I do with that money? What would I spend it on?"

Yeah, the kid had a point. And frankly, in the same situation, Andrew would've probably asked for the same thing. For an eighteen-year-old dude, there was nothing more important than finding out what sex was all about.

40

NATHALIE

*I*n the kitchen, slicing bread for the sandwich she was putting together, Nathalie thought about what Jackson had told her about Kian. He'd called him a leader, but a leader of what? And what had he meant when he'd said that Kian was working hard for the family? Syssi and Kian were newlyweds and had no children, so Jackson must have been referring to the extended one. Some kind of a family business that needed strong leadership. She wondered what it might be. Andrew would surely know, she could ask him. Or Jackson, for that matter.

She liked the concept, though. All the cousins and probably also the aunts and uncles working together, watching each other's backs. Must be wonderful to have a security blanket like that.

And Jackson holding Kian in such high regard meant that they all appreciated it.

Nathalie glanced at her father. How different their life could've been if they were part of a tight-knit family.

So marry Andrew already and become part of it.

Before Sage had spoken, Nathalie had felt a slight pressure in her head and wondered if he'd done it on purpose, giving her a warning so she wouldn't startle and cut herself.

No, I wish I could take credit for being so thoughtful, but I had nothing to do with it.

Nathalie finished the sandwich, put it on a plate, and handed it to Vlad. "Could you take this order to Jackson for me? I'm going upstairs for a little break."

"No problem."

Vlad was okay with her talking to herself, but she preferred not to do it in front of anyone when it could be avoided. Still, it was nice to know that she was safe in case something slipped. After all, they all had secrets that needed protecting.

Nathalie took off her apron, hung it on its peg by the door and climbed the stairs. Sage must've understood that she wanted to talk to him somewhere private that wasn't in her head, and he waited patiently until she entered her bedroom and closed the door behind her.

"I need you to do something for me."

He chuckled, which sounded very weird coming from a ghost. *There isn't really much I can do unless you want me to spook someone.*

"Can you do it? Can you make anyone but me hear you?"

I don't think so. But I can send messages on their computers, that will freak anyone out.

She laughed. "I bet. But that's not what I need. Though I'm going to keep it in mind if I ever seek revenge on someone. But I digress. I want you to ghost out and then try to get back in. I want to see if I can block you."

I can try, but once I leave, it might take me a while to get back. Well not from my perspective, for me it will be a few seconds. But for you it might be the next day. I'm still struggling to understand the difference in the passage of time between our realms.

Shit. She needed to test Tut's advice in case other ghosts spotted her supposed beacon and came knocking on her cranium.

"Tut said that I'm like a shining light, a beacon for ghosts. Try to focus on that so you will not drift too far away—time wise, that is."

That's it. Now I get it. Four-dimensional existence. I should be able to travel back in time if I want. Time is just another dimension. Wow! For the first time I'm excited about being a ghost!

"Sage, please focus and do as I asked."

Okay. Ghosting out.

She felt the slight pressure lift, and a moment later it pushed back, seeking entrance. But she was ready for him and slammed her imaginary gate down.

Nathalie waited a moment longer for Sage to come back, wondering if she'd succeeded in blocking him or just imagined she had. After all, Sage might have just gotten lost again, and she hadn't blocked anything.

When another quiet moment passed, she closed her eyes and imagined lifting the gate.

Then waited. And waited some more.

Ten minutes later, she was ready to give up and get back to work when she felt the pressure again. This time, Nathalie didn't resist, allowing Sage entrance.

You were right. You are like a beacon of light. As long as I kept it in my sight, I managed to hang on and not drift away.

"Great, but did it work? Did I block you?"

Yeah, you did. It felt like a door or a gate slamming in my face.

"Sorry about that. I had to test Tut's theory. But I promise not to block you unless it's a really inconvenient time, like when I'm in the bathroom... Oh, God, don't tell me you ghosted in when I was sitting on the toilet or something..."

For some reason, she'd never considered the possibility. Tut had always been good about this, leaving her alone to do her business. Though come to think of it, he might have been just keeping quiet. Shit, she hoped he'd had the decency to ghost out during her bathroom visits. If he ever showed up again, she was going to ask him about it.

She felt the slight pressure lifting. "Damn it, Sage, don't you dare leave before answering my question."

No, of course not. I wouldn't. Never. I don't remember much about my past life, but I know I was a gentleman.

So why the hell did he sound so guilty?

"Sage, if I ever feel you ghosting in while I'm taking care of business, so to speak, I'm going to kill you all over again. Is that clear?"

Yes, ma'am.

41

ANDREW

*A*ndrew banged his fist on the steering wheel. Damn that horny little prick and his crazy demands. He would need to find someone else to pick up Eva's trail. Someone who would do it for good old fashioned money.

Getting the kid a girl was just not going to happen. Even if Andrew knew one that was easy, he would never ever dare propose something like that.

Just for the hell of it, Andrew had asked Tim if he knew of a service he could call.

Not that it would've done him any good. Even if Tim delivered the girl himself, there was no way to get her into the building. And Roni wasn't allowed to go anywhere without his handler. For one crazy moment, Andrew even entertained the idea of inviting them both over and then distracting Volaski while Roni got it on in another room, but Tim said it would be a no go.

Even with an escort, the kid could only leave for doctor

appointments, family events, and the like. For all intents and purposes, Roni was indeed a prisoner.

Perhaps he should call Turner. If anyone knew how to solve this conundrum, it would be him. Fuck, he hated the idea of asking the guy for a favor, even though Turner owed him for the extremely well-paying gig Andrew had brokered for him.

He was still fuming when he opened the door to Nathalie's shop, but luckily she wasn't there. It was hard to leave the day's frustrations at the doorstep so he could show his woman a smiling face and a good time.

God knew she had enough stress in her life without him adding his crap to the mix. But he was only human and needed a few moments to cool down before interacting with her the way she deserved.

It was a shame that Nathalie had nothing stronger than wine and beer. He needed something with a kick.

"What's up, Andrew?" Jackson greeted him.

"Not much." As if he could talk about it. "How are things here?"

"Couldn't be better. It's just Vlad and me. Nathalie and Fernando are not back from his doctor appointment yet. But we are managing just fine. She worries for nothing."

"Good job, guys. You're making life easier for her, and I appreciate that."

"Yeah, she deserves a break. How about you? Can I offer you a cappuccino? A sandwich?"

"Maybe later. Right now I'm in the mood for something with a high alcohol content." Andrew tugged on his tie to loosen it a bit. "You don't happen to have some by any chance? I won't tell if you do."

"Sorry, man. You know we don't have an alcohol license. Nathalie has a few bottles of beer in the fridge for her private consumption, but that's it. I can't even let you drink it in here. You'll have to take it upstairs."

"You know what? I'll do just that. Could you bring me a sandwich there? I didn't have a real lunch today, and I'm hungry."

"Sure. The usual?"

"You got it."

On his way up, Andrew grabbed two Stellas from the fridge and tucked them in his jacket pockets, then reached for a container of what looked like leftover spaghetti and a jar of pickles. A fork went into one pocket, joining the Stellas, and a napkin went into the other one.

Just something to tide him over until Jackson delivered the sandwich.

In the den, he unfolded one of the tray tables and set it in front of the couch. The Stella was a weak beer, but it was cold and refreshing, and the leftover spaghetti was pesto, which he liked. The pickles didn't really go with any of it, but Andrew was hungry, and he wasn't picky.

A few minutes later, he heard Jackson's light footsteps as the kid jogged up the stairs. He showed up with two plates heaped like small mountains.

"If you don't mind, I'm going to join you."

Andrew scooted to the side, making room on the couch, and put the empty container of pasta on the floor under the tray table.

The three hefty sandwiches Jackson had stacked on each plate were resting on top of generous portions of potato salad on one side and coleslaw on the other.

"That's a bit much, but thank you."

Jackson put the plates down and grabbed a bottle.

"Hey, you're underage, and I'm a federal agent. Give it back."

Reluctantly, Jackson put the beer down.

For a few moments, the only sounds they made were crunching and chewing. But as Jackson finished his second sandwich and wiped his mouth with a napkin, he turned to Andrew. "So, you want to talk about it?"

"Are you offering to play shrink? I don't think so."

"Whatever, dude." The kid picked up the fork and attacked the potato salad on his plate.

Now Andrew felt like an ass. There was no reason to snap at the kid just because he was tired and frustrated. "I'm sorry. I had a bad day. I had what I thought was a breakthrough idea in my investigation of Nathalie's mother, but it didn't pan out."

"What was it?"

"To find a hacker to get into that Swiss bank and follow the money trail. But the guy demanded a price that was a deal breaker. Now I have to look for someone else who is more reasonable. A shame really. Because Roni is the best there is."

"You know Kian will help with the money, right?"

Andrew winced. "Roni didn't want money."

Jackson lifted a blond brow. "Oh, yeah? What was it?"

"A girl."

"So get him a girl. That's not a problem."

"For you, maybe. But we are talking about a scrawny, pimply, eighteen-year-old virgin, who is living under a microscope because he is too dangerous to let loose. The guy broke into the Pentagon's database when he was fifteen."

Jackson whistled. "Impressive."

"Yeah, well. Unfortunately, this superior intelligence comes with an equally big ego and wrapped in an unattractive gift paper."

"So you pay someone."

"I'm not a pimp. And even if I stooped so low, there is no way to smuggle a girl into the building. So unless I find a female agent who is willing to do it and is young enough to meet the guy's demands, I'm out of options."

Jackson scrunched his forehead. "I have a solution for you, but it will not be cost-free."

Andrew could just imagine… well, not really, but he knew it would be creative… "I can't wait to hear it."

"I can talk to my cousin Sylvia. She is like twenty-seven, but she looks really young, and she is not very picky." Jackson smirked. "You know how we are, we need a steady supply of sex. But the neat thing about Sylvia is that she has a very unique ability. Besides thralling humans, she can cause glitches in computers and short out other electronic equipment. Kind of like a jinx, but on purpose."

"I don't think Kian would agree to pay one of his own to prostitute herself. And knowing Bhathian, he wouldn't do anything without getting Kian's approval either."

Jackson waved a hand. "Sylvia will not want money."

"You said that there will be costs. And why would your cousin Sylvia agree to help us if there is nothing in it for her? I understand not being picky, but no one would volunteer for this out of the goodness of their heart."

"I'll call her and see what it would take. Worst case scenario she'd say no."

ANDREW

"You sure you want to do this?" Andrew asked Sylvia for the umpteenth time.

She was nothing like he imagined she'd be. When Jackson had said she wasn't picky, Andrew had created an unflattering picture in his head. But Sylvia was pretty, and not an airhead either.

"As I've said before, I've got it. If he is gross or stinky or behaves like a jerk, I'm just going to thrall him to believe that we did it. But if he is okay, I'll gladly help the boy get rid of his virginity." She shrugged. "It's exciting. I've never had a virgin before."

Andrew still had trouble accepting the nonchalant attitude of immortals toward sex. But he understood. There was something special about being someone's first.

As far as gross or stinky, she had nothing to worry about, but the jerky remained to be seen. Roni had promised that everything would be spotless and fragrant, including himself, and to be on his best behavior. But the kid was full of himself and had been isolated from people his age for years, which meant that his social skills probably left a lot to be desired.

"Okay, let's do it." Andrew got out of the car and went to the other side to open the door for Sylvia.

"Thank you."

"Are you sure the cameras are out?"

She smiled. "Wherever I go, everything is going to glitch and then go back to normal once I'm a few feet away."

"I hope you're right."

"Worst case scenario, security will stop us, and we'll tell them the story we prepared. Don't worry; it's going to be fine." She patted his arm.

In case they were caught, the cover story was that Sylvia was with Andrew, and they stopped to retrieve something he'd forgotten in his office on the way to their date.

Not kosher, but not a huge offense either. The worst he'd get would be a slap on the hand.

But Sylvia's magic must've been working because no one stopped them on their way to the seventh floor.

Roni opened the door and blushed like the virgin he was, but just as he'd promised, he was freshly showered and shaved, and soft music was playing in the background.

Sylvia smiled a dazzling smile and reached her hand to his cheek, cupping it gently. "It's okay. No need to be shy, Roni. I'm Sylvia."

The kid didn't move, holding the door open but blocking the way.

Sylvia chuckled. "Aren't you going to let us in?"

He shook his head as if trying to clear it and stepped back. "Please, come in."

Andrew looked around the small living room in wonder.

The place that just yesterday had looked and smelled like a filthy college dorm was spotless and smelled clean. It had probably taken an entire container of air freshener to achieve that.

The question was, what now? Should he wait in the other room? Out in the corridor?

Going down to his office was a no-no. Sylvia's magic didn't work long distance. He had to stay nearby until they were done.

His dilemma was solved when Sylvia took Roni by the hand and said, "Let's go to the other room." She winked at Andrew before closing the door to Roni's bedroom.

These immortals were unbelievable—in so many ways. Sylvia hadn't been embarrassed in the slightest.

Maybe they had it right. After all, consensual sex between adults shouldn't be something to be embarrassed about. Except, Roni barely qualified as one. He was just a kid... one who was old enough to serve in the army, carry a machine gun, and risk his life for his country.

So, yeah, Roni was old enough.

All that self-talk, however, didn't make hearing the sounds that started coming out of the bedroom any less awkward. He'd been secretly hoping that Sylvia would thrall the kid instead of actually having sex with him, but apparently Roni had passed her test, and she was taking care of him for real.

Thankfully, Andrew had come prepared. In his pocket, he still had the set of professional quality earplugs he'd bought for that awful music concert.

43

NATHALIE

*A*fter helping her father settle in for the night, making sure he took all his medications and had a fresh bottle of water on the nightstand, Nathalie came back to the den and sat next to Andrew. "You seem in a peculiar mood," she said, hoping he'd tell her what was bothering him.

Earlier today, Andrew had called to let her know he would be coming late, and that she shouldn't wait up for him. Not that she had any intentions of going to sleep without Andrew. Nathalie hated letting a day go by without seeing him. But he'd ended up showing up earlier than she'd anticipated. It was just a little past ten.

He wrapped his arm around her and pulled her in for a kiss. "I had a weird day today, at work, but now that I'm here, with you, it's all better."

She wondered what he'd meant by weird. Usually, when Andrew was tired or irritated or both, he would say that it had been a rough or tough day. Weird was a new expression for him. But she knew better than to ask him about it. He didn't like to talk about his work, or perhaps couldn't.

She wished he could talk to her, share his burdens with her the way she shared hers with him. That's what couples were supposed to do, weren't they? Would he still keep secrets from her when they were married?

"Will you always shut me out?" she asked.

Andrew frowned. "What are you talking about?"

"You never tell me anything about your day. Only that it was rough, or tough, or boring. And today it was weird. Is everything you do top secret?"

"No, not everything. But a lot of it is. And the rest is either boring, administrative stuff, or things that would ruin your mood."

Andrew's eyes shone with love as he stroked her hair. "Sharing is overrated. There is no benefit in dumping your crap on the person you love. You know what I imagine when I open the door to your place every evening?"

"What?"

"That I'm like a farmer who removes his muck-covered work boots and leaves them outside on the porch, then uses the hose to wash his dirty hands before he enters his home. That's me leaving all the crap where it belongs. When I come to you, I want us to talk about pleasant things, or better yet, make love." Waggling his brows, Andrew moved his hand up her inner thigh.

And just like that, Nathalie felt a trickle of moisture between her legs.

She slapped his shoulder. "Stop distracting me. We're having a serious conversation here."

"Okay, but make it short. I'm feeling frisky."

As if he ever felt differently.

"I want you to tell me more. If something is troubling you, talking about it may help. I know that it helps me. And I want to be there for you when you need to unburden yourself. But if you're not allowed to talk about the serious stuff, I'll settle for office gossip; like who sleeps with whom, who just had a baby, or who is getting a divorce. Things like that. It doesn't have to be the top secret stuff. Just trivia. And I'm sure there is plenty of that going on. People are the same everywhere, and they like to gossip. Federal agents included."

He smirked. "I've always frowned upon gossip and tried to ignore it. But if it'll make you happy, I'll make a point of collecting all the juicy bits for you."

"Ugh. You make it sound so bad. Just tell me things you talk about with your fellow agents. I'm sure not all of it is work related."

"Deal. Can I take you to bed now?"

"Yes."

As Andrew tightened his hold on her and pushed up and away from the couch, his abdominals strained against his dress shirt and his strong thigh muscles bunched under her butt. It never ceased to impress her, the way he lifted her so effortlessly—as if she weighed nothing.

He wasn't even winded when he lowered her to her bed.

"I love how strong you are." Nathalie cast Andrew a come hither look, batting her eyelashes.

His smile was all male pride. "You do? That makes all those hours in the gym worthwhile."

She snorted. "What gym? You haven't exercised in weeks."

"You're right. I used to go to the one in our office building after work, but now I come straight here. I guess I'm going to grow fat and flabby now that I'm no longer on the market."

Nathalie wanted to say something snarky in return, but forgot all about it as he took off his jacket and hung it over the back of her desk chair. She knew he'd go for the shirt next, and waiting for that reveal was all she could concentrate on.

Andrew had a magnificent body, even though he didn't think so. The silly man was bothered by his many scars and by skin that wasn't as smooth and pliable as that of a twenty-year-old. But to her he was perfect. So much so that she couldn't believe he was hers to keep.

Unbuttoning his shirt slowly, he was tormenting her on purpose, prolonging her anticipation. But Nathalie knew how to speed things up. Grabbing the hem of her T-shirt, she pulled it over her head and threw it on the floor, then unhooked her bra.

Andrew sucked in a breath, his fingers fumbling and missing the small buttons on his shirt.

As her pants and panties joined the rest of her clothes on the floor, Andrew stilled completely, the bulge in his pants growing bigger as he stared at her nude body with hungry eyes.

"Come here," she beckoned him with her finger. "I'll help you get out of your clothes. Fast."

"You are so beautiful, my Nathalie, you take my breath away."

She smiled, knowing that he meant every word. "You're not so bad yourself. I can't wait for you to get naked."

He chuckled. "I've noticed."

Switching from slow motion to fast forward, Andrew was out of his clothes in about a second and a half.

Yup, her man was magnificent.

As he climbed on top of the bed and covered her body with his, she spread her legs to cradle him between her thighs, then wrapped her arms around his neck and kissed him long and hard.

44

ANDREW

*A*s Nathalie held Andrew tight, kissing him like she couldn't get enough, he thought how lucky he was to be loved by her. It was hard to believe that this sexually assertive woman had been a virgin up until recently, or that his little striptease had been enough to get her so aroused.

Nathalie was so wonderfully responsive.

Rubbing against her wet heat, he was more than ready to push inside her, and by the way her hips were gyrating under him, she was impatient for him to get on with it. Except, he didn't want to rush their love making.

First, he was going to worship her sweet nipples with his tongue, then he was going to slide down her body and pay homage to the little nub that was the seat of her pleasure.

"I want you inside me," she protested as he started his downward trek.

"Patience, my love. Let me enjoy your body at leisure."

With a sigh, she let go of his shoulders as if conceding to a big sacrifice. But as his hands cupped her breasts and his thumbs started thrumming her nipples, her breathy moan was all about pleasure.

He took his time, tonguing one nipple and then the other, relishing Nathalie's stifled moans and gasps. With Fernando sleeping in the next room, they had to be extra quiet, but Andrew had gotten used to that, and it no longer bothered him.

If this was the only way he could have her, he'd take it.

With his Nathalie, even stealthy, guerrilla sex was better than any sex he'd ever had with anyone else.

Was it love that made it so special? The metaphysical connection of their souls? The knowledge that from now on it would be only her for him and him for her? Or was it just an extraordinarily good pairing of compatible pheromones? Nature and chemistry, nothing more.

Before he had met Nathalie, he would have said that it was the latter, but on a visceral level, Andrew knew that it was more than that.

As he abandoned her lovely breasts to slide further down, Nathalie cupped his cheeks and lifted his head. "I love you, Andrew. So much. And even though I get impatient sometimes, I love that you're so gentle with me, so focused on my pleasure."

He kissed her belly. "That's because I love you and treasure you. You're my life, my everything."

A tear slid down her cheek, and she wiped it away. "Now look what you've done. You made me all mushy and emotional in the middle of sex."

Yeah, he had. Although she'd started it.

"I know how to get you back in the mood."

"I didn't mean that I lost it...I'm still wet and needy."

"I know." Andrew pushed back to his knees, straddling her legs. "Turn around," he commanded in a whisper.

"Oh, you naughty boy, I like how you think," she breathed and flipped onto her belly.

Gripping her hips, he pulled her back until her ample behind was up and perfectly positioned, while her front remained down on the bed with her head turned to the side and her cheek resting on her pillow.

He pushed into her slowly, even though she was wet enough for him to thrust all the way in effortlessly. But what was the fun in that? Andrew savored the sweet torture of delayed gratification. It made the climax even more explosive.

At first, Nathalie let Andrew dictate the slow penetration, but soon she began pushing back against him, taking as much of him as he allowed her to.

Greedy, little minx.

Bending over her, he whispered in her ear. "You want it all the way inside you, don't you?"

"Oh, yes, please…"

"Well, if you're asking so nicely…" He pushed in with one strong thrust.

"Oh, God, yes…" Her cry was muffled by the pillow she buried her face in.

With a strong grip on her hips, Andrew started pounding into her, his hips smacking her beautiful ass every time he pushed in.

Given her barely contained moans and whimpers, Nathalie was loving this, her copious juices easing the glide of his pistoning shaft and dripping down her inner thighs.

They were making a racket, but there was no helping it.

He was not stopping this freight train until it got to the end of the line. Gritting his teeth, Andrew held on until he felt Nathalie's inner muscles contracting around him. Only then did he let go, shooting his seed inside her with a stifled groan.

For a moment, they stayed connected, their bodies rocked by the aftershocks of the powerful climax. Not willing to let go of her yet, Andrew held Nathalie glued to him with a strong grip on her hips. But even though she seemed content to fall asleep with him seated deep inside her, he reluctantly pulled out.

Nathalie remained in the same position, her sexy butt up in the air and her face still buried in the pillow she'd used to muffle her moans.

He patted one upturned butt cheek. "Come on, sweetheart, let's get you cleaned up."

"You go, I need a minute," she mumbled into the pillow.

He chuckled. "As you wish. Do you want me to bring you a washcloth?"

"Yes, please."

"Okay." He planted a soft kiss on that creamy cheek and grabbed his clothes off the chair he'd left them folded over. Opening the door, he peeked at the corridor first, checking that it was clear before making a dash for the bathroom, which was mercifully only a couple of steps away.

He took a quick shower, got dressed, and wetted two washcloths with warm water. Adding a dry towel from the linen closet, he returned to Nathalie's bedroom.

Andrew found her in exactly the same position he'd left her.

Well, it worked to his advantage. Everything was where he could easily reach it with the washcloth.

Nathalie moaned softly as the warm thing touched her sensitive flesh. Andrew was very careful to pat instead of rub, cleaning her as gently as he could and getting hard all over again. It was so sexy, the way she trusted him, the way she wasn't shy about anything with him.

He wished he could be as open with her. It wasn't that he didn't trust her, but he was too ashamed of what he'd done for Roni to tell her about it. And then he'd made it worse by pretending he couldn't talk about it because it was work related.

He hated the lies, and yet he kept piling them on.

45

BHATHIAN

"*S*ylvia? How did you persuade her to help?" Bhathian switched the phone to his other ear.

Sylvia was young, and he didn't know her well. But he knew her mother. Ruth was still keeping her grown daughter at home, refusing to let go of her only child.

Bhathian used to sneer at Ruth's dependence on Sylvia, but now that he'd found Nathalie, had become a parent, he understood her a little better. The only times he felt truly at peace were when he was near his Nathalie. For someone who had been resigned to spending his life alone, having a daughter of his own was priceless. Even if she had no idea that she was his.

"She wanted a trip to Hawaii."

That was odd. He didn't know that Ruth or Sylvia had financial troubles. "Did she say why she needed it? Why she couldn't afford it on her own?"

He heard Andrew chuckle. "Her problem isn't money; it's an overly clingy mother. The deal was that I'd arrange for her to *win* an organized trip to Hawaii so the mother wouldn't be able to join her. The girl is desperate for some time away from her. But given her special talent to render electronic devices useless, she could've asked for much more. The whole stunt wouldn't have worked without it."

"I had no idea she could do it." As far as Bhathian knew, no other clan member had this ability. Therefore it was extremely valuable. He should tell Kian and Onegus about Sylvia. The girl was much more useful in this capacity than as a seductress of a virgin hacker.

And yet, he was extremely grateful for her cooperation. If not for Sylvia, the hacker wouldn't have agreed to infiltrate the computers of the Swiss bank and find Eva's money trail.

"Interesting. You guys should keep track of these things. Who knows what other useful talents your people may have."

"You're absolutely right. I'm going to talk to Kian about it."

"While you're at it, you should ask him for some time off to go look for your Eva. Now that we have a tail of a trail, we should pounce on it right away."

Bhathian rubbed his hand on the back of his skull. "I can't do it. Not when we are gearing up for a major offensive. Kian needs me here."

True, many of the retired Guardians had already responded to the call, and more were arriving soon. Kian's latest count exceeded eighty, which was more than enough to storm the Doomers' stronghold. Problem was, the last time these old timers had seen battle was in some cases centuries ago. They needed training, and Kian needed each and every one of the active Guardians to help out with that.

At a time like this, Bhathian couldn't abandon Kian and the rest of his people to go chasing Eva's trail in South America. After more than thirty years, a few more days would not make a difference.

"I'll go talk to him. But I'm not even going to suggest leaving before Carol's rescue is over and she is safely back."

"I understand. You do what you have to do. In the meantime, I'll try to gather as much information as I can."

"Thank you. I don't know what I would've done without your help. I owe you big time."

"You owe me nothing, Bhathian. I'm doing this for Nathalie and for me. You know why it's crucial that we find Eva. I need to make sure that Nathalie is indeed a Dormant. Your feelings for Eva are just one part of this."

"Yeah, I know. Though to tell you the truth, I'm afraid for both you and Nathalie. Syssi was only twenty-five, and she barely made it. You are forty, and my Nathalie is thirty. As much as I hope and pray for her to be a Dormant so she could transition and stay with me forever, I'm afraid of losing her just when I've found her. And I'm afraid for you too."

There was a moment of silence on the line before Andrew sighed. "You of all people should know that life doesn't come with guarantees, and sometimes taking a risk is necessary. But time is a crucial element here. That's why I want you to go searching for Eva as soon as possible."

"I'm going to call Kian right now and discuss it with him." There was no chance Kian would let him go, but it was worth a try.

"Good luck."

46

SYSSI

The vision hit Syssi fast and hard, coming out of nowhere. Absent was the usual forewarning of the spinning, swirling sensation. One moment she was talking with her test subject and scribbling notes on her tablet, the next she was transported into the twilight zone.

The vision lasted only mere seconds and ended as abruptly as it had started. But the impact was profound.

Coming out of it, she heard someone's panicked voice. "Oh, my God, she is having a seizure! I don't know what to do! Help!"

Gasping, Syssi opened her eyes, the terrified test subject's face hovering mere inches in front of her.

"I'm okay," she croaked and gestured for the young woman to back away.

"Are you sure? You don't look good." The woman remained uncomfortably close, Amanda and Hanna's worried faces peering over her shoulders.

Syssi pushed up to her shaky feet and attempted a reassuring smile. "I'm fine. I just need some fresh air. We'll continue in a few minutes." She patted the woman's arm.

"Nonsense. I'll finish for you." Amanda waved a hand. "Get yourself a cup of coffee and a bite to eat. You need a break."

"Thank you." Syssi cast Amanda a grateful look.

"You're welcome. Now go." Amanda took Syssi's seat and flashed her blinding smile at the rattled test subject. "What's your name, dear?"

Syssi grabbed her purse and hurried to the kitchenette, which was the nearest place that offered a modicum of privacy.

Leaning against the counter, she pulled her phone out of her purse. Calling Andrew would've been more expedient, but texts were his preference when at work. Problem was, she was still shaken by the disturbing vision, and typing the simple message had taken several tries because the stupid autocorrect kept messing it up for her.

Call me as soon as you can.

Her phone rang a few minutes later.

"What happened?" By the sound of Andrew's labored breaths and that of his footfalls echoing from the walls, he was running with the phone in hand.

"Nothing yet. I had a vision."

"Damn it, Syssi; you almost gave me a stroke with that message. I thought you guys were under attack."

"I'm sorry. But I needed to tell you right away. It was about you."

"You could've said so in your text." Andrew's breathing had slowed down to normal, but then his voice sounded as if it was coming from an echo chamber.

"Are you in the bathroom?"

"Yeah. Where else in this building can I have a semi-private conversation with my psychic sister?"

"I'm not psychic. I'm a seer. The two are not the same."

"If you say so. Want to tell me about your vision?"

The mocking sound of his voice irked, especially given the gravity of what she needed to tell him.

"It wasn't good. There were ticking clocks and a funeral procession."

"What does it even mean?"

"It wasn't clear, but the feeling I got was that it would be you in that coffin if you don't act soon. You need to transition, Andrew. If you want to survive it, you can't delay this any longer."

"I don't think it makes much of a difference if I do it even a year from now. I'm already in the red danger zone. The chances of me making it are not good."

"You're wrong. First of all, there are the clocks. If the funeral were a done deal, there would've been no clocks. Second, what about my other vision? You still need to become a father."

He snorted. "I don't need to change to father a child."

"True. But what about the clocks?"

"Yeah. I don't know. But anyway, this is not a conversation for the phone. Can you meet me somewhere for lunch? Where are you now?"

"I'm at the lab. How about Gino's? Is it too far away for you?"

"No, it's fine. I can be there in fifteen minutes."

"See you there."

Syssi rubbed her chest. The talk with Andrew hadn't

helped alleviate her anxiety. He was still unconvinced that he needed to act now. She'd have to do her best to persuade him over lunch. And if that didn't work, she would ask Kian to talk to her stubborn brother. Maybe a man to man talk would help push him in the right direction. And she wasn't above asking Kian to shame Andrew into it.

Her gut was telling her that he would survive the transition, but only if he acted now.

In the lab's main room, Syssi walked over to Amanda who was still busy testing the young woman she'd been working with when the vision had hit. "I have to go. I'm meeting Andrew at Gino's in fifteen minutes."

Shit, she hadn't taken into account that Amanda might feel offended that Syssi wasn't inviting her to join them. But she hadn't given her sister-in-law enough credit.

Amanda narrowed her eyes. "Was it about him?"

"Yes."

She nodded. "Are you coming back?"

"Of course."

"You can go home, you know. I can do the rest of the testing for you today."

It was tempting. The vision had taken a lot out of her, and Syssi wanted nothing more than to head home to Kian, have him wrap his arms around her and tell her that everything was going to be okay. After she'd done her best convincing Andrew to go for the transition, that is. Come to think of it, talking with Andrew would probably exhaust the last of her reserves.

"Perhaps I'll take you up on your offer. I'll call and let you know."

On the way to Gino's, Syssi rehearsed her arguments,

feeling torn between wanting to convince Andrew to transition and being afraid he would actually listen to her. Despite what her gut was telling her loud and clear, she was still terrified that he might not make it. She would rather die than live with the knowledge that she was the one who had pushed Andrew to take this step, and it had led to his death.

Except, cowering on the sidelines was not an option, for either of them. The vision had made it clear that Andrew needed to do it, and the sooner, the better.

47

ANDREW

Walking into Gino's, Andrew searched for his sister's blonde head. Her blue BMW was already parked in the restaurant's parking when he'd got there.

"May I help you, sir?" the host smiled.

"I'm looking for my sister." Andrew peeked behind the guy's shoulders. "Never mind, I see her." He strode to where she was sitting.

The smile she gave him was strained, and as she pushed to her feet and hugged him, her embrace was bone-crushing.

"I love you too," he whispered in her ear. "But my ribs are about to crack."

She let go of him immediately. "Sorry, I keep forgetting." There were tears in her eyes, and she wiped them off hurriedly. "I ordered us wine. Hope it's okay with you."

Andrew was in the mood for a beer, but wine was fine. He was in the middle of his work day, and it would be better if he had none. But one glass of wine wasn't going to impair his thinking or his reflexes. He took the seat across from his sister and snatched one of the fragrant rolls from the basket.

Syssi seemed to be searching for what to say, or rather how to say it, and he was content to give her all the time she needed. She took a few sips of water, then put her glass down.

"Are you making any progress with finding Nathalie's mother?"

Andrew chuckled, tempted to tell her about the teenage hacker he'd bribed, but then reconsidered. Syssi might not approve. Better to skip the details. "We've picked up the money trail. Eva is still receiving her government pension every month, but the money is automatically transferred to a Swiss bank account. And those fuckers are nearly impossible to break into. But I finally managed to find someone who could. The money is rerouted to a bank in Rio, and there is activity there. Sparse, no more than once a month, but withdrawals are made, so we know Eva must be in the area."

Syssi's eyes sparkled. "Is Bhathian going after her?"

"As soon as Carol's situation is resolved."

Her face fell a little. "I see."

Andrew reached across the table for her hand. "Don't look so forlorn. Turner is getting closer. We'll have the location in a matter of days."

"I know. It's just that thinking about what Carol is going through…" Syssi shuddered. "There was no suspicious activity at the keep yet. So she is not giving in. I can't imagine how horrible it is for her, and I feel guilty as hell for sitting here with you at Gino's and enjoying lunch. But there is nothing I can do."

"I know, sweetheart. It's difficult just to sit and wait, but there is no way around it. We are doing everything in our power to rescue her. Kian is mobilizing all of the old Guardians and is planning the first attack the clan has ever launched against the Doomers."

She sighed. "And that worries me too. I know Guardians are nearly indestructible, but so are the Doomers."

Andrew gave her hand a little squeeze. "What is your intuition telling you?"

"In my gut, I know they will be successful. But success can be relative. They may win the battle but lose Carol, or rescue Carol and lose the battle. Guardians may be lost. It's like my foretelling about you. I know that to survive the transition you need to do it very soon. But that doesn't mean I'm not terrified for you."

"What if I never attempt it? Because if Nathalie is not a Dormant, I have no reason to do it. I'd rather spend my life with her, getting old together, than risk dying for the promise of immortality, or surviving but having to leave her because I don't age."

Syssi regarded him for a moment with questioning eyes. "What if it takes Bhathian months or even years to find Eva? And when he finds her, Eva proves to be an immortal, which she most likely is, but by then it will be too late for you to transition? Will you deny Nathalie her immortality because you can't join her?"

Damn, she was right. "I don't know what to do." Andrew ran his fingers through his short hair.

"You said that there are other indications that Nathalie is a Dormant. That she hears ghosts in her head."

"Yeah, but that is not conclusive either. She might have a

mental disorder for all I know. The only definite proof is Eva. She is either an immortal or she is not."

"Unfortunately, Andrew, you don't have the luxury of waiting for her to be found. You'll have to take a leap of faith."

"Yeah, you might be right."

"You know I am."

48

NATHALIE

*S*omething was troubling Andrew. Ever since he'd arrived after work today, he'd been broody, preoccupied. It was disconcerting. Nathalie had seen Andrew upset and frustrated about things at work before, but he'd always done his best to leave his troubles at the threshold, as he was fond of saying, and give her his undivided attention.

Not this evening, though. He was letting her do all the talking, and given that his responses were limited to an occasional grunt, she suspected that he wasn't really listening to anything she was saying.

Evidently, Scheherazade needed some fresh material if she wanted to capture her surly mate's attention. Her stories needed to be entertaining enough to take Andrew's mind off whatever was troubling him. Something funny and lighthearted to cheer him up and chase away the dark clouds he'd brought with him from work.

The trouble was, however, that nothing overly exciting had happened in the coffee shop during the day, and she doubted Andrew would be interested in anecdotes from the romance novel she read a few chapters from during her breaks... apart from the sex scenes, that is. Some of them were quite racy. That could be fun, reading him the juicy parts and watching him getting all turned on.

Maybe some other time... when they were alone in bed... but then there would be no need for it. They'd be making scenes of their own. And besides, she was still a little embarrassed to admit how much of her sexual inspiration had come from these books.

Oh, boy, was she really that boring? The woman who heard voices of dead people in her head had no stories to tell? Pathetic.

Well, even though she was still reluctant to talk about her ghosts, nothing else came to mind.

She really needed to broaden her interests. Trouble was, the little free time she had she was spending with Andrew. And during her short breaks, she wasn't in the mood for anything complicated. More demanding subjects would have to wait until she had more free time. Perhaps when she retired...

"So, the other day, I managed to block Sage."

"Uh-huh."

Obviously, Andrew wasn't listening.

"He saw me naked in the mirror, Tut too."

"Uh-huh... Wait, what?"

"Gotcha. I knew that would get your attention. Just joking, though. About the naked part, that is. But not the blocking. Do you want me to tell you about it? Or do you want to be left alone to brood? I don't mind, you know, if you want to." Yes, she did, but it sounded better. She wanted

Andrew to feel that he was free to be himself, even when he was in a bad mood, and that she'd be understanding and give him his space.

He pulled her into his arms and kissed the top of her head. "I'm sorry, sweetheart. It was rude of me not to pay attention. Please tell me all about it."

Now that Andrew was hugging her, all was good with her world, and Nathalie felt a weariness that she hadn't been aware of evaporate from her system.

"I don't remember if I told you about it, but Tut suggested that I practice blocking Sage."

"No, you haven't."

"So, Tut is on his way out. He says that he has pulled away and that he wants me to learn how to block the onslaught of voices that he's been blocking for me. He suggested I practice on Sage."

"Go on."

Even though it wasn't the first time she'd mentioned the voices to him, Nathalie was still struck by how seriously Andrew took her ghost stories. Without even a hint of mocking or doubt in his tone, he responded as if she'd been recounting a conversation with a real person.

"Sage is nice, and he listens to me. If I ask him to leave, he does. He was more than willing to help me with that. I told him to ghost out and after a few minutes to try and ghost back in. But when he returned, I imagined a heavy gate slamming shut in front of him, not allowing him entrance."

"Did it work?"

"Yeah, it really did. But because he was so nice about it, I promised Sage that I'd never block him unless it was a really inconvenient time."

"I'm sure he was glad to hear that."

Again, she listened carefully for any signs of mocking or condescending, but there were none.

"I can't believe how open-minded you are. Anyone else would have had me committed for telling stories like these, or at least think that I'm totally insane. You're such a great guy for believing me, Andrew. I'm the luckiest girl in the world to have snagged you."

For some reason, he grimaced at the compliment. "I have to believe you, love."

Was that it? Did he believe her because he was in love with her? She'd take it. "Well, loving me doesn't necessitate believing. Sometimes I myself am not sure that these are not hallucinations, so I can't expect you to take my word for it."

He sighed. "Let's go upstairs. There are some things I need to tell you."

As she took Andrew's offered hand and followed him up to the den, Nathalie's heart was pounding a frantic beat against her ribcage. She'd known this was all too good to be true, and now Andrew was about to tell her something that was going to prove her right.

Sitting next to him on the couch, she was anxious to hear what Andrew had to say, but at the same time reluctant to listen to it. Perhaps they could hit the rewind button, and this conversation would never happen. But at least he was holding on to her hand, so maybe it wouldn't be as bad as she was afraid it would. She could handle almost anything, other than him telling her that he had to leave her for some reason. Andrew loved her; she had no doubt about that. But sometimes love wasn't enough. Andrew had secrets that he'd refused to share with her, and now she regretted ever pressing him to reveal them.

"The reason I believe you, is that no one can lie to me. I always know when people tell the truth or lie when I am face to face with them. I'm better than a lie detector. That's my special ability that can't be explained."

She was still waiting for him to drop the bad news on her, but it seemed that this was all he was going to say. "Your special ability can be explained by sensitivity to minute clues that are invisible to others. Mine, on the other hand, can be only explained as a mental disorder." Or the genetic mutation he'd told her about. Though, frankly, she was starting to think that it had been all a load of crap to get her off his back and stop asking too many questions.

"But both will be wrong. I know lies when I hear them, and you know ghosts when you hear them."

"How can you be so sure? Isn't there a saying that claims that the simplest explanation is the right one? Why look for a paranormal cause when a simple one can do?"

Andrew smiled. "There is another saying, by Einstein, that everything should be made as simple as possible but not simpler."

It seemed Andrew truly believed that there was something mystical about their abilities. "Okay, so maybe we are both crazy. I'm good with that. It certainly beats being crazy by myself. On the other hand, it kind of casts doubts on whether we should have children. That genetic mutation you alluded to would be doubly potent in them. Poor kids. We really shouldn't have any. It's a shame, though. I wanted a whole brood of them."

Andrew mussed her hair. "Don't be silly. They'll be double blessed. I consider our talents gifts, not curses. But I need you to define brood. How many are we talking about?"

"Oh, I don't know. Five? Maybe six? I hated being an only child. I want a large family."

He kissed her nose. "We'll see. Talk to me again after the first one. I have some experience with raising babies. And I can tell you that it's tough. And as for our respective talents, you're not crazy and neither am I. Mine was proven beyond a shadow of a doubt. And as for yours, all you need to do is to ask your ghosts to tell you something that can be proven."

"Don't you think I haven't done that already? Tut says he's been dead for too long to have something that isn't written somewhere proven, and Sage is still too confused about who he used to be."

"Hm…" was Andrew's response.

"Yeah, so as you can see, I don't have a way to prove or disprove my ghosts."

"Not true. There is something else I haven't told you. But if you thought me crazy before, this will cement your opinion."

"Oh, yeah?" What else could he tell her that was crazier than her ghosts and his lie-detecting? That he'd been abducted by aliens?

"Oh, yeah, and then some."

49

ANDREW

*S*yssi's vision had been just the push Andrew had needed to get him off the seesaw of indecision. His mind was made up. As soon as this latest crisis was over, he was going to ask Kian to assign him an initiator—the male immortal who would induce his transition.

The first who came to mind was Bhathian. Out of all the immortals, the guy was the one Andrew spent the most time with. But as Nathalie's father, it seemed somewhat inappropriate. His second choice was Kian. But as Regent, the guy might be precluded from becoming anyone's initiator.

Surprisingly, Andrew's third choice was Dalhu. As one outsider to another, offering Dalhu the honor of becoming his initiator seemed like the right thing to do. And besides, he kind of liked the guy. His old rival for Amanda's affections had become a friend. Come to think of it, if Andrew hadn't been spending every free moment with Nathalie, he would have been hanging out with the dude more often.

Still, the choice of initiator might not be up to the initiate.

One might be chosen for him.

Probably one of the Guardians. Damn, he wasn't going to last long against one of these males. All he could hope for was to lose with dignity and not look like a wimp. It would be humiliating enough to be subdued like that, with the guy's fangs embedded in his neck and delivering the right dose of venom to help him transition. Hopefully, successfully.

Syssi might think that he was using the upcoming battle as an excuse to postpone the inevitable, but this truly wasn't the time for ceremonies. Everyone was gearing up for a fight, and with the levels of aggression all these males were ramping up, the one nominated as his 'initiator' may get overexcited and overdose him accidentally. The process was dangerous enough without factoring in Guardians on a testosterone overload.

The thing was, Andrew couldn't do it without telling Nathalie. Putting his life in danger like that wasn't something he could keep from her. She deserved to know. And if he was breaking the rules by spilling it all, so be it. Anyway, there wasn't much Kian could do to him in retribution without upsetting Syssi, and luckily for Andrew, the guy cherished his wife's regard above all else. Rules included.

So yeah, it wasn't very noble of Andrew to rely on his sister's protection, but considering the alternative, this was the lesser evil.

He needed to tell Nathalie everything.

"So what was it that you wanted to tell me?" Nathalie sounded anxious.

"I think we should open a bottle of wine for this. Wait here. I'll get it."

She held on to his hand. "Just tell me if it's good or bad before you go. I can't stand the suspense."

Whether it was good or bad depended on the outcome, but Nathalie looked nervous, and Andrew had no problem with bending the truth a little to assuage her fears. He gave her hand a reassuring squeeze and leaned to kiss her cheek. "It's all good, love."

Nathalie released a breath and let go of his hand. "Okay. But hurry, I don't like waiting to hear news, good or bad."

So he hadn't fooled her.

A few moments later, he was back with a bottle of red wine and two glasses. When he was done pouring, Andrew handed one tall glass to Nathalie.

Looking at how much he'd given her, she lifted a shapely brow. "Now I know this is really serious. Are you planning on getting me drunk before or after you tell me?"

"It's up to you. But I think you'll probably want a hefty dose after I'm done."

She took a sip, then another one, and put the glass down on the foldout tray table. "I'm ready. Shoot."

Damn, where to start?

"I'll try to explain the same way my sister and her husband explained it to me."

"Your sister?"

"Yeah. She was the first one to fall down the rabbit hole. Syssi has an uncanny talent to predict all kinds of things, and while attending architecture school at the University, she volunteered for testing at a neuroscience lab researching paranormal abilities. The professor running it was impressed with her results and offered her a job as a lab assistant. It wasn't Syssi's field, and she had an architectural internship lined up, but the guy died unexpectedly, so she took the offer."

"You didn't tell me that your sister could make predictions, and that you're not the only one in the family with a special talent."

"There was a reason for my omission. It'll become clear once I finish my story."

"Sorry. Go on."

Andrew ran a hand over the back of his neck. "Yeah, from now on the story gets really unbelievable, but every last bit is true. Syssi found out that her boss, Professor Amanda Dokani, is a member of a small clan of immortals— the descendants of the mythological gods that turned out to be not so mythological. They were real, and they took human mates, just as it's written in the Bible, and mixed children were born of those unions. The half-human half-god children were immortal, but when those immortals took human mates, their offspring were born mortal. Those born to the immortal females carried the dormant immortal genes that could be activated, but those born to the males didn't. The unique genetics transfer from mother to both daughters and sons, but only the daughter can transfer it to her children—the heredity is matrilineal."

As Nathalie listened intently, her eyes were focused on Andrew's face. His serious expression must've convinced her that he wasn't joking or telling her tall tales. "You were right. I do need this." She picked up the wine glass and drank half of it in one shot.

She made a face and shook her head before putting it down. "Assuming that this is all real, what does this story have to do with the voices I hear?"

"It will all be clear in just a moment. It wasn't a coincidence that Dr. Dokani was conducting research on paranormal abilities. Her hypothesis was that dormant carriers of the immortal genes might be more likely to manifest these talents. Syssi was one of Amanda's strongest subjects, and she decided to test that hypothesis on my sister."

"How?"

"One of the unique physical attributes of the male immortals are fangs and specialized venom glands. Those glands produce venom in two situations; when aggressing on other males and during sex. A dose or two of this venom facilitates the transition in a Dormant. Amanda asked Kian, who is her brother, to attempt Syssi's activation. At first, he refused because he considered it immoral to do so without Syssi's consent, but all his reservations flew out the window when he met her. Long story short, Amanda was right, and Syssi turned."

Nathalie could no longer hide her incredulity. "You want to tell me that Kian and Syssi are immortals?"

"Yes. But that's not all. As Syssi's brother, I'm also a Dormant, and the only reason I didn't attempt the transition is that it might be dangerous for someone my age. Evidently, the older the body, the tougher the transition."

Her eyebrows riding high on her forehead, Nathalie snorted. "So let me get it straight. You need to have sex with an immortal to transition? A male immortal?"

He laughed. "No. I think this would've been a dealbreaker for me. All I have to do is fight one of them and lose, which is not a problem since they are freakishly strong. As I've mentioned before, they also produce venom when aggressing on other males. All I have to do is resist until the guy fighting me produces enough to dose me."

Nathalie crossed her arms over her chest. "Okay...As fantastic as all of this sounds, I still don't get how any of it is related to my ghosts."

He smiled. "Think about it for a moment. Dormants exhibit paranormal abilities. I can detect lies, Syssi can predict outcomes, and you can hear ghosts."

It was almost comical, the way Nathalie's eyes widened and her jaw dropped. "You can't be serious. You think I'm a Dormant? This was the genetic mutation you were talking about?"

"I'm almost positive. And I think that your mother is an immortal."

"Oh my God." Her hands dropped to her sides. "As crazy as all of this sounds, it kind of makes sense. My mom never really aged. And she tried to hide it by wearing baggy clothes and putting on makeup to make herself look older." Nathalie gasped. "Yeah, and probably that's why she felt she had to disappear. She was probably afraid she'd be discovered and then experimented on. But how could it be? Her parents weren't immortal, they are both dead..."

"The only explanation I have is that she encountered an immortal male, by some incredible coincidence, and had sex with him. The males bite during sex but then thrall their partners to forget it. He didn't know that she was a Dormant and that he facilitated her transition. Because if he did, he would've never let her go."

"Why?"

"Because until my sister, they've never found one. It's a long story and even longer explanation, but Kian's clan is small, and because they are all closely related they can't mate with each other. The disparity in lifespans and risk of exposure prevents any long-term relationships, so they are basically doomed to one night stands. The females can at least have immortal children by having sex with humans. The males cannot. Finding Dormants that they are not related to is their only chance of having a life partner."

"Wow, that's sad. So Kian and his clan are the only immortals left? What happened to all the gods and the other immortals?"

"There was a big war over succession. One of the gods was pissed that the daughter of the leading couple refused to marry him, killing his chances of becoming their next leader. In retribution, or maybe because he was bat-shit crazy, he dropped a nuclear bomb on their assembly, killing all the other gods. But he didn't take into account the nuclear wind that followed, killing him and most of the mortal and immortal population of the region. The only goddess who survived was Kian's mother, the one who refused to marry a god she didn't love. She started the clan by taking human lovers and having immortal children. Her daughters continued her mission, and their daughters after them. A small group of the murderer god's descendants also survived, and to this day they are bitter enemies of Kian and his clan."

"How come they survived, and the rest of the immortals didn't?"

"Mortdh's compound, that's the name of the rogue god, was located several hundred miles north of the impact site, and the nuclear wind flew east, where basically all of the others lived."

"How tragic."

"After I heard the story, I did a little reading and found a Sumerian lament that describes it in eerie detail. To us, who are familiar with the type of destruction a nuclear bomb produces, the descriptions make it blatantly obvious that this is what it's talking about. But imagine all of those who came before—they must've thought that the wind of death the poem described was the product of someone's imagination, a myth."

She looked up at him with sad eyes. "Could you show it to me sometime?"

"Sure. I have the book at home."

In the silence that followed, Andrew watched Nathalie processing the incredible things he'd told her.

She shook her head. "This is a lot to take in."

"I know. And you're taking it all really well."

Nathalie sighed. "For a long time, I suspected that your motive for getting close to me was finding my mother's whereabouts. Is that true?"

"No. It's true that I originally came to your shop because I was searching for Eva, but my attraction to you was immediate and completely unrelated to her."

"Why were you looking for her? Did you suspect that she was an immortal?"

"At first, I searched for her because Bhathian asked me to help him find his long-lost love."

Her eyes grew wide again. "Bhathian? He is…"

"Yes, of course, he's a member of Kian's clan. He met Eva a long time ago, when she was still single and worked for the drug enforcement agency. She left an impression on him, but he lost track of her. I work for the government and have access to information he didn't. I found her file quite easily."

"So you came here searching for her? Didn't you know that she was missing?"

"I did. But Bhathian also wanted to see you."

"Why?"

"That, unfortunately, is not my story to tell. It's his. I think we should call him and have him come over."

"Wait. So if Bhathian and Kian are immortals, then so is Jackson?"

Andrew nodded. "And Vlad, and Kri and Michael, and many of the others who Jackson has been inviting to come taste your creations."

She slumped back into the couch cushions. "Wow. Just wow. But you know what? I had my suspicions. I told you about Vlad, right? Picking up a heavy piece of equipment with one hand, and Jackson's hearing is definitely superhuman. Bhathian, though, other than his size, looks completely normal, and so does Syssi. But Kian is inhumanly handsome, and his eyes are strange. When we were having dinner with them, I thought I saw them glow, but then dismissed it. Contact lenses reflecting light seemed like a good enough explanation."

"They glow when he gets overexcited or is under a lot of pressure."

Nathalie remained quiet for a while, her expressive face reflecting her thoughts. "Why are you telling me all of this only now? Why not before?"

Smart girl.

Andrew clasped her hand. "I wanted to find Eva and confirm that she was an immortal, so I could be sure beyond a shadow of a doubt that you were a Dormant. But I don't have the luxury of time. At my age, attempting transition is an iffy proposition, and I'm not getting any younger. If you are a Dormant, I want to be the one who facilitates your transition, but to do so, I have to go through it first. But if you're not a Dormant, then I want to remain mortal and live out the rest of my life with you."

She squeezed his hand. "That's so sweet." Her voice sounded choked. "You would give up your chance of immortality for me?"

"In a heartbeat. I don't want to live a day without you. It's just not worth it."

There were tears in her eyes when she pounced on him and peppered his face with kisses. "I love you so much. Let's forget about this immortal thing and just be together. You said that it's risky. I don't want you to do it."

Her face was buried in his neck, and he stroked her hair gently. "I couldn't live with myself if you could gain immortality and didn't because of me. Not going to happen. And there is no chance in hell I'll let another immortal have sex with you. So that's settled."

Nathalie chuckled and then sniffled. "But why now?"

"Syssi had a vision. She said I needed to do it as soon as possible. My sister loves me. She would've never pushed me if she believed the risk to be too high. She thinks I'll be fine if I do it now. And just to reassure you, Syssi's visions are never wrong."

Andrew hadn't mentioned that the foretelling was vague. There was no need to worry Nathalie unnecessarily. After all, if the message was to hurry, it must've meant that he would survive the transition if he did. True?

50

NATHALIE

*C*uriosity was eating Nathalie alive. What was Bhathian's story? Why had Andrew insisted that it wasn't his to tell? With all the fantastic things he had told her, what more could Bhathian reveal?

But Andrew wouldn't budge, and Bhathian was on his way. She could survive a few more minutes.

"Please, could you at least give me a clue? I can't take the suspense."

"I'm sorry. I can't. But I can distract you while we wait." He waggled his brows.

She slapped his shoulder. "How can you think about sex at a time like this?"

"Sweetheart, I'm a man, sex is always on my mind."

Usually, that would have been enough to get her all hot and bothered. Nathalie wasn't one to say no to some hanky-panky. But she was too distraught. Andrew's revelations had been shocking, and she was anxious to hear what else Bhathian had to add to the story.

"Could you pour me some more wine?"

"Are you sure? You've had quite a lot."

"Yeah, and I want more." The nerve of the guy. Dumping an outrageous story like this on her and then expecting her to be all reasonable and drink in moderation. Right now, Nathalie wished she had something much stronger than wine.

"Fine. But don't you want to be sober to hear what Bhathian has to say?"

"No, not really. I need something to take the edge off the turmoil that's going on inside my head."

Andrew shook his head and poured, but only half a glass.

Agh. She loved him to distraction, but he was pissing her off. "All the way to the top."

Reluctantly, he did as she asked.

"Maybe I should go downstairs and make coffee." Andrew began pushing up to his feet.

She tugged on his hand and pulled him back down. "No, you're not leaving me here alone. You can keep telling me things while we wait. I'm sure there is a ton of stuff you haven't told me yet."

Andrew wrapped one arm around her shoulders, the other one under her knees, and pulled her onto his lap. "Better?"

Cocooned in his warmth, she felt the tightness in her belly ease. "When you hug me like this, it always is."

He kissed the top of her head. "I'm glad."

"So the goddess, Kian's mother, what happened to her?"

"She is still here. I've met her."

Nathalie turned to look up at him. "You did? What's she like?"

Andrew snorted. "She looks like a teenager. Tiny, maybe

an inch over five feet, skinny, with long flaming red hair and an incredible presence. She has a way to tamp down her powers, but when she doesn't, it radiates. She glows in the dark."

"Really? Like fluorescent?"

"Something like that. But it's a gentle glow. She is stunning. The most beautiful woman I've ever seen. And that's saying a lot. Before I met Annani, I thought her daughter, Amanda, was the most beautiful."

"Now I'm jealous. Were you attracted to either of them?"

She felt Andrew's thigh muscles tighten under her. So the answer was yes. Would he fess up to it?

"Although friendly, Annani was too intimidating. But for a little while, I had a crush on Amanda."

"Oh yeah? What ended it?" Hopefully, it was over. If not, she would have to find the woman and scratch her pretty eyes out.

Andrew laughed, his strong body shaking. "First of all, she had her eye on someone else, which might have been part of the allure, since I'm a competitive bastard. But when I realized that I was more excited about going out on a mission than winning Amanda's heart, I had to admit to myself that what I felt for her wasn't real. I even became good friends with the guy she ended up with, my old rival."

Interesting, this was a facet of Andrew she was unfamiliar with. Was he a thrill seeker? A daredevil?

"How about me? Would you be more excited about going on some adventure than spending time with me?"

He hugged her closer. "Never. In fact, there is a big thing brewing right now, and Kian asked me to be in charge of it.

But I gladly fobbed it off on someone else. Other than helping Bhathian look for your mother, all I want to do is spend time with you."

As if summoned by the mentioning of his name, Andrew's phone buzzed with a message.

"Bhathian is downstairs. I need to go open up for him." Andrew lifted Nathalie up and deposited her back on the couch. "I'll be right back." He kissed her cheek.

A moment later, two sets of footsteps and a hushed conversation sounded from the staircase.

Nathalie tensed.

But then, as Bhathian entered the den with a vulnerable expression on his rugged face, Nathalie felt her heart soften. Whatever he had to say, it wasn't easy for the big guy. She patted the spot next to her. "Come sit with me."

He cast a glance at Andrew, who nodded his encouragement.

With a sigh, Bhathian walked over and carefully lowered himself down as if afraid he might break the couch with his bulk.

"Do you want me to stay?" Andrew asked gently.

"Yeah, I do." Bhathian sounded insecure. Did Andrew tell him that she knew he was an immortal? That must've been what they had whispered about on their way up. She'd listened when Andrew called Bhathian, and he hadn't told him much. Just that it was time to tell Nathalie everything.

Bhathian lifted his head and looked at her with soft eyes. "How much did Andrew tell you?" he asked.

"That you're an immortal, about him and me being Dormants, the transition and how it works, the clan, the goddess. That you guys suspect my mother is an immortal, and that a long time ago you were in love with her."

He chuckled nervously. "Yeah, that about sums it up. But there is more."

"I figured. Do you want to tell me the rest?"

With a sigh, he nodded.

BHATHIAN

*B*hathian had known that this day would come, but he hadn't expected it to come so soon. He wasn't ready.

Andrew should've given him a warning, time to prepare his story, to find the right words to tell Nathalie the truth gently. Damn, it wasn't going to be easy no matter how carefully he chose his words.

As she waited for him to start, looking at him so expectantly, there was no judgment in her expression, no apprehension, just kindness. Nathalie trusted him. Which made him even more anxious, and the words just wouldn't come.

Nathalie took his rough hand, sandwiching it between her small palms. "I can tell that this is difficult for you. You may find it easier if you start at the beginning."

Good advice.

He nodded. "I met Eva, or Patricia—the undercover name she used—over thirty years ago, at a bar frequented by pilots and flight attendants on layovers. She was stunning, the most beautiful, hottest woman I've ever met. And there had been plenty throughout my long life. We spent the night together, and the next day we said our goodbyes. I thought I would never see her again."

Keeping his eyes trained on Nathalie's face, he was relieved that she didn't seem to mind the hookup style encounter he had had with her mother. "I assume that Andrew told you about our lifestyle; the one night stands, the impossibility of lasting companionship."

When she nodded, he continued. "Until Eva, I never had a problem with that. It suited me just fine. But she was different. Saying goodbye to her hurt." He rubbed his chest. "I should've known that there was more to it than a simple attraction to a beautiful woman. The one glaring tell was that I couldn't thrall her. It's very rare to encounter resistance. Usually, human minds are easily manipulated. Luckily, though, I found out in time and refrained from biting her."

He paused his story and glanced at Andrew who was sitting on the other foldout table across from them. "Did Andrew tell you about the fangs?"

"Yeah, he did." She tipped her head, trying to look into his mouth. "Though to tell you the truth, I don't see how you can do anything with these—they are just slightly longer than normal incisors."

His lips twitched. "With the right stimulation, they become much longer."

"I see." Nathalie's cheeks reddened as his meaning sank in.

"A month later, I met Eva again at the same place, and she invited me to her hotel room." Bhathian dropped his head and rubbed his hand over the back of his neck. "I thought we were going to hook up again, which was fine with me, but she had another reason for seeking me out that night, and inviting me over."

Fuck, this was the toughest part, and Bhathian felt like a coward for avoiding Nathalie's eyes. Forcing himself to man up, he lifted his head and gazed at his daughter's beautiful face. "She told me that she was pregnant and that I was the father."

From her expression, it was clear that Nathalie hadn't connected the dots yet. Which was good. Bhathian preferred to tell her the rest of the story first.

"I'm ashamed to admit it, but I asked her to have an abortion. She refused, saying that the pregnancy was a miracle at her age, which was shockingly forty-five. She looked twenty years younger. I told her that I couldn't be a father to her child and offered to help her financially, which, frankly, was the only thing I could provide her with. It wasn't as if I could be with her, or even sign my name on the birth certificate."

"Did she end up aborting the pregnancy?" There was a slight tremor in Nathalie's voice. Was she starting to suspect?

"I don't think so. She told me she would think about it and get back to me. But she never did. In fact, she disappeared. I've searched for her for years, not knowing if I had a child or not, if Patricia, I'm sorry, Eva, was doing okay on her own or not. It's been eating me up for the past thirty years. But I'd hit a brick wall in my search and basically given up hope of ever finding out. Until Andrew joined the clan, that is."

He glanced at Andrew. "I owe this man more than I could ever repay him."

"We've been over this before. You owe me nothing," Andrew dismissed him.

Nathalie let go of his hand to cross her arms over her chest. "I guess she must've either aborted the baby or lost it because I'm her only child."

Bhathian shook his head. "No, she didn't."

Nathalie's eyes grew wide. "Oh my God, did she give it up for adoption? Do I have a half-brother or a sister somewhere?"

"No, sweetheart, Eva didn't give the baby up."

"I don't understand," she whispered with tears glistening in her eyes.

"I think you do. You are my daughter, Nathalie."

"No, I'm not. Papi is my father."

It hurt, but what had he expected? Nathalie loved her adoptive father. Fernando had been an amazing parent, probably better than most biological ones. Maybe he didn't know? Maybe Eva never told him that she was pregnant when they had met? And had fooled him into believing that Nathalie was his?

"Fernando is your father in all the ways that count, and he always will be. Because he loved you and raised you in the best possible way. I'm not even sure he knows you're not his. But I have no doubt that I'm your biological father. Just look in the mirror, Nathalie. Now that you know, you won't be able to deny the resemblance."

The tears sliding down her cheeks felt like daggers to his heart. The last thing he wanted was to make Nathalie cry.

Damn, how was he going to make it better for her? What could he say to take away her pain?

Why was it so horrible for her to find out that he was her father?

With a resigned sigh, Bhathian dropped his head on his fists. This wasn't how he'd imagined it would go. In his fantasies, Nathalie would be surprised, even shocked a little, but then jump into his arms with happy tears in her eyes. Not sad ones that were tearing at his gut.

He wished he could take it back.

If finding out he was her father made Nathalie so miserable, then maybe it would've been better if she had never found out. For him, it sufficed that he knew.

But then, there was a way to press rewind, wasn't there? He could thrall the memory away, and everything would be back to normal.

"If you wish, I can make you forget this whole conversation," he whispered. "Hurting you was the last thing I wanted. I love you, and I'm so proud that you're my daughter. But it's enough for me that I know. You can go back to believing that Fernando is your biological dad. Just say the words and it'll be done."

"What? No!" Nathalie grabbed his hand. "I'm sorry." She wiped her eyes with her sleeve. "Poor Bhathian, I must've hurt your feelings so bad with my stupid tears. It's just that it's such a shock. I love my father, I mean my Papi. Oh, God, this is difficult. I love the man who's been my father for the past thirty years, and I always will, but I have room in my heart for you too." She lifted her hand and touched a finger to his brows. "The shape is the same, but mine are not as bushy."

Bhathian chuckled. "Thank the merciful Fates. Imagine the pain of plucking all of that on a regular basis."

Her laughter was like salve on the raw endings of his frazzled nerves.

"Be careful, Bhathian, I might be tempted to pluck out some of yours. I bet you'll look much less scary if I tame these a bit."

"So what are you saying? That I'm intimidating? Me? I'm nothing but a big teddy bear."

Andrew chuckled. "A teddy ogre is more like it."

"Hey, don't insult my father." Nathalie winked at Bhathian.

Her words melted his heart, and he couldn't help but pull her up and into an ogre hug. "That's the nicest thing anyone ever said to me."

Andrew tapped his shoulder. "Easy there, big guy, you are squishing my fiancée."

"Sorry." Reluctantly, Bhathian let go of Nathalie. If it was up to him, he would've cradled her in his arms like a baby, making up for lost time. But he was sure she wouldn't appreciate it. Nathalie was a grown woman, a beautiful, smart, accomplished woman, who was about to be married to a great guy that Bhathian felt privileged to call a friend.

Nathalie stretched up to her toes and kissed his cheek. "That's okay. You didn't squeeze too hard. But I think I'll have to keep calling you Bhathian. First of all, you look younger than me, and it will be beyond weird to call you daddy. People might get the wrong idea. And anyway, I can't do it as long as Papi is still around and still aware."

Even though he was disappointed, Bhathian couldn't argue with her logic.

Andrew must've noticed his crestfallen face. "Don't look so glum, my friend. When we find Eva, you guys can pick up from where you left off thirty years ago, and make a brother or sister for Nathalie. That way you'll have someone to call you daddy after all."

Bhathian felt his ears heat up. "First, I need to find her. And when I do, she might not want to have anything to do with me."

Wrapping his arm around Nathalie's waist, Andrew clasped Bhathian's shoulder. With the three of them standing clustered together, he said, "I promise you both. We are going to find Eva and make this family whole again."

ANDREW

*I*t was after midnight when Bhathian hugged Nathalie one last time and said goodnight.

With a sigh, she dropped on the couch next to Andrew. "I'm exhausted, but I don't think I'll be able to sleep."

He lifted her up onto his lap. "I can sing you a lullaby."

"The obscene one that your grandpa taught you?"

"That's the only one I know."

"Maybe some other time."

"Deal." He kissed her forehead. "Are you okay?"

"Yeah, I am. It was a lot to take in, but at the same time, it clarified so many things. I no longer think I'm crazy, which is great. It's like a great weight has lifted off my chest. And I can understand why my mother felt like she needed to disappear. I've spent such a long time being angry at her, feeling abandoned, unloved. It's good to know that she didn't do it on a whim. That she had a very good reason for going into hiding. But what was even worse was imagining that something awful had happened to her. It made me feel guilty for being angry at her. Now I'm more hopeful that she is alive and well."

"She is. I've traced where her pension money goes. She has it routed to a Swiss account, and from there to a bank in Rio."

Nathalie perked up. "So we can find her?"

"Not we, Bhathian. He is going to Brazil as soon as this big thing I've told you about is over."

"Can you tell me more about it? Or is it a secret?"

"I no longer have a reason to keep anything from you. Other than anything related to my work and national security that I'm sworn not to reveal, that is. A female immortal has been captured by the clan's enemies, and they are planning a rescue. It's going to be an all-out assault on the enemy stronghold. Just as soon as we find where they are holding her."

Nathalie's face grew pale. "Are you going to take part in it?"

He chuckled. "No. As a human, I'll be more of an impediment than help. These guys are powerful."

"But Bhathian is going, right?"

He nodded. "Bhathian is a Guardian. One of only seven."

"What's a Guardian? Like a bodyguard?"

"Something like that. They used to be warriors, but during peacetime, they are more like an internal police force. Kian called in the reserves, all the old Guardians who left the force, but they need each one of the seven currently serving to train the others and make them battle ready."

He felt Nathalie shiver. "That's so scary. And I thought I had problems before. They seem so trivial compared to this."

"You have nothing to worry about. The Guardian Force is formidable. They'll overpower their enemies and rescue the female with ease." Well, there were no guarantees. But it was likely. Enough so Andrew could assuage Nathalie's fears with a clear conscience.

Chewing on her lower lip, she looked up at him with sad eyes. "It's not only Bhathian that I fear for. I fear for Kian. And I fear for Syssi who must be going crazy with anxiety as she thinks about her husband going into battle. But most of all I fear for you."

"Why? I told you I'm not taking part in this one."

"Yeah, I know. But you are going to attempt the transition, risking your life for pie in the sky. I don't want it. I'd rather have you with me for the span of our mortal lives than lose you over this. We can be so happy, Andrew. We could have children and grandchildren and age together, and it would be wonderful. Why risk it?"

He couldn't refute or dismiss her concerns. Echoing his own thoughts, Nathalie was right on every count. Except one. She had the chance of becoming immortal and he would be damned forever if she gave it up for him. "We can have all of this but for much longer. The kids and the grandkids and their grandkids. It will all work out. I promise. I'll transition just fine. A stubborn bastard like me is not going to give up on a life with a woman he loves. I'll fight for it with all I have, and I'll survive."

"How can you promise something that you can't control? You don't know how your body will react. You're strong and healthy, but don't tell me not to worry. I know that you do. Otherwise, you would've done it a long time ago, right after your sister's transition."

Again, she was spot on. "Look, Nathalie. I won't deny the risk, and I've waited till now because, frankly, I didn't have a strong enough reason to go for it. Not until I met you. You are everything to me. You are my reason for wanting to live for as long as possible, so I can spend as much time with you as I can. But I wanted to make sure that you're a Dormant before I went for it. That was the only precaution I cared about. But after Syssi's vision, I no longer want to wait. Besides, you being a Dormant is almost a certainty."

She cupped his cheek. "Don't you see, my love? If something happens to you, I don't want to go on without you. Especially since you are doing this for me. I wouldn't be able to live with myself."

"Oh, sweetheart." He gathered her closer and kissed her trembling lips. "Sometimes we need to take a risk. Life doesn't come with guarantees, and if we let fear deter us from reaching for what we want, we would never achieve anything. The safest thing is to sit on the couch and watch the dumb box, but that's not living. And besides, there are risks involved even in that. Like muscle atrophy, getting fat, etc., etc."

She slapped his arm. "Don't make fun of it. This is serious. I'm not talking about complete inactivity. But you'd agree with me that there is a big difference between going for a walk and skydiving. One is a pleasant activity; the other is life-threatening."

He chuckled. "But much more fun."

Nathalie crossed her arms over her chest. "Not everything is about having fun."

"Oh, yeah? I thought it was. Don't knock it until you try it."

"What? Skydiving?"

"Yeah. It's a great rush."

"Never. Not in a million years."

Andrew bent his neck and rubbed his nose on Nathalie's. "How about in a million and one?"

Her lips twitched. "Stop it. I know what you're doing."

"I'm rubbing your cute little nose."

"You're trying to distract me."

"True. But you worry too much, my love. Everything is going to be alright."

"How can you say that? I have a feeling that I'm marrying an incorrigible thrill seeker."

"Yes, you are."

"So you're not even trying to deny it?"

"Why would I? It's the truth. I love adventure, I thrive on danger, always have."

"Oh, boy."

"But I promise always to be careful."

"You're full of promises tonight."

"I am. And I intend to deliver on each and every one."

The end...for now...

THE STORY CONTINUES IN
DARK WARRIOR'S DESTINY

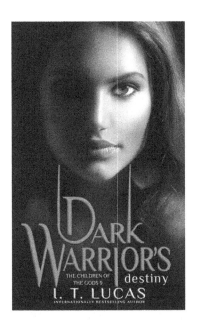

Dear reader,

Thank you for reading the ***Children of the Gods series.***

If you enjoyed the story, I would be grateful if you could leave a review for Dark Warrior's Promise on Amazon. (With a few words, you'll make me very happy. :-)

Also by I. T. Lucas

PERFECT MATCH

VAMPIRE'S CONSORT

KING'S CHOSEN

CAPTAIN'S CONQUEST

THE THIEF WHO LOVED ME

THE CHILDREN OF THE GODS SERIES SETS

BOOKS 17-19: DARK OPERATIVE TRILOGY
BOOKS 20-22: DARK SURVIVOR TRILOGY
BOOKS 23-25: DARK WIDOW TRILOGY
BOOKS 26-28: DARK DREAM TRILOGY
BOOKS 29-31: DARK PRINCE TRILOGY
BOOKS 32-34: DARK QUEEN TRILOGY
BOOKS 35-37: DARK SPY TRILOGY
BOOKS 38-40: DARK OVERLORD TRILOGY
BOOKS 41-43: DARK CHOICES TRILOGY
BOOKS 44-46: DARK SECRETS TRILOGY
BOOKS 47-49: DARK HAVEN TRILOGY
BOOKS 50-52: DARK POWER TRILOGY
BOOKS 53-55: DARK MEMORIES TRILOGY
BOOKS 56-58: DARK HUNTER TRILOGY
BOOKS 59-61: DARK GOD TRILOGY
BOOKS 62-64: DARK WHISPERS TRILOGY
BOOKS 65-67: DARK GAMBIT TRILOGY

MEGA SETS

INCLUDE CHARACTER LISTS

THE CHILDREN OF THE GODS: BOOKS 1-6
THE CHILDREN OF THE GODS: BOOKS 6.5-10

TRY THE CHILDREN OF THE GODS SERIES ON AUDIBLE

2 FREE audiobooks with your new Audible subscription!

FOR EXCLUSIVE PEEKS AT UPCOMING RELEASES & A FREE COMPANION BOOK

JOIN MY *VIP CLUB* AND GAIN ACCESS TO THE VIP PORTAL AT ITLUCAS.COM

INCLUDED IN YOUR FREE MEMBERSHIP:

YOUR VIP PORTAL

- READ PREVIEW CHAPTERS OF UPCOMING RELEASES.
- LISTEN TO GODDESS'S CHOICE NARRATION BY CHARLES LAWRENCE
- EXCLUSIVE CONTENT OFFERED ONLY TO MY VIPS.

FREE I.T. LUCAS COMPANION INCLUDES:

- GODDESS'S CHOICE PART 1
- PERFECT MATCH: VAMPIRE'S CONSORT (A STANDALONE NOVELLA)
- INTERVIEW Q & A
- CHARACTER CHARTS

IF YOU'RE ALREADY A SUBSCRIBER, YOU'LL RECEIVE A DOWN-LOAD LINK FOR MY NEXT BOOK'S PREVIEW CHAPTERS IN THE NEW RELEASE ANNOUNCEMENT EMAIL. IF YOU ARE NOT GETTING MY EMAILS, YOUR PROVIDER IS SENDING THEM TO YOUR JUNK FOLDER, AND YOU ARE MISSING OUT ON **IMPORTANT UPDATES, SIDE CHARACTERS' PORTRAITS, ADDITIONAL**

FOR EXCLUSIVE PEEKS

CONTENT, AND OTHER GOODIES. To FIX THAT, ADD isabell@ itlucas.com TO YOUR EMAIL CONTACTS OR YOUR EMAIL VIP LIST.

Made in United States
Orlando, FL
04 October 2023

37561692R00183